# AN UNHOLY SACRIFICE

The Shrine was heavy with the scent of flowers. Light came in from the north side, where the doors to the cloister had been folded back. Motes of dust revolved lazily in the air.

Out of the reach of daylight the Lady of Promise shone dark and light. In the flickering candlelight she seemed to be moving slightly.

The scream that pierced the air seemed to hang there for a long moment and then collapse of its own weight to the floor. To the floor where a girl lay in a sprawl of blue chiffon, arms and legs at gawky angles, and the back of her head a mess of hair and bone and blood and a terrible ooze that was none of those things.

### Agatha Christie

Death on the Nile
A Holiday for Murder
The Mousetrap and Other Plays
The Mysterious Affair at Styles
Poirot Investigates
Postern of Fate
The Secret Adversary
The Seven Dials Mystery
Sleeping Murder

### Dorothy Simpson

Last Seen Alive
The Night She Died
Puppet for a Corpse
Six Feet Under
Close Her Eyes
Element of Doubt
Dead on Arrival
Suspicious Death
Dead by Morning

### Elizabeth George

A Great Deliverance
Payment in Blood
Well-Schooled in Murder
*Coming soon:*
A Suitable Vengeance

### Colin Dexter

Last Bus to Woodstock
The Riddle of the Third Mile
The Silent World of Nicholas
  Quinn
Service of All the Dead
The Dead of Jericho
The Secret of Annexe 3
Last Seen Wearing
*Coming soon:*
The Wench is Dead

### Michael Dibdin

Ratking

### Liza Cody

Stalker
Head Case
Under Contract

### S. T. Haymon

Death of a God
Death and the Pregnant Virgin
A Very Particular Murder

### Ruth Rendell

A Dark-Adapted Eye
  (writing as Barbara Vine)
A Fatal Inversion
  (writing as Barbara Vine)

### Marian Babson

Death in Fashion
Reel Murder
Murder, Murder, Little Star
Murder on a Mystery Tour
Murder Sails at Midnight
The Stalking Lamb
Murder at the Cat Show
*Coming soon:*
Tourists are for Trapping

### Dorothy Cannell

The Widows Club
Down the Garden Path
Mum's the Word
*Coming soon:*
Femmes Fatal

### Antonia Fraser

Jemima Shore's First Case
Your Royal Hostage
Oxford Blood
A Splash of Red
Quiet as a Nun
Cavalier Case
*Coming soon:*
Cool Repentance

### Margery Allingham

Police at the Funeral
Flowers for the Judge
Tether's End
Pearls Before Swine
Traitor's Purse
Dancers in Mourning
Mystery Mile

# Death
# and the
# Pregnant
# Virgin

S. T. Haymon

BANTAM BOOKS
NEW YORK • TORONTO • LONDON • SYDNEY • AUCKLAND

*This edition contains the complete text
of the original hardcover edition.*
NOT ONE WORD HAS BEEN OMITTED.

DEATH AND THE PREGNANT VIRGIN

*A Bantam Book / published by arrangement with
St. Martin's Press Inc.*

PRINTING HISTORY

*St. Martin's edition published December 1980
Bantam edition / February 1984*

*CRIME LINE and the portrayal of a boxed "cl" are trademarks of Bantam
Books, a division of Bantam Doubleday Dell Publishing Group, Inc.*

ISBN 0-553-18513-6

*Published simultaneously in the United States and Canada*

---

*Bantam Books are published by Bantam Books, a division of Bantam
Doubleday Dell Publishing Group, Inc. Its trademark, consisting of the
words "Bantam Books" and the portrayal of a rooster, is Registered in U.S.
Patent and Trademark Office and in other countries. Marca Registrada.
Bantam Books, 666 Fifth Avenue, New York, New York 10103.*

---

PRINTED IN THE UNITED STATES OF AMERICA

OPM    11   10   9   8   7   6   5   4   3   2

# 1

Three miles outside the village they ran into a traffic jam.

Philip Cass braked the car to a halt and twisted round in the driving seat.

"I said we should give it a miss this weekend! What was that again about nobody arriving before tonight?"

"I can't believe it!" exclaimed Joanna Cass, her eyes on the rear of the coach that towered immediately ahead of them. "Felucca Coaches, Penrith. Penrith! That's somewhere in the Lake District, isn't it? It must be hundreds of miles! And why Felucca? Isn't that some kind of Arab rowing boat?"

"Amphibious," Philip returned acidly. "They've heard about Norfolk, more often under water than visible to the naked eye, and they've come prepared."

"Oh good!" said Joanna. "You're not really angry."

Her husband favoured her with a baleful look that on his chubby, freckled face carried no conviction at all.

"That merely goes to show, even after all these years, how little you know me. Do you realise that, leaving town the time we did, we could have been lying in the sun for hours on top of the Chilterns or the South Downs, monarchs of all we survey?"

"Subtopia!" said his wife, her voice brimful of scorn. "Crawling with gents in business suits commuting from Henley or Haywards Heath."

"I'm a gent in a business suit myself five days a week." The traffic oozed forward another yard. Philip Cass reached for his wife's hand and squeezed it. "Don't mind me," he said.

"I never do." She leaned over and kissed him, with more warmth than might have been expected after ten years of marriage. Her husband returned the salutation with delight and a never-failing astonishment that such a beautiful and intelligent creature should hold him in esteem. A blast from the horn of the BMW behind them called to his attention the fact that the line of cars was once more on the move: a good forty feet this time.

"Things are looking up," said Philip Cass. "Not far now to Our Lady of Promise, God rot her."

1

* * *

Joanna said with unexpected asperity: "I wish you wouldn't talk like that about the Lady."

Philip Cass regarded his wife with some alarm.

"Don't tell me! First Rachel, now you."

"Nothing of the kind. It's just—well, you can't see a tremendous crowd like this, all these people, converging on this one spot out of the whole of England, without feeling a kind of respect, a—a sort of awe. Even if you don't believe in it yourself, you oughtn't to make fun of it."

"My dear girl, fun is the last thing I would dream of making. I regard the whole business as much too dangerous for that." The cavalcade began to move again. "You know perfectly well," Philip Cass went on, his features compressed into a seriousness which sat oddly on their cherubic contours, "that, face to face with any of these true believers, I wouldn't dream of hurting their feelings by telling them what I really think of our local idol. But as to feeling 'a kind of respect, a sort of awe' because hundreds, thousands, or, for all I know, millions of misguided people have suddenly taken it into their heads to descend on the village of Mauthen Barbary like a swarm of locusts, you might as well expect me to feel a kind of respect, a sort of awe, every Saturday a howling mob descends on Tottenham Hotspur or Manchester United. Foolishness multiplied doesn't make it any less foolish. On the contrary, it makes it worse. Enthusiasts, whether they're football hooligans or religious nuts, take fire from each other, so that the resultant lunacy is infinitely greater than the sum of its parts."

From the coach came the sound of singing: a hymn so pathetically tuneless that Philip Cass, in spite of himself, burst out laughing.

"I'll admit they hardly sound like dangerous fanatics. All in all, probably the worst we have to fear this weekend is that they'll go trampling our lettuces in the dark, looking for somewhere to answer the calls of nature."

"How revolting!" cried Joanna. "Anyway, it won't happen. Rachel told me over the phone they're putting up chemical things on the Rond, down by the river."

"Sweet Maut, run softly till I end my—" Philip slipped the car into gear and edged forward another yard. "Poor little stream, polluted to make a Christian holiday. I must say, though, I'm amazed that Rachel, so enraptured with higher things, should have thought to impart such earthy information."

"As a matter of fact," Joanna admitted, dimpling, "I was the one to raise the subject. You aren't the only one to have thought of the lettuces! And don't be so horribly brotherly. Your sister has unsuspected talents. They've put her in charge of all the accommodation arrangements—"

"You must be joking! That girl couldn't arrange a game of tiddlywinks if her life depended on it."

"You haven't been looking. Rachel's changed a great deal in the past year."

"Oh, I've been looking all right," said Philip Cass, his voice suddenly bleak and uncharacteristic. "Charlie Griffin has a lot to answer for."

At Priory Farm, the outlying homestead of the village of Mauthen Barbary, they were directed into a field by a policeman unimpressed by the fact that the Casses were not transient pilgrims but bona-fide residents on their way to their country home, Forge Cottage, on the Green.

"Sorry, sir. My orders are that all vehicular traffic into the village is banned until after midnight tomorrow."

"Then may I please have a word with whoever gave you your orders?"

"Certainly, sir," returned the police officer. "Only thing— he's back at Headquarters. Thirty-seven and a half miles. Now may I ask you, sir, either park your vehicle as requested, or else reverse in the turning space provided. You're keeping others waiting."

Philip played his last card.

"Where's P. C. White?"

The stolid Norfolk face broke into a grin.

"Oh, he's off to Norwich, the lucky so-and-so. You don't think they'd be daft enough to leave the local copper on the job on a day like this?"

"Never mind, darling. At least we're here," Joanna said soothingly as they bumped over the grass towards a white-coated figure beckoning in the distance.

"Where's here? How are we going to get that half-ton of household goods in the boot up the Green? It's a five-mile hike just to get back to the road."

"Don't exaggerate. There's a gate through to the further

field, and from there you can get into Back Lane and home in no time. Rachel and I often walk this way."

"Thank heaven for small mercies." Philip backed the car into the space indicated by Bert Gamlin, the dairyman at Priory Farm, resolutely turning off the ignition and paying no attention to the man's repeated admonition: "Back a bit more, bor! Back a bit more!"

"When you take a bagging hook to those brambles in the hedge I'll go back as far as you like," he stated calmly when Bert, aggrieved, appeared at the driver's window. "Not until. Packing them in a bit, aren't you?"

"Five pun a coach, two-fifty a caravan or dormobile, an' a pun a car," answered Bert, his face alight with happy disbelief. "Beats sugar-beet any day."

"If you park 'em any closer people won't have room to get their hands into their pockets to get their money out. You don't mean to say you're going to have the gall to charge me a pound for leaving my car here when I've no blessed choice in the matter?"

"Guvner did say it were on'y strangers—" the man sounded doubtful.

"And as we've only been at Forge Cottage for going on five years," Philip finished for him, "you're not sure that we really qualify as in-people. This is Norfolk all right! Twenty-five years before anyone says good morning and another twenty-five to say good night!"

The farm-hand leaned his arm on the window-frame and winked across at Joanna.

"'E allus go on like that?"

"Bert," said Joanna, favouring the man with a dazzling smile, "could you be a angel and organise those young rascals of yours to bring the stuff in the boot up to the Forge? Tell them there's 50p in it for each of them, and an extra twenty if they don't break anything."

Bert hesitated.

"Young Jack's in, last I seen 'm, but I doubt 'e'll come for 50p. No offence meant, but the competition today's something fierce. 'E's already made 'isself twenty-five bob setting out litter baskets along the High Street and down on the Rond. Young Willie's got a load of papers Miss Massingham give 'im to give away outside the Shrine. Two pounds she's paying 'im— half in advance, half when they're all gone, jest to make sure 'e don't go an' chuck the lot in the river when 'er back's turned."

e let out a whoop of laughter. "She don't know young Willie!
'ha's the betting 'e's flogging the ruddy things to the trippers
2p a go?"

The chill was all but palpable as Joanna Cass said: "I
rtainly couldn't hope to compete with Miss Massingham."

"Tell yer what," said the farm-hand. "Leave yer boot
locked. I'm due for my tea in ten minutes. Soon as I get in
l send young Jack over. If 'e's gone out, 'is Ma'll know where
find 'im. Thinks the world of you, 'is Ma does—"

As if embarrassed by the revelation, he moved away towards
e car next in line, bellowing ferociously as he went. "What
u want, bor, the whole bloody field to park in? Move 'er out
ain an' come in closer. Closer!"

## 2

igh above Back Lane a lark was singing. Bees swerved
urposefully about their business. Ancient oaks, wrapped in
y like old women in their shawls, punctuated the earthen
ack with grateful intervals of shade. Somewhere a calf gave
oice and was comforted by the melodious lowing of its
other.

"You see," said Joanna, tilting her face to the sun. "It hasn't
hanged. It's just the same as it always was."

Philip Cass put his arm round his wife's waist.

"Don't kid yourself, old girl. It's changed. But don't get the
ind up. I'm not putting Forge Cottage on the agents' books.
ot yet, anyway."

He looked about him appreciatively.

"What's more, I'm willing to admit that, after five years of it,
orfolk has grown on me. It's on the same scale I am. No
iagaras, no hills higher than hills in decency ought to be.
oderation in all things." He frowned, and began to kick along
pebble he found in the road. "Which, I suppose, is basically
hy I'm so against the Lady. She no more fits into a Norfolk
illage than a mountain would. The trouble is, if you live in
authen Barbary, it's a mountain you're compelled to climb,
ke it or not."

Joanna stopped looking upward and bent her gaze thought-
lly on the fragment of flint at her husband's foot.

"But if she worked a miracle and I bore you a child, wou
that make you change your mind about her?"

Philip Cass kissed his wife with passion and exasperatio

"How many times do I have to tell you? How can o
possible wish for more when one already has everything"

They found Paul Falkener stretched out full length in the fro
garden of Forge Cottage. He was a big man and it was a sm.
garden.

"Take your ruddy great fetlocks out of my delphiniums," sa
Philip, by way of greeting.

The man sat up smiling, then got to his feet; a noble figu
with a breadth of shoulder, a neatness of hip, that would ha
looked more suitably accommodated on an Attic vase than
the torn shirt and jeans that in fact covered them. His hair w
bronze, leonine; his beard bushy and strong. A red cotte
handkerchief, patterned with white, was knotted loose
round his massive neck. His feet were bare.

Philip Cass looked his visitor over with an admiratie
seasoned with a spice of mischief.

"When they made you and Augustus John," he announce
"they threw away the mould."

Paul Falkener laughed, a handsome man who could afford
take a joke. "Some host!" he exclaimed. "You ask me over for
drink and you're hours late."

"Yes, we're late, and I don't remember asking you over fe
any such thing. Did you, Joanna?"

Joanna shook her head.

"Just as I thought. He's making it up. Anything to cadg
some booze."

"I am not making it up," Paul Falkener stated with unruffle
humour, "and I've already helped myself to the booze, than
you very much. Don't bother finding the key, Joanna—" h
looked across to where she stood at the cottage door, rumma
ing in her handbag—"Rachel must have forgotten to lock it
He turned to Philip. "Can't say I think much of that ne
Scotch you've got in. The Glenlivet was in a different clas
altogether. And you really ought to speak to Rachel," h
finished virtuously. "All these outsiders milling about, yo
never know who might get in."

"Come indoors, you clown," said Philip. "I've still got
bottle of the Glenlivet where I bet even you couldn't put you
hands on it."

\* \* \*

'orge Cottage was a pleasant place: brick and flint without,
nd within, downstairs, a long, low room that served as
itchen, dining, living room all in one. French windows gave
n to a rear garden which, apart from an immaculate vegetable
atch, stretched weedy and inviting to a plantation of Corsican
ines bounded by Back Lane. In front, across a narrow
arriageway, was the village pond, resort of a pair of swans.
Beyond, the Green heaved itself into a grass-covered mound
vhich some said was an ancient barrow and others, less
omantic, the spoil left behind by the Irish navvies of Queen
'ictoria's day. They had built along the south side of the Green
he fine road which, by taking all the through traffic thereafter,
ad confirmed Forge Cottage and its neighbours, Maypole
Cottage and the row of almshouses endowed in the sixteenth
entury by Sir Amyas Griffin, in their blissful quietude.

The mound acted as a baffle, so that as the two men sat
omfortably over their drinks, only a barely perceptible
usurration reminded them of the crowds on the further side of
he Green.

"No ice-cream chimes?" Philip remarked. "Somebody's
nissed an opportunity."

"Don't you believe it. Rachel's got Neil Woodgate down
here with a stand, doing a roaring trade. Hot dogs too. She
lidn't see why the Shrine shouldn't get the money instead of
ome commercial firm. She's right on the ball, that little sister
of yours."

"I'm beginning to think I must ask for an introduction. She
loesn't sound like anybody I know."

"You've no idea! She wangled a freezer out of old Beslow,
nd you know what he's like—wouldn't give you the skin on a
ausage if he could figure out some way to keep the damn thing
rom falling apart without it—and she got Len Foulcher, who
vorks for the Electricity Board, to borrow miles of cable so
hey could plug it in back at the Hospice. I think she even
talked some firm in Lynn into donating the ice-cream."

Philip commented drily: "No doubt promised them their
reward in Heaven."

Falkener got up from his chair and padded across to the
french window. The rush matting that overlaid the old quarry
tiles moved sibilantly under his bare feet. He stood for a

moment looking out at the garden, his bulk perceptibl
diminishing the amount of light in the room.

Then he said quietly: "You oughtn't to go on like tha
Rachel's a saint, do you know that? A saint."

Philip Cass put down his glass as though its contents wer
suddenly not to his taste.

"You mean you couldn't get her to hop into bed with you?"

At that the man at the window wheeled round.

"You certainly do need an introduction! My God, Cas
you're a bastard! You've got it in so bad for the Lady you can
see straight. You certainly can't see Rachel. You can't recognis
marvellous, unadulterated goodness when it's stuck rigl
under your bloody nose."

"I'm responsible for Rachel. I'm all she's got."

"All she's got!" Paul Falkener repeated. "Brother, hov
wrong can you get? Let me tell you, Rachel's got more tha
you'll ever have if you live to be a thousand. And believe me
you don't have to feel responsible for her any longer. She's free
white and eighteen and she's the most responsible person
expect to meet in my whole misguided life."

"Amazing," Philip Cass commented, light of tone bu
without humour, "how powerful the Lady is. She wins over th
unlikeliest prospects." He rose from his chair in his turn. Th
two stood confronting each other, a confrontation not withou
its element of the ridiculous. Cass was a good six inches th
shorter of the two, and the light from the window, falling fu'
on his round schoolboy countenance, only emphasised that hi
was not a face intended for scenes. "Who could hav
prophesied that Paul Falkener, that personification of the *vi
de Bohème*, would fall so completely under her spell?"

"I'm here to do a job of work—it's as simple as that. Just sto
badgering Rachel, that's all."

"If it's badgering to use whatever influence I may possess te
wean her away from an unhealthy cult, then, whether I have
your approval or not, I shall go on badgering."

"Unhealthy cult!" cried Falkener, throwing out his arms
"Know what, Cass? You're sick. You need help. There's a nam
for what you feel about your sister, only I won't mention it."

"And exactly what do you mean by that?"

"Are you two quarrelling again?" asked Joanna, comin
down the stairs. She had changed into jeans and blouse and
looked prettier, and younger, than ever, if a trifle pale. She had
pulled her hair back from her face and tied it with a red

ribbon. She held in her hand a sheet of notepaper which she thrust into a pocket, and she spoke almost absently.

"I wouldn't say quarrelling," answered her husband, his tone instantly lightening, as if the presence of his wife were of itself enough to provide solutions. "Paul's just accused me of harbouring an incestuous love for Rachel, that's all."

"What a relief! I was afraid he'd been accusing me of an unnatural passion for Oscar. He's outside banging on the gate with his beak and hissing for his bread. Until Jack brings the groceries no one's going to get out of the door, so it's no use showing it to Paul. Come to that, how's Jack going to get in?"

The question was answered by a sudden piercing cacophony, amid which only the anguished protest of an unoiled wheelbarrow was immediately identifiable. In another moment young Jack Gamlin, unscathed and imperturbable, was at the door with the groceries.

"Give him a pound, dear," said Joanna. "Conduct beyond the call of duty." She looked on in unfeigned admiration as the boy, a small edition of Bert, unloaded his cargo on to the doormat. "However did you get past Oscar?"

"Give 'im my Injun war-cry an' kicked 'im up the arse-'ole."

Joanna looked across to where Paul Falkener stood, still by the window.

"What somebody ought to do to you, Paul," she said. "You drink too much. One of these days you'll say something you'll really be sorry for."

"I suppose I asked for it. I shouldn't have accused him of trying to make it with Rachel," Philip said later, leaning over the garden gate—a posture without risk once Joanna had given the swan his bread. The bird, with an air of having conferred, rather than received, a favour, had waddled with aldermanic deliberation over the road and back to the pond verge, where he sat disposed in an elegant bundle, head coiled away under a wing, apparently absorbed in transcendental meditation or the processes of digestion.

Joanna eyed him with a certain anxiety.

"I can't help feeling that flabby sliced stuff is bad for him. But he won't touch wholemeal."

"Spoiled by the *dolce vita*, like the rest of us. He doesn't deserve anything. Look what he's done to the gate." After a moment Philip resumed: "I believe Paul was telling the truth don't you? About him and Rachel, I mean."

Joanna regarded her husband with kindness, but her voice held a hint of impatience. Her face had not lost its pallor, its air of abstraction.

"Of course he was! But it wouldn't make any difference what you two were on about. You always find some excuse for starting a row."

"We do, don't we?" Philip sounded as though he had just that minute made the discovery, and was not displeased by it. "Do you think it's because I'm jealous he's so beautiful and I'm such a little runt?"

"That's probably it."

"Also because he spends his time playing at being an artist while I have to waste the best years of my life making ball-bearings."

"That too," Joanna conceded. "Except you might bear in mind that ball-bearings stop friction, which must make them a good thing, while Paul, artist though he may be, is a dismally fifth-rate one."

"He is, isn't he?" Philip grinned. "Poor bugger. It's a great comfort. I haven't been vouchsafed a preview of the master-work that's to be unveiled tomorrow, but if those panels in the Shrine are anything to go by—"

"Sub-William Morris with a dash of Winnie the Pooh." Joanna's tone was that of the uncompromising professional.

"Meow!" said Philip, and nibbled her ear. "Charlie should have given you the job."

"No thanks! I'll stick to my wallpaper designing. I know my limitations. But it's funny—" Joanna looked out over the Green—"at St. Martin's, all those years ago, he won all the prizes. He was going to be the new Michelangelo."

"What went wrong?"

"I don't think anything, particularly. I suppose everyone has only so much talent, or genius—and, as things have turned out, Paul's ration hasn't stretched very far. Some of his early things—" She stopped.

"Good, were they? Personally, I've never seen anything of his I'd give a fiver for. What happened to the others?"

"Sold them, I suppose." She seemed to have lost interest in the subject. "Charlie mentioned something about having seen something of his in a gallery up in town, and that was what made him decide to give him the commission—"

"Coincidence, wasn't it, Charlie picking out one of your old playmates?"

Joanna moved away a little to study an insect deep in a delphinium floweret.

"Not all that much of one. There aren't all that many people working in wood. But Charlie reminds me—" she looked at her husband, not wholly at ease—"I promised him last week we'd go over to the Manor this evening."

"You did what!" Philip Cass made no pretence of being pleased. "I thought we took this place to get away from the social grind. And for God's sake, Charlie of all people!"

"He's a lonely old man, Philip."

"Lonely my foot! He's a tiresome old busybody who's having the time of his life playing havoc with the life-style of a rural community."

"That isn't the way he sees it. From his point of view he's restoring Mauthen Barbary to what it used to be."

"Used to be when, for Pete's sake? Things have moved on a bit since Henry the Eighth was king of England."

Over the rounded crest of the Green a second swan appeared, its whiteness tipped gold by the late afternoon sun. It was Nellie, Oscar's mate.

Philip Cass's ill-temper, never deep-rooted, dissolved in delighted recognition.

"I've been wondering who she reminded me of! Look at that paunch, practically scraping the ground. Charlie to the life!"

Nellie gained the water and launched herself upon it with what seemed to her two observers something close to a sigh of relief. Her cargo buoyed, she sailed rapidly across the pond to where Oscar remained lost to the world. She allowed herself to drift alongside, and gave her mate a vicious peck on the back.

The male swan came out of his reverie, neck weaving, head thrust forward in threat. Then he recognised his assailant, flapped his great wings with a mighty to-do, and promptly folded them out of harm's way. The two moved off amicably side by side.

Philip Cass lifted his wife's heavy hair and kissed the nape of her neck.

"I'm sure there's a moral in that somewhere. I too have made my token demonstration. Now I can give in without loss of face. Charlie it is, warm Martinis and all. I'll even take him a bottle of that new whisky, and I hope it corrodes his ancient guts."

His wife turned towards him with an intensity of love that, as always, while every fibre in his body responded to it, dismayed him a little, so little did he feel deserving of it. But all she said was:

"I'll go inside and put the kettle on."

Philip followed her up the flagged path.

"Is that honestly the best you can think of doing, inside?"

Later, much later, as, aglow with the warmth of love given and received, they sat at the refectory table eating a healthful country tea whose ingredients had been purchased a stone's throw from Oxford Street, Philip conceded: "I suppose he's not such a bad old bastard *au fond*—and what a *fond*! Wasn't it Chaucer's Clerk of Oxenford who was lean as a rake? At Cambridge, have you noticed, they run to bellies and buttocks. Must be the layers of blubber they're forced to develop to survive the East Anglian winter."

"How many Cambridge dons do you know?" Joanna giggled. "And it's donkey's years since Charlie was there. Really, darling—"taking advantage of his mood—"you have to be reasonable. It isn't as if he set out deliberately to find the Lady. You might as well blame Chloe for getting trapped in that badger sett."

"What makes you think I don't, the silly bitch? I *don't* blame Charlie for finding the damn thing. If you're out with your half-wit dog and it goes down a hole and hasn't the sense to get itself out again, you've got to start digging. I accept that. What I'll never forgive him for is that having once uncovered the Lady and taken a good look at her, he didn't shovel the earth back PDQ and never let on to a living soul what he'd stumbled on."

"That's nonsense," she protested. "It was a marvellous discovery. How could anyone have done that?"

"*I* could," Philip asserted grimly. "I only wish I'd had the chance. Ah well! At least, with luck, we'll see Rachel over at the Manor."

"Afraid not," said Joanna. "She left a note. Upstairs on the dressing-table. She's going to be busy till late and doesn't know what time she'll be in. She's got her key and we're not to wait up for her."

"Can I see it?"

"I put it down somewhere. It was just a hurried scrawl. Mostly about the eggs and milk in the fridge, and not being able to get any cream."

Philip Cass poured himself another cup. The pleasant room,

grown shadowy as the sun moved down the sky, helped to reinforce a natural optimism.

"At least she intends coming in some time. That's something. I was afraid she'd have some crackpot idea about keeping vigil, or some such nonsense."

"After the kind of day she must be having I'm sure she realises she'll need her sleep if she's to be fit for anything tomorrow. You know how she needs her eight hours."

Philip commented with affection: "She's just a kid. D'you know what Falkener called her?—A saint. I don't know that I approve of saints in the family. Or anywhere else. There isn't one in the whole martyrology that wasn't more trouble than he was worth."

"Trust Paul to be theatrical." When Joanna spoke again it was with some uncertainty, almost as if she regretted her words even as she uttered them. "I know what he means, though. In the past few weeks there's been something—a light, an inner illumination. Sometimes her face—it looks transfigured—"

"Every time there's a pop festival on the telly you can see thousands of young girls looking precisely the same." Philip's tone was robustly unsympathetic. "I'll tell you one thing. I won't have *you* worried because my impressionable young sister happens to be going through a religious phase, and, through no fault of our own, we've provided her with an outlet for her fantasies bang on our own doorstep."

"I'm not worried."

"You don't think *I'm* too concerned? Ought I to see a psychoanalyst? Paul's put me on the defensive."

"Don't be silly."

"Thinking it over, I'm glad you said we'd go the Charlie's. You know what the conversation will be—Lady, Lady, Lady from the moment we step in at the door till the moment we say good night. Well, good!"

He got up from the table.

"I was cracked to imagine you could get away from her in Mauthen Barbary this weekend. So OK. Let's go to the other extreme. Immerse ourselves. Find out what makes Our Lady of Promise tick—"

"If you can't fight her, join her. Is that it?"

"I'll join. But who says I can't fight?"

# 3

Along the High Street and the south side of the Green, down to the Shrine and the Rond across the road from it, the pilgrims flowed in a gentle, never-ending stream. Nobody was in a hurry. Buyers waited patiently for their turn at the revolving stands of postcards which Mrs. Crowe, the post-mistress, had cannily set up outside the post-office. The goods in the window at Watlington's—Groceries & Provisions, estab. 1847—were scrutinised with a leisurely conscientiousness by all who passed by on that side of the street. The fully clothed plaster pig with which, at closing time, Mr. Beslow the butcher replaced his trays of meat, came in for considerable comment, and would doubtless have come in for more had the strangers been in a position to know how closely it resembled Mr. Beslow.

The visitors, it was clear, were in a mood to admire everything. Not that Mauthen Barbary was a difficult place about which to find something pleasant to say. Colour photographs of the Market Cross, the houses in the High Street, and that fine old coaching inn, The Barbary Pirate, graced many a *Come to Britain* brochure.

It was a village all of one piece—which was to say it consisted of a miscellaneous collection of buildings, scarcely one of which, by a stroke of luck, had gone up later than 1850. There *was* a small council estate hidden away like a secret sin in a cul-de-sac behind Back Lane; but as it was, in fact, a few yards outside the parish boundary, not even the families who lived there had the cheek to claim Mauthen Barbary as their address.

When The Barbary Pirate opened for business there was no great rush of custom. The locals had stayed away, fearing an alien invasion, but the pilgrims appeared to be in little need of strong liquor.

It was a crowd which differed in marked ways from the typical gathering to be expected upon an English religious occasion. Not a single elderly person was to be seen; nor was there the usual preponderance of women. Instead, the throng consisted of couples, a good many of them black, almost all of

14

them in their twenties or early thirties. The young women eyed each other shyly. The young men were attentive and loving.

The only exceptions to this general pairing were two groups of unaccompanied women; one, West Indian, dressed all alike in long white dresses with wide sleeves, and white veils covering their heads, marching along under a banner inscribed, BRIXTON BAND OF HOPEFULS: the other a phalanx of earnest females who had taken up positions on the steps of the Market Cross beneath an enormous blow-up of a stick-limbed, swollen-bellied child, captioned in blood-red capitals: AREN'T THERE ENOUGH ALREADY? THINK IT OVER.

The young people applauded the passage of the white-robed Brixtonians. They went by the women at the Market Cross as if they were not there.

Willie Gamlin nevertheless did well with his stack of leaflets. In that assemblage above all others a child was assured of a friendly reception, and while Willie did not actually assert that he was selling the official programme of the weekend's arrangements, he did not actually say he was not. When his customers discovered what they had bought for their two pence they crumpled the leaflets without anger and disposed of them in the nearest litter basket. Thus did one young Gamlin's work unwittingly complement the other's.

A little past the Market Cross, where the hillock of the Green divided the new road from the old, the pseudo-Tudor chimneys of the Hospice contorted themselves skyward. It must have been a dreary abode even in its heyday when it had served as Mauthen Barbary vicarage, with curtains of Nottingham lace at the windows and an army of maids to service its insatiable grates. As architecture it had recently come back into fashion. It had its devotees, not one of whom would have risked a night under its cheerless roof.

Certainly, as lodging for the pilgrims, the house was a total loss. Those who, applying early, had counted themselves fortunate to be assigned a bed there, looked thoughtful before they were well past the laurels that lined the drive to the front door, and emerged weighing the feasibility of sleeping in the car.

All Rachel's skills had been unable to turn the spartan dormitories, with their rows of camp beds, into the bowers of Eros which the circumstances plainly called for. If the pilgrims knew anything at all, they knew that in Mauthen Barbary of all places, on that night of all nights, a man and his woman needed to lie together. Even to book in at one of the hotels five miles away on the coast was chancy, for who could say how far round the village the magic circle extended? Time alone would show whether the Lady's promise was something that could be carried home like a rose picked in bud, to open far from its parent bush. The crowd flowed past the Hospice, down the road to the Rond, in hopes of finding accommodation more suited to the occasion.

There, a good many had better luck. The girl who couldn't organise a game of tiddlywinks had, it appeared, contrived to get the army at her beck and call; sweating men in black berets who still, as the day drew towards evening, laboured cheerfully to erect tents of camouflage material wherever, in the already congested meadow, they could find space to support yet another one.

There was an endearing amateurishness about the allocation of these makeshift sleeping quarters. Hand in hand, couples went from tent to tent, lifting the door flaps with many pleasantries, until they found one that was unoccupied. Those who were unsuccessful made no undue fuss about it. The sun shone, the little river ran glinting between willows, the air was full of the bruised sweetness of wild parsley. Being townspeople for the most part, they thought well of the prospect of sleeping out in the open, embraced beneath the stars. They gave no thought to the mists which, when dusk fell, would rise from the river, the dews that would drop out of the darkening sky. They queued merrily for ice-creams and frankfurters; took the unlikely mixture down to the river bank where they took off their sandals and sat eating, their feet dangling in the water.

The Rond was a triangular piece of land, bounded along one of its sides by the Maut, along a second by the wall enclosing the Manor grounds, and along the third by the road. On the opposite side of the road stood the Shrine, a large construction of pantiled flint which a casual glance might easily have taken for another of those fortress-like Norfolk barns capacious enough to house the corn of the seven years of plenty with room to spare.

No outward sign disclosed the building's special function: no cross on the roof peak, no statue above the porch; not even one of those notice boards whereon houses of worship are wont to advertise their services. Only, along one side, an unobtrusive colonnade or cloister, built of brick and opening upon a lawn pierced here and there by jagged encrustations of masonry like the molars of some primeval monster, hinted at something vaguely ecclesiastical.

The masonry was all that remained of the Priory and the original shrine, a process of dissolution begun in 1539 and continued thereafter whenever anyone in Mauthen Barbary had need of building stone. The ladies from Brixton had appropriated one of the flatter segments of this residue to serve as a picnic table, setting out on it their packets of sandwiches and tins of coke. White teeth flashing in the sun, they bit into their sandwiches with an enjoyment it was a pleasure to behold. Other pilgrims, stretched out on the grass, watched them with admiration, their own self-confidence bolstered by the reflection that even such splendid creatures as these had need of the Lady's good offices.

Barnabas, the Guardian of the Shrine, a barrel-chested man in a friar's habit, with a shock of grey hair and a cheerful, rugged face, had shut and locked the Shrine door at seven, explaining apologetically to any within earshot that there were preparations to be made which rendered it necessary to break the rule that the Lady must be accessible twenty-four hours a day. Few professed themselves inconvenienced. Like children who reserve the best sweet for last, they were keeping the Lady for the morrow, her birthday, the fifth anniversary of her resurrection and, for that very reason, a day of power. To approach her in advance of that meridian, or, alternatively, to nag her twice over, was as impolite as it was patently impolitic.

"My understanding," Charles Griffin was saying, as Anguish, his manservant, ushered the Casses through the Great Hall and out on to the terrace, "is that Barnabas is shutting the Shrine early. Which means the others shouldn't be long."

He moved with pleasure to greet the new arrivals, propelling his low-slung bulk, clothed in a shantung suit of antique cut, in a way that reminded Philip and Joanna anew of Nellie dragging herself down the slope to the pond. The feelings of guilt the image engendered increased proportionately the warmth of their salutations. Philip presented his bottle. Joanna brushed her lips against the old man's cheek.

"My dear child!" he responded, evidently touched. "I can't tell you how happy I am to see you. Both of you, though—" smiling at Philip—"I ought, I suppose, to fear the Greeks, even when they come bearing gifts." He handed the bottle to Anguish, and turning again to Joanna, cradled her hand between his own two, splotched with the rust-stains of age. "I was so afraid this brute husband of yours would keep you in town."

'I never can resist a party," Philip protested easily. "I hope Anguish has baked a cake with five candles on it."

"Five!" exclaimed a voice with an American intonation. "I've just this minute been complaining to Mr. Griffin about that very thing. I guess you couldn't bake a cake big enough to carry the candles, one for every year of the Lady's true age."

Charles Griffin said: "I don't believe you've met Professor and Mrs. Diefenhaus, from the University of Navaho, California." The Americans, rangy and distinguished-looking, rose from their chairs and shook hands enthusiastically.

"Perhaps I should warn you," Griffin went on, "they've come from Walsingham, about which the Professor, who, I may mention in passing, is probably the greatest living authority in the United States on medieval cults of the Virgin, has written a distinguished monograph."

The Professor waved away the compliment with a deprecatory gesture. His wife said comfortably: "Eliot's specialty certainly gets us to visit some gorgeous places." She gazed about her with the appreciation of the dedicated sightseer: at the great south front of the Manor with its turrets and pinnacles, atop which heraldic beasts gazed out arrogantly upon the countryside; at the terrace that ran the length of the house, stone-balustered save where a flight of time-worn steps descended between banks of rosemary to a parkland dotted with sheep. Endearing herself to Joanna, she announced: "I never realised Norfolk was so beautiful."

"And out of the whole of England," appended the Professor, "to boast, in this day and age, in a Protestant country what's more, not just one but two shrines dedicated to the Virgin! It's truly amazing!"

Philip took the drink proffered by Anguish, sipped gingerly and found it all he had feared.

"Nothing amazing about it," he countered, "if you know your Norfolk. The very county motto is 'Do Different.' And different is what Norfolk people invariably do. Everyone born within the county boundaries has a built-in gene that makes him—or her—" he grinned at Joanna, "automatically, unavoidably contrary. You can't blame them for it. It's their karma, the East Anglian version of kismet."

Charles Griffin chuckled.

"He's not entirely wrong, the rascal! The tradition of dissent in Norfolk is very deep-rooted. In the Middle Ages, when the English Church acknowledged the Pope as its head, Norfolk was a hotbed of Lollardry. But after the Reformation were the natives any more satisfied? Not a bit of it! They became Puritans, Levellers, Fifth Monarchy Men, anything that differed from what, in the context of the time, happened to be the Establishment. And so today, when it has become perfectly respectable for bishops to publish books which throw doubt on the very existence of the Deity, Norfolk, true to form, moves in the opposite direction—towards Walsingham, towards Mauthen Barbary. As you say, Philip—incorrigibly contrary."

At that moment Anguish, who had disappeared in response to some summons audible to him alone, returned with another guest, a young man with an inbuilt air of discouragement. In clerical grey with dog collar, the Reverend Lionel Persimmer, vicar of St. Blaise's, the parish church of Mauthen Barbary, seemed to be finding the weather trying. Sweat beaded his forehead and glistened on his thin nose.

He had come from the Rond, he explained, as if he felt some explanation called for; and the crowds! He wiped his face with a crumpled handkerchief and accepted a drink as if it were an insult he was doomed to swallow.

"I know," Mrs. Diefenhaus sympathised. She was a kind person who felt under an obligation to put people at their ease. "Eliot and I were down there just a while ago. But it is kind of consciousness-raising, don't you think?"

"You mustn't expect Lionel to look at it the way you do," Charles Griffin interposed with a touch of elderly spite. The living was in his gift and it offended his self-love to have picked a loser. "Like Philip, our good vicar disapproves of everything to do with the Lady."

Persimmer drained his glass and proclaimed loudly: "A heathen travesty!"

Professor Diefenhaus was plainly shocked by the intemperate ejaculation.

"I'm an Episcopalian myself," he declared in resonant tones. "I mention that, sir, simply to make it clear that I have no personal spiritual axe to grind. And I'm not speaking as a medievalist either, although of course Mr. Griffin's discovery—or should I call it rediscovery?—of the Lady of Promise ranks as just about the most exciting find in that field this century.

I'm no art critic either. Alice here will testify to that. If I take exception to what you say, sir, and, I have to say it, I do take exception—it's simply as a guy who finds that ancient hunk of tree one of the most eloquent and poignant symbols he's ever laid eyes on."

"Yes," breathed Joanna. "That's it exactly."

Presently, at Griffin's suggestion, since the contingent from the Shrine had still not put in an appearance, the party descended the stone steps and walked across the park to visit the copse where the Lady had lain in hiding for more than four hundred years. They walked slowly, accommodating themselves to the pace of their host, and to the slow, sweet ending of the day.

They spoke little. Even Mr. Persimmer looked as if life might have a brighter side. The fractiousness went out of his face, and one could see, in the fine-drawn features, something of what Charles Griffin had hoped for from him.

As they reached the clump of trees for which they were making, Chloe, a large dog of indeterminate pedigree, came bounding over the grass. She nudged her skull into Griffin's hips in an ecstasy of greeting that all but toppled him. Carefully readjusting the balance of his belly upon his inadequate legs, he explained fondly: "Getting her picture in the papers has gone to her head. She never allows me to show off the grotto without her."

Philip pricked up his ears.

"Grotto? You haven't gone and dreamed up a second Lourdes or something?"

"No, no. A foolish word to choose. I've had the brambles cut back, that's all, and a load of pebbles put down to discourage the weeds. I've kept it very simple."

"The way you've done the Shrine," Professor Diefenhaus commented approvingly. "It's one of the things that particularly impressed us—its utter austerity. Would you say, Mr. Griffin, it's a case of that Norfolk puritanism you spoke of, making its influence felt?"

"No, I would not!" Griffin replied, a little tartly. "It was money pure and simple—or rather, the lack of it. If I had my way—which is to say, if I had the money—I'd cover the Shrine with gold leaf, the way it used to be in the old days."

"I think," Alice Diefenhaus said firmly, "I prefer it the way it is."

"That's because you haven't visualised how it used to be, and now it could be again." Griffin spoke with an unaccustomed intensity. "The place was a blaze of gems and precious metals. A traveller who was there in Richard the Third's time wrote that he had to shield his eyes from the glare. Poetic overstatement undoubtedly, but just imagine it!"

Joanna said: "The Lady never needed all that."

"No, indeed. But how it must have set her off! Why, Henry the Eighth alone, when he came here with Jane Seymour, brought a life-size effigy of the Holy Infant in solid gold!"

Philip whistled.

"Quite a gift! What happened to it after the place was pulled down?"

"Melted down, I expect. Unless the Professor has some specific information?"

Professor Diefenhaus shook his head.

"As of now I've done very little work in depth on Mauthen Barbary. That's why, at your kind invitation, I'm here at this moment, to puruse the contents of your Muniment Room. But may I ask, sir—" excitement sharpening his tone—"seeing they buried the Lady right here on the Manor lands—may I inquire if you've ever thought of having someone go over this whole acreage with a metal detector?"

"A metal detector?" The old man came to a halt in the middle of the grassy ride that had been cut into the heart of the wood. "It seems a queer way to go seeking the Son of God. To say nothing of the fact that it would be a complete waste of time."

"With all respect, sir, how can you be so sure? The outlay involved would be picayune compared with the value of the Infant itself, should it be found."

"Which it never will." Griffin chuckled. "Once you've found your way about my archives, Professor, you'll understand why I'm so certain none of the plunder from the Shrine lies here. You said 'they' buried the Lady. Now, who do you think those mysterious 'they' were?"

"Why surely," said the Professor, "those who held to the old faith. The devotees who couldn't bear to have their madonna destroyed."

"That's the accepted story," Griffin agreed, "but I'm quite sure it isn't the true one. I myself am quite satisfied Our Lady of Promise was buried some fifty yards from where we are standing by that notorious scoundrel and my esteemed ancestor, Sir Amyas Griffin."

At that, even Lionel Persimmer was moved to take part in the conversation.

"But Sir Amyas Griffin was the royal commissioner charged with the despoliation of the Shrine!"

"Precisely! The person in the best position to do it. Consider the evidence. We know that in July, 1538, the Lady of Walsingham was burnt at Chelsea. The government wanted to give the event maximum publicity, and so they brought the image up to London where the greatest number of people could watch her go up in smoke. Blasphemy not only done but seen to be done. Exactly the same end was planned for Our Lady of Promise. But what happens?"

Happy in the telling of his story, Griffin regarded his little audience with an eagerness that invited them to share his enthusiasm.

"When Sir Amyas arrives in Mauthen Barbary what does he find? That the zealots of the community have been at work ahead of him; that they have already dismantled the Shrine roof and made a bonfire of the beams, a holocaust into which they have cast the sacred image for good measure. I have a letter—that is, a copy: the original, obviously, was sent off to London—a letter from Sir Amyas to Thomas Cromwell, Henry's chief minister, in which Sir Amyas describes graphically how, when he rode into the village, he found the fire still burning, and how he ordered his men to rake the image out of the flames using long iron hooks. But alas, he concludes, it was too far gone and fell away to ashes." He looked round expectantly. "Now, what do you make of that?"

The Professor was the first to respond.

"To me, knowing what we now know, it sounds like a plausible cover story to safeguard his position with the king. In fact, the Lady must have been spirited away before the royal party even turned up."

Philip remarked, in deplorable taste: "In other words, the bird had flown."

Charles Griffin clacked his false teeth, an indication he was not amused.

"Hardly flown. To move the Lady, as we ourselves discovered in our turn, called for heavy tackle and the effort of a number of strong men. Still—" returning to his theme—"we can agree, can we not, that Sir Amyas, in his letter to Cromwell, was lying; though not, I suggest, in quite the way that the Professor has indicated. As it happens, I have just this past week uncovered some manuscripts that look promising. Literally uncovered: they were in an alcove that had been bricked up some two hundred years ago when a staircase to the west wing was realigned. One item consists of a quantity of odds and ends of parchment crudely stitched together to form what I can best describe as a temporary account book wherein Sir Amyas, or more likely his steward, jotted down items of expenditure which at a later date would need to be entered up in a more respectable ledger. Well—" the old man paused, savouring the attention his words had aroused—"one entry in this makeshift record reads as follows: '*Received of John Heydon, pewterer of Lynn, for the lead from off the roof of the Virgin's house, seventeen pounds and nine pence.*'" A longer pause ensued. Then: "You see the implication?"

"The old scoundrel!" cried the Professor, and promptly blushed.

"My dear sir," said Charles Griffin, "no apology is called for. On the subject of Sir Amyas I have no illusions. From that entry it's clear he couldn't have found the beams burning as he wrote, or he couldn't have stripped off the lead."

"Seventeen pounds, nine pence," said the Professor. "That was quite a sum in those days."

"A sum which obviously did not find its way into the royal coffers! The letter, then, more than covered up the non-appearance of the Lady. It explained why the royal commissioner had no lead to send up to London along with the other loot."

Philip put in sharply: "You've made Sir Amyas out a liar and a thief. You've still to prove he actually hid the Lady."

"To do that I need only cite the parish records, which fortunately begin just at this very period. Sir Amyas came to Mauthen Barbary in early August. The only deaths listed during that month were of two old women, a newborn infant, and a man who fell out of a hayloft. If Sir Amyas had really believed that persons in the village had secreted the Lady, there would have been a great many more than that, none of them natural! He would have had the truth if he had to wipe out the entire village to get it." The heavy dewlaps quivered, the hooded eyes brightened with a perverse pride. "He held the royal authority, and he was not the man to let a little thing like a massacre stop him."

Joanna objected: "What I can't see is why he should want to hide her."

"Admittedly it's harder to proceed from 'if' to 'why'—decide what's in a man's mind; even the mind of a man with whom, for all his villainies, I must admit I feel a kinship that bestrides the years which divide us."

Philip laughed.

"My dear Charlie, you're out of your time. Inside that scholarly exterior there's a swashbuckling Tudor adventurer trying to get out."

Charles Griffin liked that.

"My dear boy, I half believe you're right! And besides—" looking about him with complacency—"wouldn't you say I owed the old reprobate a debt of gratitude? If he hadn't concealed the Lady, and let the suspicion fall on the Barbrés, the old lords of this manor, so that Henry dispossessed them and gave their lands to his faithful Sir Amyas, I shouldn't be lording it here today."

Alice Diefenhaus exclaimed: "So that's why you think he did it!"

"I feel sure that was one reason."

"There were others?"

"I think it also likely he had in mind that the Lady Mary, Henry's daughter by Katherine of Aragon, was a Catholic who might yet, one day, come to the throne. In which event, what a passport to royal favour to be in a position to pose as the preserver of the most sacred image in the realm! And so it would have happened, for Mary Tudor did indeed become queen, if he hadn't died the year before her accession. I'm sure that was part of it, too."

Joanna prompted gently: "Was there something more?"

"I do not believe any man of my blood, having once set eyes on the Lady, could do other than defend her, if necessary against the whole world."

# 4

Joanna shivered, and placed her hand on her husband's arm.

"I don't like it, Charlie," she said. "You've turned it into a grave."

"It always was a grave," Charles Griffin returned. "I'll admit that old Randall, being the sexton and used to his way of doing things, may have tidied it up more than was strictly necessary. But this is one of the stopping places tomorrow. I couldn't leave it looking like a place one had dug a dog out of."

Chloe circled the excavation nose to ground, and finding that it no longer offered anything of interest to that sensitive organ, disappeared into the surrounding undergrowth.

"It looks awful," Joanna persisted.

Griffin's mouth set in a sulky line, an ancient child.

"I had Randall fill it with those pine boughs. Very pleasant and aromatic. You women must have everything pretty! It will look quite different when the barberry has had a chance to spread." He pointed to some meagre clumps of a low shrub set among small mounds of pebbles.

"Not the most inviting-looking plant in the world," Diefenhaus remarked. "I shouldn't care to be stuck with one of those spines. But I guess that's the original barberry of Mauthen Barbary."

Lionel Persimmer bent over the bushes with an assumption of expertise which made Griffin go quite pink with annoyance.

"I know it's on the Barbré coat of arms." The vicar straightened up, a tuft of the spiny leaves in his hand. "But I think really it's just one of those punning conceits the College of Arms goes in for. All the time I've been in Mauthen Barbary I've never once seen barberry actually growing."

"I sent for them from Surrey," Charles Griffin growled, then broke into a smile at his own absurdity: really an old man with much to be said for him. He favoured the clergyman with the friendliest glance he had bent on him in many a day. "As you say, a punning conceit, as far-fetched as The Barbary Pirate up the road, with his turban and scimitar." And to Diefenhaus: "There are some who hold that Barbary should, by rights, be Barbari, the barbarians; Norsemen who landed their longboats on the coast and then pushed inland until they came to this valley. The Barbrés, on the other hand, came over with the Conqueror and were here until the bad, bold Griffins supplanted them. As a Griffin, I would be the last to wish to strip them of the sole remaining vestige of their past glory."

"And the Mauthen bit?" asked the Professor.

"That's much easier. In the Norfolk dialect a young girl is a mauther."

"Our mauther of Promise," Philip Cass said lightly, and then, surprised: "Strange how much it sounds like 'mother.'"

"Not at all strange," said Charles Griffin.

\* \* \*

The evening had become at once hushed and noisy. In the foreground, across which the little party moved sedately back towards the house, the lambs had quietened, the birds sung their last song for the day.

From the Rond, on the other hand, at the far end of the Manor grounds, the distant murmur had enlarged itself into laughter, a snatch of song, the twang of a guitar. Sound sharpened in the clear air, freshening towards night.

It served to remind the Reverend Lionel Persimmer.

He said to Philip Cass: "I saw your sister."

"Everybody seems to have seen Rachel except me. What did she have to say for herself?"

"She offered me an ice-cream." Paradoxically, the recollection appeared to make the clergyman feel hot. He fished out his handkerchief and wiped his face. "It was horrible."

"What was wrong with it? I understand it came from a reputable firm in Lynn."

"Not the ice-cream. You're making fun of me, Mr. Cass," Lionel Persimmer said, not without dignity. "Making fun when all I'm trying to do is urge you to get Rachel away from this accursed place—"

Professor Diefenhaus's voice boomed cheerfully over the grass.

"I shall keep working on you to get that metal detector. I'm willing to bet my bottom dollar it will more than pay for itself."

Mr. Griffin, concentrating his attention on placing one foot in front of the other, refused to be drawn.

"Come now, sir!" the Professor persisted. "On your own showing Sir Amyas wasn't the most scrupulous of men. Surely you don't believe he turned all the treasure in the Shrine over to the government?"

"I'm quite sure he didn't. The golden Child, yes—it was, after all, little more than a year since Henry had presented it, and Amyas would have been hard put to it to account for its absence from the inventory. The Lady's jewels, on the other hand, and the precious materials used so lavishly in the decoration of the Shrine—of these I know quite well he helped himself to as much as he felt able to get away with."

"Well, then—"

"Well, then! No metal detector is needed to discover where

they went. They're in plain view!" He pointed a pudgy finger towards the Manor House. "Transformed into bricks and mortar. They paid for pulling down the stone barracks which had served the Barbrés since Norman times, and for the erection of that gingerbread masterpiece in its place. It took all Sir Amyas had—a good deal more than he had. The man died up to his ears in debt. If there'd been any valuables still lying buried in his backyard you may be sure he would have dug them up, if only to get himself out of the hands of the money-lenders." His eyes on the south front of the Manor, rosy as a pippin in the evening light, the old man removed the battered panama which, together with his silk suit, gave him the appearance of a survivor of the British Raj. It was an unconscious salute to the past.

"Sir Amyas and the Lady of Promise. A rogue and—what did you call her, Professor?—a hunk of ancient tree. A strange pair to be indebted to for everything I have." His eyes followed the lines of his house the way a younger man might note the curves of a woman. "When I'm dead the Manor will belong to the Shrine." He replaced his hat, and chuckled. "In the Hall my portrait will hang alongside that of Sir Amyas. What a pair we'll make, eh? But over the road—" the voice became grave, reverential—"I hope the Lady will feel the juxtaposition not inappropriate, and that she will find it in herself to intercede for both our souls."

Anguish had lit the fire in the library. A table along one wall was set out with salads and a lordly salmon on a bed of lettuce. Upon a trolley bright with crystal were trifles and syllabubs. The warmth, the shadows dancing over the walls, made the walkers aware for the first time that they were chilly. It was, after all, barely June.

During their absence, Anguish informed his master, Miss Massingham had called.

"Oh dear!" exclaimed Charles Griffin. "I hope she didn't see these festive preparations. I shouldn't like her to take offence. Miss Massingham," he explained to his American guests, "plays an extraordinarily strong game of bridge. Lionel will bear me out. You fly-by-nights—" he smiled at Philip and Joanna—"have no idea what expedients we who are stuck here week in and week out are reduced to in order to pass the *longueurs* between your visits."

"If you're down to Lydia Massingham," said Joanna, "you certainly are reduced."

"Really, darling," her husband protested, "that's not very neighbourly of you." For the benefit of Professor and Mrs. Diefenhaus he explained that Lydia Massingham lived at The Maypole, next door to Forge Cottage. "She's not a bad old stick, really. Just a teeny, weeny bit Lesbian."

"Butch, I'm told, is the word," Charles Griffin put in with scholarly precision. "The vicar and I, and Dr. Teago who makes up our fourth, find it immensely reassuring, don't we, Lionel? We feel quite safe with one who so obviously has no lewd designs on our virtue. Anguish—you didn't show her in here, I trust?"

Without moving a muscle, Anguish contrived to convey his contempt that such a possibility should even be mooted.

"She remained in the outer hall, sir."

"Excellent!"

"Guessed all the same you were having people in. Asked me to tell you what you can do with your bloody bridge pencils— I'm quoting what Miss Massingham said."

"I'm sure you are. Did she say anything else?"

"Yes, sir. That is, wrote it down, my not having a piece of paper handy, on the back of a leaflet she had with her, telling you where to get an abortion."

"Where is it?"

"It was some address in London, sir. Oh, the note! It inadvertently fell into the fire when I was putting another log on." The man withdrew to the library door, and finished, with a hand on the door-knob: "Far as I remember, it was suggestions about what you could do with the score cards and the playing cards in addition, sir."

When he had gone, Alice Diefenhaus, weak with mirth, asked: "Is his name really Anguish?"

"Indeed it is. A very good name too. One of his forbears was Mayor of Norwich in the seventeenth century. He was my college servant for years, and no one could have served me better." He sighed. "Of course, that was before television."

"Television?"

"It has been Anguish's ruination. All those Forsyte Sagas, full of hierarchies below stairs, have confused him as to which of us is master and which man. It is his consuming grievance that, times being what they are, we have no servants' hall at the Manor. He is the sole domestic residing on the premises."

Alice Diefenhaus remarked matter-of-factly: "I guess if I had to keep a place this size clean without any other help I'd have a bit of a consuming grievance myself."

"Oh, he doesn't have to do that! We employ a regular platoon of village housewives whom he slave-drives abominably."

Professor Diefenhaus asked: "D'you think Miss Massingham really said what he said she did?"

"I suspect she said a good deal more which Anguish suppressed out of consideration for the ladies. Lydia's a liberated woman in every sense of the word. Fortunately, she's not one to harbour a grudge, and she enjoys a rubber as much as the rest of us. Just the same," he finished, "I'm glad she didn't run into the Shrine people as she went down the drive."

The long twilight had yielded to night before "the Shrine people" arrived at Charles Griffin's party. They crowded into the library laughing, only six but seeming more, invigorated by a sense of participating in great events.

They attacked the food provided for them with so much gusto that the others, who had already eaten, rediscovered their appetites and helped themselves afresh. Philip Cass, who had drawn a little apart, made only a token protest before accepting the plate Joanna had piled up for him. As for the Reverend Lionel Persimmer, the access of melancholy occasioned by the new arrivals so stimulated his salivary juices that he bore away from the trolley a bowl of sherry trifle intended to serve eight. Standing on the hearthrug in the posture of one defying the world, he spooned up the delicious mess as if it were some form of ritual challenge—an attitude somewhat deflated when Mrs. Diefenhaus observed kindly: "Oh dear! You've got some on your nice suit," and, getting up from her seat, proceeded to rub away at the offending stain with her napkin.

"Go to the bathroom and put some water on it," she admonished in a motherly way that brooked no denial.

She returned to the sofa where she had been sitting, to find Barnabas, the Guardian of the Shrine, occupying the other half of it, a small table in front of him to support his loaded plate and a glass of water. He had folded back the sleeves of his habit, revealing a gallery of tattoos up either forearm: HMS *Victory* nudging a notably pneumatic mermaid; a Chinese dragon with one scaly paw goosing a Queen Victoria looking far from amused.

Barnabas wielded his knife and fork and remarked, between chews: "Funny, in't it? I could eat beans in a force ten gale and never lose a one, but I'm hanged if I can get the hang of this plate-on-your-knee ploy. I always seem about three arms short."

Mrs. Diefenhaus turned an admiring glance on the tattoos. "You've made pretty good use of the two you have."

"Oh ah!" he laughed. "Now you know why Mr. Griffin has me go round in this here fancy dress. Wouldn't want me run in for porn. Not that I mind the rig as a general rule. But today! If it hasn't been 'Father' it's been 'Brother,' with a couple of 'Your Holinesses' thrown in—for me, the blooming caretaker! Made me feel a right fraud. One chap come up and asked me 'Got a match, mate?' I was so grateful I give him the box."

Charles Griffin leaned back in his chair, looking happy but a little fatigued by the sight of so much eating. His own digestion had long outlived such excesses, his corpulency, apparently, being sustained by the memory of past feasts.

"Barnabas grumbling again? Pay no attention. No one with that pair of arms can tell me he doesn't understand the necessity of dressing up once in a while. Take our two Maidens here—"the old man sketched a little bow towards two girls, dressed in simple blue shifts, who hovered shyly next to a solid woman with white hair stiffly coiffed. "Carol and Marilyn, isn't it?—"

"Jennifer—"the mis-named one whispered.

"Of course. Carol and Jennifer. What could be more *à propos* than those frocks of theirs, blue, the Virgin's colour? And for tomorrow, I'm told, they have some that are even more special."

"Chiffon, full length and very full, edged with silver braid," said the solid woman, who was a widow named Mrs. Chitty, in charge of the Maidens of the Shrine. "Oh, they'll look lovely!"

Philip asked: "Twelve of them, aren't there, in all?" Mrs. Chitty nodded. "Twelve virgins to attend the Virgin. What puzzles me is how you make sure they're what they hold themselves out to be."

"You're embarrassing the girls," Griffin protested. "Our Maidens are volunteers from whom no vow of chastity is demanded. All we ask is that, should they cease to be virgins, they resign. Nothing more."

"Guide's honour, eh? D'you really think a girl's going to advertise her fall from grace—let the whole village into the secret?"

"You don't understand, Mr. Cass," said Jennifer, voice trembling, face fiery red. "It'd never happen. But if it did, we'd never pretend. Not with the Lady we wouldn't."

Carol, equally disturbed, added: "Why don't you ask Rachel?"

"I'd be glad to, if I could get within speaking distance."

Neil Woodgate, a young man who, beyond the first introductions, had contributed nothing to the conversation, being healthily occupied with eating, now interposed, his skin flushing like the girls'.

"She came to the Rond for the ice-cream money. A hundred and thirty-seven pounds and thirty-five pence. All for ice-cream and hot dogs!" His voice softened as, Philip had noticed, people's voices tended to soften when they spoke of Rachel. "She was over the moon."

"She came to the Shrine earlier on." Mrs. Chitty's voice, too, took on a more mellifluous tone. "She brought flowers, a whole vanload of them. Some florists in Sheringham and Cromer—nobody can say no to Rachel! Some we set out in bowls and the girls have made the rest up into posies for people to carry—"

"Have *you* seen Rachel this evening?" Philip asked Paul Falkener.

The artist was looking extraordinarily handsome, and extraordinarily dishevelled. He had eaten less than the others, but drunk more of the Rhine wine Charles Griffin had provided as accompaniment to the repast. Barefoot as ever, his neckerchief awry, his shirt open to the waist, he padded backwards and forwards across the room, as if possessed by some excitement that could only be worked off by the expenditure of physical energy.

Alice Diefenhaus watched his comings and goings with unfeigned admiration. She liked people to look like what they were: it simplified life. She liked professors to look professorial and artists to look artistic.

"Was the Lady easy to copy?" she asked him.

"Impossible. You'd have thought, with such purity of line, it'd be a piece of cake. But such subtlety, such damnable subtlety—" He broke off, and resumed on a lighter note: "It's a complete flop, but Mrs. Chitty's dreamed up a beautiful robe to conceal the fact from the odd spectator with a seeing eye."

Mrs. Chitty reddened with pleasure.

"Mr. Falkener's much too modest. I'm sure if you didn't

know which was which you couldn't hardly tell one from t'other."

Professor Diefenhaus inquired of Griffin: "Will the people along the route of the procession be aware that the figure they're seeing is not the Lady of Promise, but only a stand-in for her?"

"They will if they read the papers. We've made no secret of it. We're only doing exactly what they did in the old days. There are several references to *imago imaginis*, the image of the image. The sheer weight of the Lady makes a perambulation with her all but impossible. When it's all over the real Lady of Promise will be waiting in her Shrine for all who wish to approach her—where she was, where she is, and where, but for the immeasurable folly of man, she would always have been."

5

At eleven o'clock promptly Mrs. Chitty took her girls off to get, as she said, many times over, their beauty sleep before the great day. Neil Woodgate went along cheerfully to escort them, and Philip watched him go with a wry regret. Such an eminently suitable husband for Rachel: hard-working, clean-limbed, so obviously in love—and so obviously fated to make do with a Carol or a Jennifer!

Joanna said: "Give me a hand with this, will you? We're going over to the Shrine."

"I don't think I want to."

"Please."

He settled the lacy shawl round her shoulders without further demur. She brushed his cheek fleetingly with her hand, and he felt rewarded.

Anguish leading the way, they left the Manor by the front door, which opened on to a courtyard enclosed, at right angles to the main building, by low wings housing, on one side, the estate bailiff's offices, and, on the other, stabling converted into shelters for agricultural machinery. The fourth side lay open to the drive, curving away between horse chestnuts whose white candles gleamed in the dark.

The manservant opened a door and extracted an enormous bathchair of ancient design.

"You mustn't think I'm an invalid," Charles Griffin insisted, as Anguish settled him into the contraption and covered his legs with a rug. "I'm simply old enough to feel confident one or other of you young stalwarts will offer to push me. Anguish, I know, would prefer to stay behind to stack the dishes ready for the cleaning women in the morning, as well as to finish up any wine we have been so foolish as to leave undrunk."

"Three and a half bottles," said Anguish. "More than enough, sir."

"I'll take it," said Barnabas, placing his hands on the handlebar of the bathchair. "I know its little ways."

"Are you sure it's safe?" Alice Diefenhaus asked. "It looks kind of insubstantial."

"It carried the Prince Regent when he stayed here just after the Battle of Waterloo, and when he weighed twenty-two stone: so it should certainly suffice for me. Actually, thanks to Philip here, it's now better than new. Philip, as you may or may not know, makes little metal marbles which, in some way not far short of miraculous, make things run smoothly. If only they could do as much for our lives, our loves, our digestions, and the government of the country! Well, Philip took this dear old chariot down to his factory and they poured marbles into every nook and cranny, with the result that I have had to have a handbrake fitted to stop me exceeding the speed limit!"

"Are we ready?" Barnabas asked.

Joanna said: "I don't see Mr. Persimmer."

"He accidentally used too much water," Anguish put in respectfully. "He's still drying off in the kitchen."

"Share the wine with him," said Griffin. "He wouldn't have come along anyhow. Lionel would as soon enter the Shrine as the portals of Hell."

The two women moved off companionably down the drive, Joanna's shawl ghostly beneath the trees.

"I surely admire you," Professor Diefenhaus remarked to Paul Falkener striding alongside. "Walking barefoot over stuff like this. Some of those flints look sharp as swords."

"Nothing to it. Practice, that's all. My feet, you might say, are my ultimate masterpiece. Been working on 'em for years. Can't remember when I last wore a pair of shoes.

> *Giovanezza, giovanezza,*
> *Primavera di bellezza!"*

Falkener broke into song and ran on ahead.

"Mr. Falkener seems in great spirits," the Professor commented.

Charles Griffin poked his head out from under the wicker hood of the bathchair.

"Liebfraumilch," he said succinctly. "He hasn't much else to celebrate. You've seen his panels in the Shrine?"

"I must have, I suppose. I must confess I didn't notice them."

"Exactly! Yet it's odd. If you'd seen the piece that made me decide to get him down here—" Griffin brooded for a moment, then ended: "Perhaps it's all for the best. The Shrine is only big enough for one work of genius."

At the Manor lodge, a little Gothic folly with boarded-up windows and a general air of decay, the road fell away steeply to the Shrine and the river. The sky had clouded over, but the roadway was bright with lights strung from tree to tree.

Philip muttered: "Little Miss Fix-it at it again!" And aloud: "It looks like Piccadilly Circus."

"I don't care much for them either." Charles Griffin squinted upward. "But we have to think of the pilgrims. City people are so ill at ease without street lighting. I insisted the Shrine be left in shadow. I like to see it bulking dark against the sky."

"When Alice and I were here before," the Professor recalled, "we drove up and down the street several times before we realised that was it."

"If I'd had the money for that gold leaf for the roof you wouldn't have missed it."

"I guess we were expecting something instantly identifiable. A crucifix. Something like that."

"Never, here!"

They had arrived at the Shrine, where Alice Diefenhaus and Joanna Cass awaited them, and Paul Falkener paced impatiently up and down the little forecourt. Barnabas extricated Mr. Griffin from his conveyance.

"Never a cross here!" the old man repeated. "This is a temple to life. No place here for that symbol of a savage and shameful death!"

He took Mrs. Diefenhaus's arm and moved slowly towards the porch, lit by a small lantern.

Philip Cass murmured to his wife, his arm round her shoulders: "You're cold. The shawl isn't enough for you."

Joanna shook her head and asked brightly: "Can we go in now?"

Barnabas took out his key and unlocked the door.

Inside, a small vestibule with a lavatory on one side and a storeroom on the other, led, through double doors, into a long, lofty hall containing, at the end farthest from the entrance, a small inner room, a kind of three-sided box. The walls of the hall were rough-plastered, hung with a few faded tapestries, their detail obscure in the low-keyed light of a single chandelier.

By day, a skylight gave additional illumination and, along a section of the wall giving on to the cloister, there were doors which could be folded back to give a view of the Priory ruins. At night, as the little party filed in behind Barnabas, the place was a cave: seeming, if anything, darker for such light as there was.

"Just a tick," said Barnabas.

He moved away into the gloom. Alice Diefenhaus exclaimed: "Will you smell those flowers!"

A switch clicked and the inner room came to light, its two facing walls lined from floor to ceiling with a ladder-like construction of iron rails, spiked with prickets upon which stumpy candles were impaled. The end wall, at either side, was hung with Paul Falkener's panels. Between them the wall curved into a shallow alcove where, upon a pedestal banked with flowers and softly illuminated from below, stood the Lady of Promise.

The statue was more than life-size, of some dense black wood lively with the burnishing of age. To an eye trained to the sight of Madonnas sweet or simpering, it was an astonishing apparition—a woman in her last days of pregnancy, enormous belly thrusting against her robe, her breasts ready to give suck; the body tilted backwards, legs apart, the better to support her burden.

What was more astonishing, if not shocking, was that the Virgin was naked.

Not technically naked. Draperies fell in folds from her hooded head down to her feet: yet they left explicit every smallest detail of that body great with the hope of the world. Shadows emphasised the enlarged nipples, the distended navel, the dark mound beneath that domed overhang.

The Lady's hands were spread, fingers splayed, on either side of her belly; and it was plain, from the expression on her face, that the Child had just that instant moved in her womb. It was plain, too, that the baby so soon to be born was no Infant with halo but a brat squalling at the end of an umbilical cord and followed by a bloody afterbirth: an unfinished son of man with no other purpose in life than to attach itself to those engorged breasts.

All this was there to be read in the Lady's face. Yet, at first sight, an overriding consideration supervened. For this Virgin of the House of David was a negress, the black wood of the face carved in wide, generous planes, the nose flat, the lips thick and protuberant.

It was this singularity which accounted for the presence of the Brixton Band of Hopefuls and for the large number of black couples among the young people in Mauthen Barbary for the Lady's birthday. Yet it was, thought Joanna, her eyes on the black face, a fact utterly without significance; as irrelevant as that the models for Rembrandt's *Holy Family* were his beloved Saskia and his son Titus, or that the guests in Veronese's *Marriage at Cana* were dolled up in the glad rags of sixteenth-century Venice.

The statue transcended colour and race as it transcended time.

It was.

For the moment everyone in the Shrine was silent and still. Everyone: even Philip Cass, even Paul Falkener. Silence and stillness were what the great black figure demanded. Here was no place for chanted prayers and choreographed processional, but for that silent communication which came from the heart and brain and went, who could say where?

Charles Griffin was the first to speak. The Americans were newcomers: they had not heard his views before, and he could not restrain himself.

Why should the Lady be a negress? Was the Professor of the opinion that the Lady's unknown creator had made a wildly inaccurate guess at the physiognomy of the inhabitants of the Holy Land? Or, conversely, did they incline to his, Griffin's, theory, that the woodcarver had seen no other possible form latent in that black tree-trunk from which she was made?

The Professor, not without difficulty, took his eyes off the Lady, and answered disappointingly that he had no idea.

But the spell was broken, and Philip demanded roughly:

'What makes you so sure she even *is* the Virgin? Virginal seems the last word to apply to a woman in that condition."

Alice Diefenhaus said, with transatlantic forthrightness: "I guess, by the time she got to her ninth month, Mary looked pretty much the same as any other pregnant woman. And if you don't see more pictures or statues like this one, maybe it's only because the Church prefers to gloss over the physical implications."

"It must have been a hard time for her." Alone of them, Joanna kept her face towards the statue. "After Gabriel's visit, how the neighbours must have talked! I bet she was positively relieved she and Joseph had to go to Bethlehem, so that she could give birth among strangers." She paused. "Though it must have been frightening," she finished, low, "to give birth among strangers."

"For Pete's sake!" Philip was obdurate. "You make it sound like a soap opera. Virgin or not, no one could call this one frightened. She looks positively triumphant."

"You should 'a seen her earlier this evening!" Barnabas joined the discussion. Paul Falkener had resumed his restless pacing. "With Len Foulcher's lights full on her. She looked like she could 've brought down thunder and lightning if she'd a mind to."

"Len Foulcher's lights?" Griffin wanted to know.

Barnabas pointed towards the inner room. "Len rigged up a couple of spots. You never saw anything like it."

"Well, switch them on, man! Let's see for ourselves."

"I can't do that. Paul here took out the bulbs."

"So I should think!" The artist padded over. "They looked bloody awful. And it's no good asking me to put them back. I took them home for safety's sake. They cost a packet and Len has to take them back on Monday."

"Just the same, I'd have liked—"

"You wouldn't, you know. They made the Lady look like a sideshow at the fair. They turned the Shrine into a television set—and you know what you think of the telly. That unit you wouldn't let in here to film has been on it again to get you to change your mind."

"Small chance of that! I can't stop them photographing on the public highways, but I've warned them if they come into the Shrine, or on to my land, I'll sue them for trespass."

Philip Cass said: "I should have thought you'd be all for the publicity."

Charles Griffin waved his arms in irritated dismissal "Television makes everything unreal."

"True enough!" Philip chuckled. "If the Second Coming came and they had it on the box, ninety per cent of the audience would switch over to another channel, grumbling 'Not another repeat, for Christ's sake!' Oops!—"at the faces still with disapproval—"Poor taste rearing its ugly head again! Put it down to my besetting facetiousness. Or rather—"he jerked his head towards the inner room—"blame it on *her*! Tell me, Mrs. Diefenhaus, what possible attraction do you think Our Lady of Promise could have for a nineteen-year-old girl, no hang-ups, just an ordinary, healthy kid?"

"Young people today see so much that's destructive—" Alice Diefenhaus spoke diffidently, feeling her way. "So much pulling down, so much putting down. If I were young again in such a world, I don't know, I imagine I'd find a whole lot about the Lady to attract me."

Philip shook his head.

"You don't convince me one bit. You haven't met my sister Rachel or you'd see the absurdity of it."

"I hope to have that pleasure—"

"Paul here says she's a saint. If she were, I wouldn't say a word. If she wanted to nurse lepers I'd say OK, if that's what you want. But she's not like that at all—just an ordinary girl who's been got at in some way I don't understand."

He looked mistrustfully about the shadowy hall.

"Oh, some of it's plain enough. This Maiden business, all that dressing up in Isadora Duncan draperies—"

"It's me he's getting at," Griffin announced with a smile, "and I'm too old to be got at. And besides, this isn't a place where it is appropriate to raise your voice other than in petition or praise. Your concern for your sister does you credit, Philip, but I'm your host, and it isn't manners to abuse your host."

Philip, as if relieved to be pulled back into the shallows, threatened playfully: "I'll take back my ball-bearings!"

"We must see Mr. Falkener's statue before we go." Alice Diefenhaus tactfully changed the subject. "Where do you keep it hidden?" she asked the artist.

"She, not it. She's in the storeroom, and no, you can't see her. Not straight after the genuine article. I've too much vanity to invite comparisons. Save your curiosity for tomorrow."

"Or else see it on the telly," Philip put in. "*Imago imaginis imaginis*. 'The image of the image of the image.'"

"That's right, lover boy." Falkener gave Cass a brilliant smile. "Too late at night for another of our life-and-death struggles." He turned to the Guardian of the Shrine, standing hands clasped in front of him, in peaceful contemplation of the Lady. "Don't worry about the cloister door. I'll lock it as I go out." To the Americans he explained: "My pad's just the other side of the Priory garden."

Charles Griffin said: "We'll wait in the porch, Barnabas, while you close up."

"That's all right, Mr. Griffin," the man replied. "I'll be staying. I'm sure Mr. Cass or the Professor won't mind pushing you home."

"Staying?"

Paul Falkener halted, halfway to the cloister.

"A vigil!" said Professor Diefenhaus, with the pleasure befitting a professional medievalist.

"That's putting it a bit grand," said Barnabas. "We usually have a rota of chaps. Like standing watch on board, more like."

"But there's no rota for tonight," Falkener pointed out. "How long are you planning on staying?"

"All night, I reckon. Truth is, I never felt comfortable shutting up the Shrine this evening, and I wouldn't feel right going off home now. Tonight, of all nights."

"You're crazy, man. You'll be dead in the morning. Better let me take turn and turn about with you."

"That's kind, and ta, but I'm kind of set on seeing the night out myself."

"Don't dissuade him," said Griffin. "He's quite right. Tonight of all nights the Lady shouldn't be left on her own."

"Crazy!" said Falkener again, and went out into the cloister without saying good night. A moment later, those inside the Shrine heard the clang of the iron and glass door that filled the centre arch, and the sound of a key turning in the lock.

"Come on, Charlie," said Philip. "Your carriage awaits."

When they had gone, Barnabas switched off every light except the one in the vestibule. The Lady of Promise loomed on her pedestal, a shape, a presence. The man approached the statue timidly, knelt for a little in front of it in an attitude of prayer; then suddenly, with a hoarse cry, flung himself full length upon the floor, and lay there, weeping.

Hand in hand Philip and Joanna Cass climbed the hump of the Green. The windows of Forge Cottage were dark.

"Could be she's come in and gone to bed." Philip spoke without conviction. "How about looking in at the Hospice to see if she's there? There were still plenty of lights on."

"She wouldn't like it. We can't treat her like a child."

"We can as long as she acts like one."

Forge Cottage seemed the darker by contrast with Maypole Cottage next door. There, every window blazed. Music blared, underpinning a babble of female voices. A smell of cooking wafted over the Green.

"Good Lord!" Philip snuffled the air, seizing, as always, the chance to take refuge in a joke. "They're burning bras!"

"Don't be silly," said Joanna. "It's bloaters."

"Bras," her husband insisted doggedly.

Thankfully the two pushed open their gate.

"You're to go straight up," Philip admonished. "You've been looking peaky all evening."

Inside the door Joanna kissed her husband with great tenderness.

"I'm fine now I'm home."

"Shall I just run up and see if she's in?"

"Do that. I'm going to put the kettle on."

She listened to his footsteps on the stairs: quick up, slow down. She had no need to ask whether he had found the girl.

"You're the one who needs to go to bed. You did all the driving."

"Perhaps I will." Suddenly he seemed exhausted. "I don't think I want any tea. Will you be long?"

"You know me. I must have my cuppa. And look at the paper."

"You're not going to wait up for her?"

"No. I'll be up soon."

"Did I ever tell you I loved you?"

"I'd prefer it in the present tense."

"Past, present, and future."

Again she listened to his footsteps. She did not pour out the tea she had made, nor unfold the newspaper. She took a cigarette out of a box on the dresser, lit it, and sat down to wait.

# 6

At 10:25 a.m. on Sunday, the fifth anniversary of the rediscovery of the Lady of Promise, Barnabas, the Guardian of the Shrine, came out of the vestibule, closing the inner doors behind him. Four men of the village awaited him, self-conscious in the white trousers and smocks made for them by the ladies of the WI. Outside in the forecourt the Brixton Band of Hopefuls, magnificent in the morning sunshine, launched into a calypso.

> "In Mauthen Barbary today
> Folks have come to love and pray.
> Lady let us fruitful be,
> Like the golden apple tree."

Eleven Maidens, aware they looked well in their blue gowns and silver sandals, passed to and fro carrying trugs filled with posies. A television cameraman, perched on the low wall which divided the forecourt from the road, had stuck a white carnation behind his ear.

The pilgrims looked rumpled and deeply content. They stood about, stretching their necks to see what was happening, but with no sense of impatience. They had sun, they had summer, they had hope.

> "Life is love and love is life.
> Man take woman, husband wife.
> Lady surely do agree
> It's child what makes the family."

"If I'd known there'd be telly," one of the white-smocked men complained as he followed Barnabas into the storeroom, "I'm hanged if I'd 'a made a ruddy ass of myself for a measly fiver."

"Can't see why not, Arthur, seeing you usually do it for free." Barnabas was in splendid spirits. "Now, remember, Mick here is in charge. When he says left you don't go right."

"Is she screwed down to that there pallet then?" Arthur

41

looked distrustfully and a little in awe at Paul Falkener's statue, which indeed was looking extremely impressive in its velvet cloak. "Wouldn't want to turn her arse over tip."

"Screwed down, and those rails you hold it by go right through the base, so short of you doing acrobatics she can't move. Ready? Then lift—and off we go!"

The appearance of the statue was greeted with cheers. The bearers, Arthur included, smiled for television, and contrived to give the impression that their burden was heavier than was in fact the case. Mrs. Chitty, wearing the lavender crimplene outfit she had got for her niece's wedding, gathered the Maidens under her wing, and chivved them into position, immediately ahead of the substitute Lady.

"Where's Rachel?" asked Jennifer. "Mrs. Chitty, Rachel's not here!"

At the same moment, Neil Woodgate, edging through the crowd, called across to Barnabas, "Seen Rachel?"

"Rachel's inside," said Barnabas, answering both inquirers. "She's staying behind to keep the Lady company."

Attaining the porch, the boy offered, red rising in his cheeks: "I don't mind staying too, if you think—"

"I don't, bor! Rachel and the Lady are fine as they are. You go on ahead and make sure the river gates are fastened back proper, if you want to make yourself useful."

The Guardian turned and locked the outer door.

"Rachel in there?" Mrs. Chitty looked confused. "Then what are you locking up for?"

"So's no one can get in while the procession's on, that's why. Rachel can get out if she needs to. She's got her key."

Flustered, Mrs. Chitty complained. "Eleven. We're all lopsided."

"You walk with the Maidens. That'll even it up."

"Right at the front? Oh, I couldn't do that."

"No one deserves it better." And to the delight of the onlookers, the television crews, and perhaps Mrs. Chitty herself, Barnabas gave the good lady a resounding kiss.

It served as a signal to get the procession moving. Mrs. Chitty and the Maidens moved out of the forecourt into the road, followed by the bearers with the statue. Barnabas and the Brixton Band of Hopefuls fell in behind, and behind them again, as the leaders turned down the hill towards the river, came, with no pretence of order, the pilgrims.

It was a procession to make the Dukes of Norfolk, hereditary holders of the office of Earl Marshal, and, as such, past-masters in the organisation of progresses, blush for their home county. Unregimented by stewards, the marchers could hardly be said to march at all. They strolled, they straggled, stopped to take pictures or remove pebbles from shoes. The Maidens, young and eager, soon found they were going too fast for the general pace. Arrived at the little stone bridge over the Maut they waited, their blue draperies fluttering like butterflies, for the rest to catch up. The bearers moved the statue off the road on to the grass of the Rond, where they posed with becoming dignity for the press photographers assembled there. The Brixton Band of Hopefuls, having time to spare, joined hands and moved round the statue in a stately pavane, their veils floating free.

> "Nazareth town in Galilee,
> Angel Gabriel came to tea.
> 'The Lord is with thee, girl,' he said.
> Mary, bless my marriage bed!"

Along the river, past willows dipping their leaves in the water, the procession took its way: across the Rond, where the men in berets who had put up the tents the day before waved cheerfully and went back to taking them down. The river gate in the boundary wall enforced some kind of order, since no more than four abreast could pass between the griffin-topped pillars which guarded the entrance to the Manor. The double gates of wrought-iron were drawn back and fastened.

The television crews, barred from proceeding further, darted about like water-beetles, taking long shots of the parkland beyond, as if they glimpsed a forbidden paradise.

Once through the gate, the procession spread itself out to the point of disintegration; men and women dotting the greensward among the baaing sheep. Only the blue-robed statue, bobbing along behind the Maidens, gave them a compass bearing, and, if they needed it, a reminder of purpose.

At sight of the advancing crowd, Oscar and Nellie came waddling up from the water. Nor was the effort wasted. Crisps and chocolate bars were offered; and accepted with that disdain which, with swans, passes for good manners. Nellie's underparts began to sag ominously.

Alice Diefenhaus, watching through field-glasses from the

Manor House terrace, commented: "They're going to kill those birds with kindness."

"Let's hope you're right," Charles Griffin returned, with the quaint little nod that was typical of him. "Hateful creatures. An avian mafia which keeps the whole village in subjection. Living testaments to the truth of the maxim that if only you're beautiful enough you can get away with murder." He gazed out over his domain with an air of satisfaction. "What do you think of it?"

Professor Diefenhaus, at his wife's side, hesitated. "Wouldn't you say it's maybe, a little haphazard?"

"You couldn't have hit on a happier word!" Griffin smiled at his guest. "I'm aware you mean it in dispraise. But, as it happens, it's the highest compliment you could pay."

"I certainly never saw a more relaxed bunch in my life."

"That's the whole point! These good people are here to beg the Lady of Promise to give them a child. Or rather—"the old man corrected himself—"they have faith that prayers offered here in Mauthen Barbary will be answered in a very special way. They arrive here predisposed to conceive, free of that tension which, when they copulate elsewhere, has an effect the direct contrary of what they most desire. The anxiety which closes up the womb has been dissipated. And there you have the clue to this haphazard progress you see passing before you. We could doubtless, with a little thought, have devised solemnities, but would they have served the pilgrims' purpose? We should merely have added a meretricious religiosity which even the sight of the Lady herself might not suffice to dispel."

"You're a very perceptive man," said Alice Diefenhaus. "And I suppose Mr. Falkener's Lady is part of this deliberate playing it cool?"

"Oh, you mustn't give me the credit! The Priory monks had it to a T six hundred years ago. Heavy as she is, had they really wanted to move the Lady, the real Lady, she could have ridden on a cart, or a dray. But no: her presence *en plein air* would have been altogether too overwhelming. And so they contrived a substitute, an approximation of the truth, not to be taken too seriously."

"Taking your line of reasoning to its logical conclusion, sir," said the Professor, "why have a procession at all?"

"No real reason, save that it is proper and agreeable to make a small obeisance to history. That, and to make an occasion.

People have come a long way, spent time and money getting here. Added to which—"the old man's eyes twinkled—"a little healthful exercise between couplings will do them no harm."

As the statue neared the copse where the Lady had lain buried, Chloe rushed out from under the trees barking a greeting. Taken by surprise, the bearers forgot their instructions. The statue tipped over on its side on to the grass. The crowds moved faster, stimulated by an accident. From behind the trees a bell began to jangle, raucous and commanding.

Alice Diefenhaus had the field-glasses to her eyes again. "There doesn't seem to be any damage. Barnabas is helping them get the statue upright. Oh dear—Chloe's run off with its cloak!"

Mr. Griffin barely nodded. Something else had his attention. He drew an old-fashioned half-hunter from his waistcoat pocket.

"A good fifteen minutes late! Unlike Lionel. He must be sulking."

"He sounds it," said Professor Diefenhaus, "if that noise is him ringing the church bell."

"He always says there's no one he can trust to do it on time, but I think he positively enjoys shattering our sabbath peace. Still, I've seldom heard it sound quite so unlovely."

Alice Diefenhaus reported: "That lady who was here last night, in charge of the girls—she's gone after Chloe."

Mrs. Chitty had not run far into the wood before she began to feel foolish. Worse, she could feel sweat in her armpits. That was the worst of synthetics: the slightest exertion and you felt like a slut. Mrs. Chitty suppressed a desire to cry, smoothed her lacquered hair unnecessarily, and waited with all the dignity she could muster for the others to catch up with her. As the statue approached, she thought how different it looked without its lovely cloak. Not even the kindly shade of the trees could disguise how far it fell short of the real Lady.

Mrs. Chitty was suddenly glad Mr. Falkener had not joined the procession as he had said he would. She could never have looked him in the face and said, as she had said last night, that you couldn't tell the difference.

Chloe had carried the cloak to the Lady's grave, where she sat, tongue lolling, waiting to be congratulated. Barnabas reached down and retrieved the garment. The bearers lowered the statue to the ground, and Mrs. Chitty rearranged the cloak about its shoulders. The Brixton ladies sang with undiminished vigour.

> "Lady sleep in cold hard ground,
> Lady sleep until she found.
> Lady waken from the tomb.
> Bless the seed within my womb!"

The pilgrims drifted through the copse, paused by the graveside, and because there was, after all, nothing much to see but a hole in the ground, drifted on again. One of the Maidens caught her dress on the spines of a barberry bush; otherwise there was no further casualties. The church bell pealed a final discordant summons and fell silent.

The church itself, where Lionel Persimmer, his face twisted with hate, preached Christian love to a congregation of eleven, stood on a knoll at the western edge of the Manor park, fronting on to Church Lane, a short byway connecting it with the High Street. The pilgrims skirted the churchyard wall quietly, silenced by the melancholy of the place. It was a sad little church, out of key with their mood, and they were glad to be past it.

Along Church Lane and the High Street spectators waited on the cobbled pavements, the natives come out to see what all the fuss was about, and, in true Norfolk fashion, giving small hint of their personal opinion of the carryings-on. Only the children had not yet mastered the immemorial East Anglian art of self-concealment, that trick of dissolving the features into a blankness so consummate as to render them virtually invisible.

"Look, Ma!" cried a little boy, stretching out his arms. "The lovely black lady!"

"Oh ah!" his mother responded, yanking him out of the way.

Enthusiasm was scarcely to be expected. Mr. Griffin owned most of Mauthen Barbary, and Mr. Griffin had let it be known that the village, if it wanted to stay in his good books, was to make no financial hay out of the accident that the Lady of Promise had been found within its boundaries. No souvenirs, no cream teas. Parking fees at Priory Farm, plus some bed and breakfast trade that would have come along anyway, it being a fine weekend, and that was about all.

"And what, sir, is your opinion of this invasion of your rural peace?" A television reporter inquired with a smile of piercing winsomeness of an elderly local.

The greybeard took his pipe out of his mouth to consider the question.

"Oh ah," he pronounced at last, with evident regret at having committed himself.

The stalwarts of the WI were more forthcoming, willing to admit to the media that all that embroidery on the Lady's cloak had been hard work, but there you are. The Maidens had made their own dresses. The good ladies' lips curled slightly as they imparted this item of information; but whether in disparagement of the Maidens' needlework, or out of some inborn scepticism of self-confessed virginity, was not disclosed.

The sight of the eleven girls, prettily flushed as they stepped along the High Street in front of the swaying statue, galvanised into action the group of women waiting, as the day before, on the steps of the Market Cross. They had exchanged their poster of the starving child for a banner which proclaimed, with classical pessimism, NOT TO BE BORN IS BETTER. They had changed their costume as well. Skeletons at the feast, they had interpreted this literally, in black kaftans painted with a skeleton fore and aft. The hoods which covered their heads and masked their faces were emblazoned with a skull.

"Lady out!" they shouted, advancing to meet the oncoming procession.

The words were hard to distinguish, coming out of the grinning death's-heads; but they stopped the Maidens dead in their tracks.

Barnabas slipped out of his place in the line.

"Need any help, Brother?" asked one of the Brixton Hopefuls, folding a sleeve back from a powerful arm.

"That's all right, love. Just keep on singing."

The Guardian of the Shrine strolled towards the demonstrators.

"Lady out! Lady out!" they greeted him, and sat down in the road.

"OK, Miss Massingham," Barnabas said mildly, addressing himself to one taller and broader than the rest. "You've made your point. The telly men have got some beautiful pictures. You don't want to spoil it, do you, by being carried off with your knickers showing? Tell your mates to move aside, there's a good girl, and let's get on with it."

"I'm not—"the hooded figure began.

"Make your speech, Lydia!" a smaller skeleton shouted. "Go on—make your speech!"

"I—," the hooded figure began again: then, surprisingly, rounded on her supporter.

"Shut up, Liz! Get up, everybody! Let 'em through!"

"But, Lydia—!"

"Get up, can't you hear me!" The voice was shrill but authoritative. The demonstrators, bewildered by the sudden turn of events, rose uncertainly and milled about in the road. Lydia Massingham shouted: "Oh, get out of the way, you blasted fools, for Christ's sake!"

The procession surged triumphantly forward.

> "Lord sit in Heaven on His golden throne.
> Lord sit in Heaven all alone.
> Where my Mama? Look down, Lord, you'll see
> She's in Mauthen Barbary!"

## 7

Detective Inspector Benjamin Jurnet could have kicked himself. He had spent Saturday by the sea, visiting an aunt who, having retired many years before to spend her twilight days on the North Norfolk coast, had found the knifing air straight from the Arctic Circle so rejuvenating that, at eighty-four, she could still walk her nephew to a standstill across the windy saltings. Wearied by his exertions, he had been happy to defer his departure until next day; and next day dawning warm and inviting, he had decided to meander back to Norwich along the network of country lanes with which Norfolk abounds.

He was in no hurry to get home. Miriam was in London visiting her parents, an absence that left him bereft yet not entirely sorry for the opportunity it afforded to evaluate their relationship away from the powerful distraction of her physical presence. The gentle landscape across which he wound his way encouraged calm thinking.

Which made it droll that he should feel a spasm of

annoyance at finding the road through Mauthen Barbary closed. He should have remembered. All the arrangements had been made back at Headquarters. Although he himself had not been involved, there had been talk about the forthcoming pilgrimage, whatever that might be, and Our Lady of something or other.

Put a chap behind a steering wheel, he explained his irritation to himself, and anything that makes him put the brake on sends up his blood pressure. It would, after all, be the matter of a minute to reverse, drive back to crossroads he remembered a mile up the road, and find a way that cut out the village completely.

Instead, he coasted to a halt where the police constable indicated, and waited for the man to appear at the driver's window.

" 'Morning, Hinchley," he greeted him. "Bit off your patch, aren't you?"

The policeman grinned.

"Makes a change, sir. Proper do, I must say."

"Any problems?"

"Peaceful as a Sunday School treat. We could 'a packed it in and gone home yesterday, for all we're needed." His good-natured young face took on a worried look. "Were you needing to go through? They'll be turning into the High Street just about now. Pretty narrow, an' there must be four thousand on 'em at least—"

"Not to worry. No rush. How long you reckon they'll be?"

"Hard to say. It's not like any march you've ever seen— stopping, starting, stopping, like they had the whole day in front of 'em."

"Four thousand, you say?"

"Just my guess." The man shook his head in a bemused astonishment. "Funny world, isn't it? Half of 'em going mad to get the Pill, the other half coming to a little village at the back of nowhere to pray to a wooden image to put 'em in the family way."

Jurnet, who was not a religious man, agreed. "You'd think they'd find it a better bet to take fertility drugs."

"I reckon myself, sir, it's the publicity's put them off. I mean, you want a kid, you want a kid, not drop a litter."

"That's probably it. Where do they end up?"

"The marchers, sir? Up the road there. That building past the big trees. That's the Shrine. That's where they keep the Lady of Promise."

"That's the name! Doesn't look much of a size to pack in four thousand."

"They plan to let 'em in a few hundred at a time. Pray your piece and then make room for the next lot."

"Four thousand. That's a lot of promises. Wonder if anyone checks to see whether the Lady of Promise keeps them all."

"Couldn't say, sir. And it'd be more like two thousand, wouldn't it? Promises, I mean. I mean, they're all in pairs."

Jurnet laughed.

"And all of opposite sexes. That's something, these days. Two thousand, then. Still a lot of promises."

At the constable's suggestion Jurnet parked his car on the bit of scrubland at the side of the Wesleyan Chapel that, shuttered and abandoned, fronted on the road a little beyond the bridge over the Maut. Not all forms of religion, he noted, flourished equally in Mauthen Barbary.

He walked to the little bridge, crossed it, and turned on to the Rond. P. C. Hinchley, watching from the roadway, smiled to himself at the sight of the patterned sports shirt, the slacks just this side of trendiness, the dark good looks that suggested the Mediterranean more than East Anglia. No prizes for guessing how Detective Inspector Jurnet had come by his nickname among the rank and file.

The constable murmured: "All right then, Valentino."

It was a restful place, Jurnet thought, down by the little river. Two swans who came over to inspect him in a bullying kind of way, finding him completely unintimidated, sailed away downstream with an air of ineffable insult.

As a police officer, Jurnet approved of religion on the whole, since, in his experience, if practised in moderation, it tended to make people behave better rather than worse. Carried to extremes, on the other hand, it was something to be distrusted, like a dog whose temper you weren't sure of. No knowing when it might not bite. Mauthen Barbary, with its statue that promised conception, savoured of extremism.

As extreme as Miriam wanting him to become a Jew before she would marry him.

Suddenly impatient to be on his way, he turned away from the river and started up the hill, towards the Shrine. The modesty of the building took him by surprise. Nothing extreme there, he had to admit.

He crossed the forecourt where photographers and cameramen stood about compulsively fingering their apparatus like musicians, waiting for the conductor, their instruments, and stepped on to the porch.

"No can do, Inspector." Jurnet recognised a reporter from the *Norfolk Mercury*. "Locked. Have to wait till the Guardian gets back."

"The who?"

"Guardian. Fellow got up like Friar Tuck who's the head cook and bottle washer."

The procession, with home in sight, had finally achieved some semblance of order. Past the Green came the Maidens, Mrs. Chitty sweaty but unbowed; and, behind and above them, the blue-robed Virgin borne high by bearers who had rediscovered their strength with an end to their labours in view.

The *Norfolk Mercury* man explained. "That's not the real Lady. Wait till you see the genuine article."

"She's black!" Jurnet exclaimed.

"That's not the only thing about her."

Jurnet watched the statue bobbing nearer. Voices sang.

"Eve she ate the apple and brought us woe.
Lady, when you bore Him, did you suffer so?
Tear my body wide apart, you won't hear me protest.
Lady, keep your promise, put a baby at my breast!"

Soon he could see the singers, and the brown-robed figure of the Guardian of the Shrine. His eyes widened.

"That's the one." The reporter pointed. "In the brown thingumajig."

"Know his name?"

"Barnabas. Don't know his last name. Brother Barnabas, that's what they call him."

Jurnet repeated softly: "Brother Barnabas."

The procession entered the forecourt, crammed into it. The flints of the Shrine wall pricked uncomfortably through the detective's shirt.

"Hallelujah!" the Brixton ladies shouted, lifting their arms, the wide sleeves falling back to their dark armpits.

Somehow the statue got lowered to the ground, somehow the Maidens and the Guardian reached the porch. Cameras whirred as Barnabas produced the key to the Shrine from the pocket of his robe. He turned it in the lock without ceremony:

a homecoming, not a performance. He pushed open the door, crossed the vestibule, and unlocked the inner doors.

The Shrine was heavy with the scent of flowers. Light came in from the north side, where the doors to the cloister had been folded back: light and heat from the great pillar of sun shafting down from the skylight; light and heat from the hundreds of candles guttering along the wall racks in the inner room. Motes of dust revolved lazily in the air.

Out of the reach of daylight the Lady of Promise shone dark and light. In the flickering candlelight she seemed to be moving slightly.

The scream that pierced the air seemed to hang there for a long moment and then collapse of its own weight to the floor. To the floor where a girl lay in a sprawl of blue chiffon, arms and legs at gawky angles, and the back of her head a mess of hair and bone and blood and a terrible ooze that was none of those things.

The Maiden who had screamed, screamed again. Detective Inspector Benjamin Jurnet, making a way for himself, thrust her aside into Mrs. Chitty's arms. Barnabas, after a moment of frozen horror on the threshold, stumbled into the Shrine with a roar that was outraged disbelief and a terrible fear rolled into one.

"Rachel!"

# 8

Jurnet looked about him with distaste. He was in the Hospice, in a dining-room that had been converted to his use. Jurnet was used to makeshift work places. He disliked them equally, even those which had been a good deal more inviting than this, with its funereal furniture and its curtains heavy with dust. The pier-glass over the mantelpiece in which from time to time, try as he did to avoid the encounter, he found himself reflected, did nothing to lighten his humour. Whenever he lifted his head without thinking, there he was, in his sporty shirt and with-it trousers. To put it bluntly, he wasn't dressed for a murder.

Given half a chance, he'd have slipped back to Norwich for a quick change. Some hope! Headquarters, delighted to discover that, by a happy chance, it had a man on the spot, wouldn't take kindly to the suggestion that there was such a thing as correct wear for a murder investigation.

The Superintendent, he had noted, not without a spark of resentment, understood it very well. Contacted at his golf club and arriving with exemplary promptitude, he had contrived somewhere en route to pick up a dark blue business suit. Could be he kept one permanently in the locker room against just such an eventuality.

It was little things like that which marked out a leader of men. The Superintendent's piercingly well-bred disregard of his subordinate's holiday get-up made Jurnet want to spit.

Not fair. The Super was a good man to work with. Willing, once put in the picture, to fade into the background and let you get on with it. They had a good relationship, he and the Super. A touch of mutual dislike only sharpened their mutual respect for each other.

Jurnet had escorted his master to the Shrine to view the body. The poor kid's face in death was so utterly null as to make it an effort of the imagination to conceive that the breath of life had ever moved that inert flesh. There had been a touch of grim amusement in observing that the Superintendent had spent more time looking at the Lady of Promise than at the corpse.

Through the cloister arches Hinchley and another constable could be seen ostentatiously searching the Priory ruins. Jurnet entertained not the slightest hope they would find a weapon, but certain things had to be done, or at least be seen to be done, when a Superintendent was on the premises. The inside of the Shrine would have to wait until Colton and the lads had done their stuff, and taken the body away. They were technicians: they knew how to tread delicately, unlike those youngsters outside falling over their own feet in their eagerness.

"Pretty little trinket, that." The Superintendent had transferred his attention to the body—specifically, to a gold cross on a short length of chain clutched in the dead girl's right hand. Jurnet had already filed it in his mind as one more question to which an answer would be required in due course. "Rather an unusual shape. *Pommée*, I believe they call it."

"Oh yes?"

"It's the way the arms end in little balls, as if they might be stylised apples. *Pommée*—that means apples. You don't often see crosses shaped like that." Straightening up, the Superintendent added: "Have you noticed it's the only one in the whole set-up?" His eyes wandered round the hall, and back to the great black image that commanded it. "This is a damned odd place altogether."

"You can say that again, sir," said Jurnet.

The Superintendent had taken himself off, satisfied, so far as Jurnet could judge, that the inquiry was in good hands. There *had* been a flicker of surprise that the pilgrims had been allowed to depart unimpeded. Allowed! That was a laugh. They had drained away like water out of a sink when you pulled the plug. Strange how the villagers, drawn by the glamour of murder, had come crowding, while those others had got away as fast as if they thought it was catching.

Yet not so strange, when you considered what they were in Mauthen Barbary for. They had come for life, not death, the poor bastards.

And, for Christ's sake, what were you supposed to do? Pen four thousand people up in the village pound while you went over them one by one with a tooth comb? The constables on duty, once word had been got to them, had taken down as many names and car numbers as possible, and the names of the coach operators. For what that was worth.

Bugger all.

There was more to his ill-humour. Sergeant Bowles, writing up his notes at a side table, knew the signs. Back in Norwich they all knew how it was with Inspector Jurnet at the beginning of a case. Bear with a sore head. Acting as if he wished to God he was anywhere but where he happened to be.

The good sergeant could not be expected to understand something Jurnet himself understood imperfectly. Was it delicacy, a reluctance to intrude upon the privacy of others, or an uncharitable shying away from other people's troubles that made it so difficult for him to set in motion that relentless stripping away of illusion which was the first step of the judicial process? Jurnet made a face, remembering the face of Philip Cass when he had brought him the news that his sister Rachel had been found with her head bashed in.

The living troubled him more than the dead, who were beyond pity; so that to return, mentally, to the Shrine and the dead girl lying like a sacrifice before that black goddess, occasioned no pain. Teago, the village doctor, called in to confirm the obvious, had refused to commit himself as to the time of death. Near to tears, he said it was the first time in thirty-five years of practice he had been called on to answer such a question.

"Oh, my God!" he had mumbled. "Rachel!"

Jurnet had not let him move the girl. That was Colton's business. "Just say if she's dead, that'll be enough to go on with."

Yes, she was dead, as if it needed saying. Killed by the blows of a blunt instrument. As to that, the old fellow hadn't hesitated to commit himself. A hammer; probably quite small.

There had been something else. Something Jurnet hadn't been able to put a finger on. A puzzled look in the doctor's eyes. The way he had made as if to speak and then pulled himself up.

"Nothing. Nothing—"

Patience. Colton should be phoning any minute now. Taciturn bugger, full of his own importance. Getting a promise of a call ahead of his written report was no mean victory.

Without the report there was blow all to go on. Jack Ellers, who had driven in with Colton, was still down at the Shrine looking for what he might find; though what he might hope to find in that great empty barn took a bit of imagining. They had found the cloister door unlocked, with the key on the outside. Any one of the twelve hundred inhabitants of Mauthen Barbary or the four thousand strangers who had come on pilgrimage could have walked through that door and killed Rachel Cass. Out of fifty million people in the UK that wasn't too bad. Nothing like narrowing the field.

Yes, there was blow all. And even as Jurnet reminded himself that, still, there was something, there was a knock at the door, and an excited young constable who could not wait to be told to come in.

"There's a man here, sir, says he done it!"

Jurnet raised his head and called out, loud enough to be heard in the outer room: "Come on, Barney, and tell us all about it."

"They must have told you I live here in the Hospice. I couldn't wait any longer."

"They didn't tell me. And couldn't wait any longer for what?"

"For you to come and get me."

"Sit down, Barney." Jurnet indicated a chair. "What makes you think I'd want to?"

Barnabas, Guardian of the Shrine, ignored the invitation. "Don't play games, Inspector. You know who I am."

"Yes," the detective answered. "I know you. Barney Smithers. We've met."

"You know what I did. What I done."

"I know you left the court a free man with your conviction quashed."

"Only because the judge misdirected the jury. You know I was guilty."

Jurnet inclined his head.

"Well, then!" The man's composure began to break up. A terrible grief pervaded his face.

"I know," said Jurnet, "that three years ago one Barney Smithers was convicted of raping and damn near killing a young woman named Mary Caston at Yarmouth. And I know that by one of those extraordinary quirks which I'm told are among the glories of English justice the conviction was quashed. I also know you were roaring drunk at the time. And what I don't know is what it has to do with the death of Rachel Cass."

Barney Smithers sat down at the dining-table which served Jurnet for desk. He leaned his elbows on the pitted mahogany and rested his head on his hands.

"She come through the cloister door, just as I was finishing the candles. I can't tell you how beautiful she was. I don't mean pretty—" he lifted his head and glared at Jurnet as if repelling a contradiction—"she weren't all that much to look at. Beautiful like—like the candle flames I was lighting. Only a candle that wouldn't burn down and go out." He was silent for a moment, then shouted: "I snuffed it out all right!"

"You were telling me."

"She said something about it being a lovely day for the procession, but she was glad to be staying with the Lady because, apart from anything else, her feet were killing her."

"Just one thing," Jurnet interposed. "How many people knew she planned to stay behind in the Shrine?"

"Everyone, after I come out an' told 'em."

"I mean before."

"I did. I don't know who else. It was her idea. When she came in with the flowers yesterday she took me to one side, so's no one else could hear. She knew Mrs. Chitty'd blow her top about there not being an even number of Maidens without her."

"And you didn't mention it to anybody else?"

"Not to anybody." Glowering: "What the hell's it matter anyway?"

"I'm sorry. You were saying she was glad she wasn't going on the procession because her feet hurt her—"

"Killing her, was what she said. And then she kicked off her sandals and did a little dance in her bare feet. She wasn't wearing any stockings. Not a proper dance—" the man seemed to feel it important to put every smallest detail beyond dispute—"just twirling round, like, and that blue frock she had on spread out like a tent. And then she laughed, not on account of anything either of us said, mind. Laughed because she was happy."

He fell silent, for so long that Jurnet prompted: "And then?"

"Then she went and stood in front of the Lady. And I stood watching her." Barney Smithers' eyes narrowed, focussing on himself watching the girl in front of the pregnant Virgin.

"You'll think I'm daft—" he resumed, his tone surprisingly normal.

"Try me."

"I wanted to go down on my knees and pray to her. Like I'd spent the night praying to the Lady."

"And did you?"

"You must be joking! She'd have split her sides. She looked at me and said wasn't it time I got going, and then she came over and kissed me. Not a sex kiss. A pure kiss, very loving." There was another silence, at the end of which the man said: "That's when I must a' killed her."

"What d'you mean, must have?" Jurnet demanded. "Why so vague all of a sudden?"

The Guardian of the Shrine turned his head this way and that.

"I don't remember."

"Don't give me that one! Killed her how? What with? What did you do with the weapon?"

"I tell you, I don't remember! What do you know about it? How many girls you done in? What I do remember, I was standing in the vestibule and it was wonderful. The world belonged to me. D'you get what I'm saying?" The man shouted, and Sergeant Bowles moved unobtrusively nearer. "I stood there feeling the way I'd felt at Yarmouth—"

"At Yarmouth you were pissed. Did you have drink in the Shrine with you last night?"

"I haven't touched a drop since that day—"

"Okay." Jurnet cut in with calculated cruelty. "You felt wonderful—which I take to be your private shorthand for saying you raped the girl and then killed her."

"Rachel!" Barney Smithers buried his face in his hands. After a little he looked up and announced quietly: "They ought to bring back hanging for people like me."

"Oh ah."

"Get the sergeant to write it up and I'll sign it. Then you can charge me."

"One thing at a time," said Jurnet. "Sergeant Bowles will take down your statement."

He reached into a drawer and took out a pair of silver sandals. They were flimsy and foolish and almost unbearably poignant. The ghost of the dead girl filled the room.

Detective Inspector Jurnet did not hold with ghosts.

"We'll wait for the lab report," he said coldly.

"You think I'm making it up."

"I never said so. Let's just say I'd look pretty silly if I charged you on your story and then it turned out there was no sexual interference."

"If that's all—You want me to wait outside?"

"You can go back to your room. You aren't going to run away."

"No. I ain't going to do that. You'll lock me in, just the same?"

"If it'll make you any happier. One other thing. You haven't told me where this fits in."

Jurnet picked up an envelope from the table; shook out its contents, a transparent polythene bag containing the golden cross *pommée* on its tiny circlet of chain.

The man looked at it with repugnance.

"The Lady don't have nothing to do with crosses."

"Rachel was holding this one in her hand. You must have seen it."

"She never would!"

"She did, though."

"A cross!" In a voice of immeasurable horror Barney Smithers exclaimed: "She knew I was going to be the death of her!"

# 9

Sergeant Bowles came back into the room and put a key down on the table.

Jurnet frowned at the sight of it. He always needed a little time to recover from the backwash of other people's emotions.

By way of antidote he deliberately went to the other extreme.

"Barney got a slop bucket up there?"

"All the appurtenances. You'll be taking him in with you tonight, sir?"

"Haven't decided. We're going to have to have another chat, and Mauthen Barbary may be the best place to have it. The Lady may jog his memory."

Sergeant Bowles observed: "Certainly could do with a bit of jogging. Still—confession first day. Not bad going."

"For what it's worth."

"You mean, all depending on what Dr. Colton has to say?"

"Up to a point. If the time of death doesn't fit in, that's it, no matter how many gory details Barney dredges up out of his subconscious. But even if it fits, and even if Colton says there was sexual interference, it still doesn't have to be Barney. The world and his brother could have got in through that cloister door."

"But why say he did it if he didn't?"

"Come now, Sarge, it won't be the first time someone's confessed to a murder he didn't commit. Maybe our old pal Barney got himself so worked up praying to that black image he can't tell truth from fantasy. Maybe his conscience is on at him to atone for that earlier crime for which, by a fluke, he got off scot free. On the other hand, I'm not saying he didn't do it, either. Could be the girl wasn't touched sexually, and still he was the one knocked her off."

"I don't see—"

"Artful, wouldn't it be, to claim to have raped a girl you killed, knowing that the very fact she'd presently be found to be *virgo intacta* would put you in the clear?"

"Phew!" Sergeant Bowles let out an appreciative whistle.

He chewed on the possibilities, then came up with: "But if it wasn't sex, what would be the motive?"

"You're out of date, Sarge." Jurnet's tone darkened. "Who needs motives any more? The act of killing's become an end in itself, a kinky kind of sex. Murder as orgasm." He shrugged the thought from him and gave a little laugh, not free of embarrassment. "Who'd be a copper, if he had his right mind?"

P. C. White, for one, could have been the answer to that. A country policeman who felt for his patch the passionate attachment of a peasant to his ancestral smallholding, he had returned to Mauthen Barbary from his enforced translation to Norwich shocked to the core at what had transpired during his absence. Ushered into Inspector Jurnet's presence he did not actually voice his conviction that it would never have happened had he been present to prevent it, but the accusation hung in the air almost tangibly.

"Glad you're back," said Jurnet. He never set out consciously to charm underlings, who consequently, once they had got over his foreign appearance, got on well with him. "You're the one can tell me all about Rachel Cass."

P. C. White looked stricken.

"The wife's got eyes like bloaters, the kids've been bawling their heads off—" He pulled himself up short and began again. "She was good, sir. That's the best word I can think of. Good meaning what it ought to mean, not the upper crust doing their Christian duty by the lower orders." He paused for reflection, then continued: "Nice to look at, but no beauty queen. But there was something—"

The police constable's face reddened so alarmingly with the effort to pin down what was special about Rachel Cass that Jurnet proffered helpfully: "It's not easy to paint a picture of someone who seems to have been a kind of local saint—"

"I wouldn't say saint." All P. C. White's East Anglian hackles rose at the suggestion. "But special. Definitely special." He looked fiercely at Jurnet. "I reckon some nut case come in with them pilgrims."

"I wouldn't bank on that." Jurnet's tone was carefully tempered to give no offence.

"It don't even have to be them. I hear Miss Massingham brought in a bunch of Women's Libbers."

"Come now, Constable. Women's Lib doesn't automatically make them nut cases."

"No, sir." The constable sounded unconvinced. "Placards of starving kids and where to get an abortion. So I hear."

"If you hear aright," Jurnet pointed out reasonably, "they'd be the last people you'd suspect. Virgins would be just up their alley."

"From what I hear," said P. C. White, who had plainly had a prejudiced informant, "if that lot was virgins it was on account no one asked 'em. And from what I hear of the look of them, no one in his right mind was likely to."

"Did anyone ask Rachel, do you know?" Jurnet leaned across the table. "Did she have a boy friend?"

"There's young Woodgate. Engineering trainee at Bolton's, out Cromer way. Decent young fellow. Not that he'd got far with her, far as I could see. Rachel liked him, I'd say, but nothing serious. Same thing with Mr. Persimmer, the vicar."

"Of the parish church?" The constable nodded. "Does he take the services at the Shrine as well?"

"Aren't no services at the Shrine. People who go there do their own praying. Not that Mr. Persimmer would go if there was. He don't hold with the Lady at all."

"That couldn't have got him far with Rachel Cass."

"I doubt he got far with her anyway. He's a right old misery. The kind o' parson that's better at a funeral than a wedding." The constable gulped as he added: "Reckon, though, he won't find it easy to bury *her*."

To distract the good fellow, as well as because he wanted to know, Jurnet turned the conversation into another channel. "Tell me what the village thinks about the Lady."

"Not much, at first. All them strangers, and it don't put a penny piece in our pockets." Jurnet smiled inwardly at the burly constable's self-identification with Mauthen Barbary. "But then, people got to thinking, it's a bit of a marvel after all, her lying buried all those hundreds of years, and then being found like that. I reckon we ended up, most of us, proud we had her instead of some other place. And she is something out of the ordinary, you got to admit that."

Jurnet having readily admitted it, the constable went on: "And all that business with the Maidens. Well, o' course, when Mr. Griffin first come up with the idea you can imagine what they had to say about it in the public at The Pirate. An' there's still some that thinks the whole idea a bit of a giggle. But most people in Mauthen Barbary now, they take the view that virgins these days aren't all that thick on the ground, worse luck, and if folks can get all worked up about protecting otters, an' seals, an' oyster-catchers, why shouldn't they feel the same about young girls that want to keep themselves pure till Mr. Right comes along?"

This novel view of virgins as a threatened natural species would have diverted Jurnet had his train of thought not been rudely interrupted. From the outer room came an angry shout and a noise as of a chair being overturned. The door burst open and Paul Falkener advanced into the room scowling.

"Will somebody tell that shit down at the Shrine to let me in!"

Behind the man Jurnet could see the young constable in the outer room leaning against a piano, a reddening handkerchief pressed to his nose. At a nod from his superior, Sergeant Bowles went outside to render what help he could; while Jurnet, taking in the extraordinary figure confronting him, said coldly: "Assaulting a police officer is an arrestable offence."

"Never touched him! Fell over his own bunions, the clumsy lout!"

Falkener leaned across the table. In the instant before P. C. White, a hand hooked into the visitor's trouser belt, hauled him backward, Jurnet smelled whisky hot on his face.

The detective looked at the village constable.

"You know this man?"

"Mr. Falkener, sir. Artist at the Shrine."

Artist! That explained everything.

Falkener's mane of hair was matted, there was dirt in his beard. His feet were bare: to Jurnet the ultimate proof of Bohemianism. The front of his shirt hung in strips below the kerchief knotted at his neck.

Into Jurnet's mind unbidden came the thought: isn't that what they did in the Bible? Rent their garments in lamentation? That was what Falkener looked like; an Old Testament prophet, possessed by a cosmic grief.

Jurnet said: "Pending the completion of our inquiries, we've been obliged to close the Shrine for the time being. Was there some special reason you wished to enter it?"

"Two." Falkener's face worked. "I want to see where Rachel was killed. And I want to ask the Lady why."

"If I may say so, gratifying your first wish won't help either Miss Cass or yourself, and as to the second, surely you can say a prayer to the Lady without actually being in her presence?"

"I want to see where she was killed," the man persisted.

"And I don't want to pray to the Lady. I want to ask her why."
He gazed at the detective with something of a child's hopeful-
ness of enlightenment. "Maybe you can explain how, out of a
village full of averagely rotten men and women, the only one
worth a row of beans has to go and get herself murdered?"

"She didn't 'go and get herself murdered,'" Jurnet corrected
him. "The murderer came to her. When we catch him, or her,
I hope to understand why he did it."

"When, not if? Cocky lot, you fuzz. Thousands of outsiders
in the village and you let them go, just like that. Including one
raging lunatic."

"Perhaps." Jurnet found it hard to decide how much,
between grief and drink, the man was actually taking in. "And
maybe we have to look nearer home."

Paul Falkener said loudly: "If you think anyone who knew
Rachel could murder her, you're crazy."

"So everyone tells me. But in my experience people get
killed for love at least as much as for hate. Suppose you tell me
how *you* loved her."

"What d'you mean, how?" Tears he seemed unaware of
trickled down the man's face. "I loved her—I was not in love
with her. There's a difference."

Jurnet inclined his head to show he appreciated as much.
"So does that cross me off your list of suspects?"

Jurnet countered smoothly: "We have no such list. Our
inquiries are very much in the initial stages."

"Wasting your time—" The tears were coming faster. Grief,
or alcohol, was getting the upper hand. "What the hell does it
matter? It won't bring her back."

"There's such a thing as justice."

"Justice!" Falkener's laugh was painful to hear. "And Rachel
dead! Where's the justice in that? Look here—" his voice
changed, became drunkenly demanding—"are you, or are you
not, going to let me into the Shrine? Apart from anything else,
there's my statue. Our Lady of Promise Mark Two. Indistin-
guishable from the real thing if you happen to have two glass
eyes."

"What about it?"

"They've left it outside, that's what about it. When I was
down there just now a dog was cocking its leg up against it.
There's art criticism for you! Must've been someone from the
*Burlington.*"

"I'm surprised you didn't leave it covered up in the first
place."

Falkener placed a wavering forefinger at the side of his nose.

"Oh, very crafty! Trying to fix me at the scene of the crime, eh?" Mimicking: "Why didn't you leave it covered up—"

"Well, why didn't you? You were there, weren't you?"

"Faulty intelligence, old fruit. Didn't anyone tell you Charlie Griffin had a party last night and I got sloshed?" His eyes narrowed with the effort of concentration. "Correction. Partly sloshed. Say, three parts out of four. Fourth part was a bottle of Cass's Glenlivet I'd knocked off against an emergency. Well, what with three parts and the fourth part I slept through the whole ruddy saturnalia—"

"Then how did you know Rachel Cass was dead?"

"Craftier 'n craftier. I can feel the noose tightening round my neck. Sorry disappoint you, officer—young Willie Gamlin came in with my milk—would you believe it, I've got an ulcer, just like a stockbroker—and he brought me the glad tidings. Anything else you'd like to know before sentence of death is passed upon me?"

"Constable—" Jurnet turned towards P. C. White, stolid with his back to the door—"accompany this gentleman to the Shrine, and have a word with Sergeant Ellers. See whether it's all right to take the statue he refers to inside, and if so, give Mr. Falkener any assistance he may require to shift it. Sergeant Ellers may wish to have a word with Mr. Falkener. I understand some of Mr. Falkener's property is down there in the storeroom—"

Horror seemed to exercise an instantly sobering effect on the artist.

"She—it wasn't done with one of my tools?"

"It might be a good idea to check if anything's missing. Was there a hammer?"

Falkener shuddered and shut his eyes. "Oh, my God!" He took a deep breath, and answered: "No. No hammer. Len Foulcher needed one yesterday when he was fixing the lights. He had to go and fetch his own."

"When did you last see Miss Cass?"

"At the Shrine, last night. She helped me fix the cloak on my Lady. She—" He swallowed convulsively, and ended, very low: "It isn't conceivable that she's dead."

Jurnet took out the cross that had been found in the dead girl's hand, and held it out across the table.

"This anything you've seen before?"

Falkener shook his head.

"Never seen it in the dead girl's possession?"

"She'd never wear anything like that."

"I'm not sure it's meant to be worn. I was hoping you, as an artist, might have some ideas about it."

Falkener shook his head again.

"Jewellery's not my thing. There's a name for a cross with little balls at the ends of the arms—"

"*Pommée?*" Jurnet suggested modestly.

Falkener looked surprised.

"That's it. Could be something to slip over a belt. Dangle from the waist, the way Catholics do with their beads."

"That's an idea."

"Ask the Reverend Persimmer. He's the only one daft enough to give Rachel a cross. If it *was* hers."

"She was clutching it in her hand."

Falkener's eyes closed again. When he opened them there was about him an air of confusion.

"Rachel would never take a cross into the Shrine."

"I've already heard they're tabu there. How do you explain it?"

Paul Faulkner shook his head. A great weariness seemed to have come over him.

"I don't. Explanations are your job, not mine."

Detective Sergeant Jack Ellers was excited. Jurnet had had many opportunities for observing that when Jack Ellers was excited he rose up on the balls of his feet, a kind of human hydrofoiling. Now he came into the dreary room at the Hospice all tippy-toe, and laid a flattish bundle in front of Jurnet with the delighted self-congratulation of a retriever who has just brought back a partridge to its master.

Jurnet bent over the offering and unwrapped it carefully.

"Stuck down the back it was," the little Welshman proclaimed importantly. "Between the statue and that niche she stands in. Didn't show up till we threw out those bloody flowers."

Jurnet regarded the wood-chopper that lay revealed with a disappointment which plainly disconcerted his subordinate, whose height diminished by a good inch and a half as his heels renewed contact with terra firma.

The chopper was old, the varnish of its handle replaced with the deeper shine of prolonged use. The blade looked bright and well cared for, save where a rusty stain to which some long blonde hairs adhered disfigured it.

"It's the wrong kind of weapon," Jurnet said. "And if it were the right one, there'd be a lot more blood on it than that."

The little Welshman defended his find with obstinate loyalty.

"What there is didn't come off the bum of that black idol, that's for sure."

"Look," said Jurnet, unaccountably irritated, "I don't care for that statue any more than you do. On the other hand, a lot of people hereabouts think it's very holy, so as long as we're in Mauthen Barbary the best thing we can do is bury our personal feelings deep enough they don't show. There's no point putting backs up the minute we open our mouths."

"Yes, sir!" said Sergeant Ellers. "Though if they're all like the boyo you sent along with that village copper, you don't even have to open your mouth."

"Artist—what d'you expect? Did he get his precious masterpiece under cover?"

"Ordered Hinchley and that other constable about like they were moving men. As if one bloody image wasn't enough, he had to make another! Then he blew us up for mucking about with his tools. All tied up in an old sack, they were, so of course we had to undo them to see what was what."

"Anything of interest?"

Ellers shook his head.

"All clean as a whistle. Stands to reason, if he's the bugger that done it. Hardly likely to roll a bloodstained hammer up again, waiting for us to come along and find it."

"But this—" Jurnet indicated the chopper—"was waiting for us to come along and find it. How d'you account for that?"

"I don't, Inspector Jurnet, sir." The Welshman favoured Jurnet with an impudent grin, getting his own back for the earlier reproof. "You're the brains, sir. I'm only the leg man."

"Come off it, Jack," Jurnet said amiably. "What do you think? Was it left there to mislead? Or are we dealing with someone thick enough to believe it wouldn't be found?"

"One thing's for sure. There's no fireplace in the Shrine. Whoever killed the girl didn't suddenly give way to an ungovernable impulse and pick up whatever happened to be handy. He came to the Shrine all kitted out for the job."

The telephone began to ring as Jurnet commented, with the

wry charm that won him friends in spite of himself: "Not bad for a leg man."

Colton was his usual pernickety self, hating to commit himself over the phone. He was a man who believed words had no reality until they were written down.

"Yes," Jurnet murmured soothingly into the mouthpiece, waiting for the list of reservations to peter out. "I understand. It'll all be in your report. If you could just let me have the essentials . . . Have you been able to pinpoint the time?" Jurnet motioned to Ellers to be ready with his notebook. "What time do you fix the killing at?"

Judging from the time the sergeant was made to wait with pencil poised, there was no easy answer even to so straightforward a question. At last Jurnet managed: "Well, then, taking into account the heat focussed through the skylight, and the candles—" and a little later, his patience rewarded, he was able to repeat, for Ellers' benefit: "Between ten-fifteen and eleven. Will that cover it?" After another interval he nodded vigorously at the sergeant to confirm it would cover it.

"And the weapon?" That was a simpler matter. "I've got something for the lab to look at. No, not a hammer. I'll be bringing it in with me tonight. What time will you be knocking off?"

The obligatory, mutually commiseratory, exchanges which followed, on the theme of a policeman's lot being not a happy one, had Jurnet scowling with impatience. Nothing of it, however, was allowed to seep into his voice. He seized the moment when he could inquire: "And was she interfered with?" listened to what Colton had to say, and then repeated, in astonishment: "Pregnant? How many months?" Then: "I see."

He held up four fingers to the watching Welshman.

"Pregnant," Jurnet repeated, anxious now to get off the line. He needed a period of quiet to revise his notion of the dead girl.

But Colton had not come to the end of what he had to say. Ellers saw Jurnet stiffen, and press the receiver closer to his ear.

"Say that again, would you, please?"

There was a long pause. Then Jurnet said: "You must be joking."

A jabber audible to Ellers made it clear that the police pathologist took the suggestion badly.

"OK," Jurnet got in finally. "You can understand how I—" He took out a handkerchief and blew his nose hard. "I'm listening," he said. And: "Yes. I've heard of the case. Didn't the succession to the peerage come up a while back? I thought so . . . Look, don't take this wrong—you know I have the highest possible confidence in you. There's absolutely no chance you've made a mistake?"

Colton's reply, for once, was sharp and to the point. Jurnet asked: "Will the report be ready for picking up tonight?" He listened, then said quietly: "I'd appreciate it. And thanks for phoning so promptly."

"When is a Maiden not a Maiden?" Ellers demanded with a grin, as Jurnet replaced the receiver on its cradle. "When she's four months pregnant, eh? This puts a different complexion on the case, sir, I must say."

Jurnet nodded slowly.

"Did Dr. Colton say she had or she hadn't been interfered with?"

"She hadn't."

"Well, that's something. We can cross the sex fiend off the list."

"Colton said that Rachel Cass hadn't been interfered with. Ever."

"Ever?" The little Welshman stared. "But you just said—"

"That she was four months pregnant. That's right."

"But then—"

"Look," said Jurnet. "I'm not making this up. I'm only repeating what I've been told. And what I've been told is that Rachel Cass was four months pregnant when she was killed, and she was still a virgin."

# 10

As soon as he had broken the news Jurnet was aware he had done it badly. But what other way was there to break news like that?

Philip Cass shouted: "It can't be true! If you'd known Rachel you'd know it can't be true!"

"I have to go by the medical report, sir."

There it was again: *if you'd known Rachel.* Jurnet was beginning to get good and sick of sentences which began *if you'd known Rachel.* Even four months pregnant, it seemed, wasn't enough to sow a doubt that perhaps, after all, they hadn't known the dead girl as well as all that.

"There appears to be no doubt your sister was four months pregnant."

Philip Cass sat on the sofa, next to his wife. The two touched from shoulder to thigh, and as if even that was not comfort enough, held hands tightly. With his free hand Cass pushed his hair back wearily from his freckled forehead.

"Let me make it clear, Inspector, I'm not acting the outraged brother. In other circumstances, I tell you frankly, I'd be throwing my hat in the air to know that Rachel, in the most practical way, was through with all that medieval mumbojumbo. It's the secrecy, the lies! Making herself out a Maiden, and going around in those dresses of Virgin blue! I tell you, she was quite incapable of it! If you'd known her—" (*there it was again!*) "you'd know if there was one thing she couldn't stand, it was lying. Either to tell a lie herself, or tolerate one from somebody else. My wife will bear me out."

"Yes," said Joanna, barely above a whisper. "Not even the kind you tell to avoid hurting people."

"I'm afraid the facts speak for themselves," Jurnet persisted stolidly. "I'll be having a word with Dr. Teago—that is, if he feels able to disclose the information—as to whether Miss Cass consulted him." Even as he spoke Jurnet was sure Rachel had not. He recalled the doctor's expression when he had examined the dead girl on the floor of the Shrine. It stood to reason she'd gone somewhere she wasn't known. "In the meantime I was hoping you or Mrs. Cass might have some idea as to who was responsible for your sister's condition."

The two on the flowery sofa looked at each other in a blank desperation. A cord stood out on Joanna's throat. It was a beautiful throat. Jurnet mentally filed away the information that when her face was not distorted by pain and grief Joanna Cass must be a good-looking woman.

"Not that it necessarily follows," he went on, "that whoever put her in the family way killed her. But if we can clear up that mystery at least, it may lead us on to the truth."

"The truth—" echoed Joanna.

Philip Cass gently disengaged himself. He kissed his wife's eyes as though no one were there to observe him, got up and walked over to the french windows open to the garden. As if by so doing he had drawn attention to a new dimension, suddenly the room was filled with an awareness of summer: a spice of pollen, a smell of grass.

His back to the others, Philip said: "When Bert turns up this evening we'd better tell him to pick the peas and take them home. No point leaving them to get coarse." He wheeled round, his mouth working. "Life goes on, eh, Inspector? Peas have to be picked no matter how many coppers go charging after the truth like elephants stampeding through the jungle, destroying everything in their path." He pulled himself up with a visible effort. "Sorry. You have your duty to do. But that Rachel could have acted out such a lie!" He shook his head in a bemused way, and even managed a caricature of a smile. "There you are—I've accepted it! In a way, it makes her murder credible. If Rachel could lie, nothing is unbelievable."

"That may well be true, sir," said Jurnet, who was only too uncomfortably aware that something even more unbelievable remained to be said. "But now, can you think of anyone it might be?"

"No!" said Joanna from the couch with unexpected ferocity. "We can't. She didn't trust us." Tears streamed down her face. "And it's all my fault. I did try, but not hard enough. I didn't try hard enough."

Philip Cass came back to the sofa and took his wife in his arms.

"Hush, my darling. Hush. You did everything anyone could possibly do."

When she had quietened, he said to Jurnet, waiting, observant: "My wife sets herself impossibly high standards. She's had to be both a mother and a sister to Rachel, and it hasn't been an easy role."

"I take it your own mother's no longer alive."

"She's dead, and so is Rachel's. Rachel was my half-sister. That's why there's such an age gap between us. My father remarried. And to complete the family history I must tell you that both my father and my stepmother—Rachel's mother, that is—were killed in a car accident when Rachel was nine. Joanna and I had been married three months when it happened. Rachel came to live with us. The three of us have been very happy together."

Was there a hint of defiance in that last sentence?

"Do you live here all the time?"

"No. Our home's in London." Philip gave the address, for Jurnet to enter in his notebook. "My wife comes from Norfolk. That's why we bought this place—for weekends and the occasional week away. We thought Rachel would enjoy being so near the sea." A bleak grin lit up his face. "When we bought Forge Cottage Mauthen Barbary was the kind of place where you could go to sleep in the middle of the High Street and not be disturbed. That was before Charlie Griffin found the Lady."

"If you're only here weekends, Rachel could have got herself pregnant in London."

Philip Cass shook his head.

"Once she got caught up in this Lady thing she started staying on here right through the week. At first we thought she was using it as an excuse to get out of a secretarial course she was making heavy weather of. Then, when she kept on refusing to come back to town, we decided it was just a phase, and the best thing to do was let her work it out of her system, even though we hated to see it."

He amended what he had just said: "Even though *I* hated to see it. All Joanna wanted was for her to be happy. And she certainly seemed that way. She never appeared to miss London. I can't even remember when she was last there. Can you, darling?"

He tightened his hold about Joanna, and kissed her dark hair. Jurnet found the man's unembarrassed display of love for his wife extraordinarily touching. He wondered how Rachel had found it: and what she had made of her sister-in-law's impassioned response.

"She came up for my birthday."

"Of course! That was in November," he added, for Jurnet's benefit. "Nearly eight months ago. So there you are. It's here in Mauthen Barbary you have to look for the culprit."

"At this stage," Jurnet demurred, "I'm not prepared to say culprit's the right word. The day's past when it was automatically assumed that any young girl who went to bed with a man must have been seduced."

"If you'd known Rachel," said Joanna (Jurnet gritted his teeth), "you'd have known she wasn't the type to sleep around. Being a Maiden was tremendously important to her. Or so we always thought—" Her voice trailed off.

"I understand there's a young man called Woodgate—"

"Neil! Oh, no! She liked him, but that's all."

"What about the vicar? Persimmer, is it?"

"Preposterous!" Philip intervened. "She couldn't even mention him without giggling."

"Barnabas? Paul Falkener?"

"Why not throw in P. C. White and old Beslow while you're at it? Not that they didn't all love her, I'll give you that. Oddly enough, only yesterday I had words with Falkener—accused him of trying to get her into bed. I don't know why I said it except that Paul and I always seem to rub each other up the wrong way. Know what he replied? He said Rachel was a saint. A saint. Oh, I don't mean I go along with that, but it shows his attitude. You pray to a saint: you don't fuck her."

Jurnet said: "A woman may sleep with a man for other reasons than love or lust. Out of loneliness, for instance, or the wish to give someone pleasure." He wondered fleetingly which reason brought Miriam to his bed.

Philip Cass shook his head.

"If you'd known Rachel, you'd have known that nothing but love would have been reason enough."

"If I'd known Rachel!" Jurnet lost his patience, not entirely without guile. "I'm beginning to think I'm the only one in Mauthen Barbary who does! The girl I know is sprawled on the floor in front of a whopping black statue with her head bashed in. Dead, very dead, but real. My God, she's real! But when I try to find out what she was like when she was alive, what do I get? *If you knew Rachel!* A conjurer's illusion, all done with mirrors. I report to you the fact—the fact, mind you!—that the dead girl was four months pregnant. At first you flatly refuse to believe it. Then, when you finally change your ideas, you can't accept there was any lover. Unthinkable! So who was it, for Christ's sake? The Holy Ghost?"

Out of a face twisted with shock Philip Cass's eyes looked at the police inspector as if seeing him for the first time. They appeared to like what they saw.

"Do policemen always talk that way?"

"I'm sorry," said Jurnet. "I apologise. I got carried away."

"I'm glad," Joanna said simply. "It means you're involved. You're not just in it for the money."

"No."

"Is it possible," she ventured, "Rachel didn't realise her own condition? You read about girls who didn't even know."

"Generally either mentally retarded or else they're children, barely pubescent. But even if she hadn't realised it," Jurnet pointed out gently, "it's the act of intercourse that's relevant, isn't it, not its consequences."

Joanna leaned back against her husband's arm, and said in a strong voice: "Of course she knew she was pregnant. I can't imagine why I never saw it."

"Had she—had her appearance altered?"

"Nothing like that. She was just—transfigured, that's the word. We even talked about it, Philip, didn't we?"

"*You* did, darling. Honestly, I couldn't see anything different."

"Her skin, her eyes—" Joanna broke off. Her face had turned a deep red. "Perhaps it's something only a woman senses—"

Jurnet asked: "And did she still look like that when you saw her this weekend?"

"I never saw her at all." Philip Cass spoke before his wife could answer. "When we got here there was a note to say not to wait up for her. As it happened, we went to the Manor and were pretty late getting in ourselves. Rachel still hadn't returned, and I went up to bed without seeing her. In the morning she'd gone before I was up."

"I saw her," Joanna said. "After Philip went to bed I stayed down for a cup of tea and a look at the paper."

"And Rachel came in while you were still up?"

Joanna nodded.

"She'd been working like a horse, apparently, but she didn't seem at all tired. And she looked wonderful." For some reason she flushed deeply again.

"Did you have any conversation?"

"She got herself a glass of milk and we sat chatting."

"What about?"

"Nothing very significant, I'm afraid. I asked her if Bert had been in to do the garden, and if she'd paid Mr. Beslow's bill I'd left the money for. And she told me about selling ice-cream, and getting flowers for the Shrine."

"Did she mention anyone by name? Anybody at all?"

"She wanted to know how Philip was. She was sorry she hadn't managed to get over to Charlie's. It was all very desultory." She ended: "It was lovely to see her looking so well and happy, but all the time part of me was worrying that it was terribly late, and I kept trying to cut her short and get her to go to bed. Finally she kissed me good night and went upstairs. I washed up her glass and my cup and saucer, bolted the front door, and went up myself."

"Did *you* see her in the morning before she left for the Shrine?"

Joanna shook her head.

"When I came down there was a packet of cornflakes on the table. That's the only way I knew she wasn't still asleep."

"What did you do after that?"

Joanna's head came up in an abrupt movement.

"Do we have to establish an alibi like everyone else?"

"Joanna!" her husband exclaimed.

"He's quite right, darling. He mustn't trust anyone." Tears were running down her face again. "Especially as we killed her."

Christ, thought Jurnet. Barney isn't the only one.

"We didn't actually smash her head in, but we might as well have. We loved her, you see, but not enough. We were too busy loving each other. If we'd loved her more she'd have told us about the baby, about everything. And then it would never have happened."

Philip Cass took out a handkerchief and wiped away his wife's tears with infinite tenderness.

Jurnet said: "I only wish I didn't have to bother you at such a time. For all I know, at this very moment, the murderer may be laughing his head off on his way home to Cornwall or the Outer Hebrides. But I can't start on that assumption. Generally speaking, a crime doesn't occur in a vacuum. Something leads up to it, and something leads away from it. And that means I have to know what everyone in any way connected with Rachel was doing this morning. Did either of you go down to the Shrine, or watch the procession?"

Cass made a face.

"The last thing we thought of doing. When we're here I always take a walk while Joanna gets breakfast ready. I went down Back Lane and leaned over a gate for a while, admiring a mare and her foal, and then came back. Joanna was waiting for me in the front garden."

Joanna had stopped crying. Her features were set in a frozen calm.

"I'd been across the road to feed Oscar and Nellie. Only they weren't there. I suppose they'd gone down to the river. I was just going back indoors when I saw Philip."

"Oscar and Nellie?"

"Swans," Philip Cass explained, "who think we come down from town for the express purpose of bringing them urban delicacies."

"I see. Did you meet anyone on your walk?"

"Only the mare and her offspring," returned Philip with the shadow of a smile. Even a shattering grief could not entirely depress his sunny nature. "I'm reasonably sure they'll bear out my story. Wait a minute, though—" he turned to his wife. "You remember, darling. Lydia came out of her door just as we were going in."

"The Inspector asked who you *met*."

"True. But we saw her. God, what a sight! Looked like she was about to take off for a meeting of the coven. All she lacked was the broomstick." For Jurnet's benefit: "From which you'll gather the state of our relations with Lydia Massingham, our next-door neighbour."

"I've heard about her."

"I can imagine."

"What's been the trouble?" the detective inquired cautiously. "Chucks her rubbish over your fence?"

"Nothing so commonplace. She's rather a pathetic creature really, for all her King Kong muscles. Butch as they come—but there, that's the way God made her, doubtless for good reason."

"What we have against Lydia Massingham—" Joanna Cass took over—"is that she made overtures, if that's the official word for it, to Rachel."

"Did Rachel tell you?"

"Rachel told me," she returned with an intense bitterness. "If that makes any difference now we know what a little liar she was. Only she wasn't lying about that. I've seen the way Lydia looked at her. Revolting! But Rachel actually felt sorry for her. I made her promise she'd never have her in here while we were in town, but I'm pretty sure she went in to Maypole Cottage, for coffee or whatever. Knowing the way I felt about the woman she never mentioned it."

"Forgive me for asking this. Are you suggesting there was any relationship between them?"

Joanna's dark eyes were devoid of all expression.

"After what you've told us, how can I pretend to have known *anything* about Rachel?"

"For God's sake, Joanna, we know that! Rachel and that old dyke—!" Philip jumped to his feet and thrust his chubby face close to the detective's dark one. "Haven't you finished with us yet?"

"Not quite. That walk you took. What time was it you got back?"

The Casses looked at each other blankly.

"I'm sorry," Philip said at last. "The whole point of a country cottage is not having to look at a clock. For a couple of days you opt out of time, or at least indulge in the illusion that you do." He thought for a moment. "There was still a lot of noise coming from the High Street, which probably means the procession hadn't moved off. But I can't be more precise than that."

Despite himself, Jurnet felt envy rising in his gullet like vomit. *Opt out of time!* All very nice for those with the means to do it!

He swallowed and said: "I'd like to take a look at Rachel's room, if you don't mind."

# 11

It was a pretty room with a tiny bathroom adjoining. More Joanna Cass's taste than the girl's, Jurnet guessed. The divan bed was neat beneath its floral cover, the furniture looked unused.

The dressing-table and the cabinet in the bathroom were alike free of the bottles and tubes Jurnet's experience had led him to expect. Nineteen-year-old girls might not need powders and paints but they all had them. But then, Rachel Cass had been transfigured. If you were transfigured the chances were you could get by without eye-shadow.

The detective slid open the dressing-table drawer, moving it carefully from underneath, a manoeuvre whose significance did not escape Philip Cass, who had accompanied him upstairs.

"You think she may have brought him back here."

Jurnet responded woodenly: "Besides Rachel's, and Mrs. Cass's and your own, are there any other fingerprints one might expect to find in the normal course of events?"

"Mrs. Gamlin comes in to clean."

"I'll pass that on." The drawer was sticking a little. At last it came open, revealing the wad of notes which had impeded its smooth running.

Philip Cass exclaimed: "Good Lord!"

There were three hundred pounds in five-pound notes, secured with a rubber band.

"Was your sister in the habit of keeping this much cash about the house?"

The other shook his head in bewilderment.

"Half the time we had to remind her to draw what she needed for day-to-day expenses."

"Did she have three hundred pounds in her account, do you know?"

"Oh, she could have had a good deal more than that. She had a few thousand of her own, her share of our father's estate. She'd been managing it herself since she turned eighteen. Joanna and I thought it the best way to teach her the value of money. I had the impression she'd put it in a building society. I can't imagine why she'd keep such a large sum here." Flushing as a possible reason immediately occurred to him: "Unless it was to pay for the confinement."

"Not an abortion, anyway. Girls planning to get rid of unwanted foetuses don't go about transfigured." Jurnet shut the drawer with its contents still inside. "We'll leave it there for now."

He caught sight of the statuette on the window sill.

It was a small replica of the Lady of Promise, no more than eighteen inches high. Jurnet picked it up, and turning it so that the light from the low casement fell directly on it, found himself shaken by a vibration he had no difficulty in accounting for. Small as it was, the piece had much the same impact as its oversize original. More, in a way: a concentrated essence of itself—that same sublime sense of fulfilment, that astonishing nakedness combined with a perfect modesty.

The detective held it for a little, moving his hands over surfaces that seemed to convey through his fingertips a meaning exciting though imperfectly understood, a braille he was insufficiently equipped to read. Then he returned it gently to its place, ashamed of his emotion.

Philip Cass observed sarcastically: "Another of Paul's works of art."

Giving nothing away as he followed Rachel Cass's brother down the stairs, Jurnet remarked: "He seems better at small things than big."

Joanna was where they had left her. She reached for her husband's hand as he resumed his place beside her.

Jurnet said: "I'd like to see the note she left you."

"I never kept it," Joanna replied. "It was just about the milk and—"

Philip intervened.

"I'll go through the bin and let you know if I come across it."

"I'd be obliged," said Jurnet. He reached into his trouser pocket. "And now perhaps you'd tell me if either of you recognise this."

Neither of them had seen the cross before.

"If you're asking whether it could have been Rachel's, the answer is definitely no. Shrine people have a thing about crosses. If it's gold—" Philip raised his eyebrows in question— "I'm fairly certain she didn't know anyone with the kind of money to buy her a present like that."

"I think it's gold," Jurnet said. "I'm taking it to a chap in Norwich who understands these things. If it is, you're quite right—it must have set someone back a bit. Rachel was holding it."

"A cross? Rachel?" exclaimed Joanna. "Impossible!"

Benjamin Jurnet subdued a sigh. He was not a reading man; or rather, he was a re-reading man, as suspicious of a new book as of a parcel that ticked. Over the years he had accumulated a narrow shelf-ful of books to which he returned for sustenance whenever the spirit moved him.

Now, Joanna's expostulation brought irresistibly to his mind the work which seemed to him to encapsulate all the absurdities of the human condition. *"One can't believe impossible things!"* Alice had maintained. To which the Queen had answered pityingly: *"I dare say you haven't had much practice."* No one could say the Casses were not getting practice in believing impossibilites. Knowing what was still to come, Jurnet had to restrain himself from quoting Lewis Carroll aloud to them: *"Why, sometimes I've believed as many as six impossible things before breakfast."*

Instead, he repeated: "She was holding it." He stowed the cross away in his pocket.

"It wasn't Rachel's," Joanna insisted stubbornly. "She always said a cross was a symbol of death." Finishing on a note of desolation: "And she was right, wasn't she?"

"X marks the spot." Philip Cass picked up his wife's words with bitter irony. "End of a Maiden—in more senses than one. Poor old Charlie! Thought he'd recruited a vestal virgin when what he'd got was a temple prostitute!"

"Not the way I'd put it myself," said Jurnet. "As it happens, I do have one other thing to tell you. Your sister was a virgin."

A shocked silence greeted this statement, before Philip Cass asked cautiously: "Could you please repeat what you just said?"

"I said, Rachel was a virgin." There! Jurnet thought: that's the *seventh* impossible thing. "She was pregnant, but she was still a virgin."

At that, Joanna Cass began to laugh hysterically, and her husband, tugging at his sandy hair as if he meant to pull it out, cried aloud: "It's too much, God damn it! It's too much!"

Jurnet gave them a minute, then shouted: "That'll do!" and startled them into quiet. "It's nothing to take on about. The examining pathologist was surprised, but not all that surprised. A physiological freak, if you like, but not unknown. There was a case you must have read about—"

"The Ampthill peerage—" Philip Cass ran his tongue over his dry lips.

"That's it. Two half-brothers, each laying claim to the title. The elder son was born of a first marriage that ended in divorce. It was said that the husband and wife had never had full intercourse with each other, and the husband always contended, therefore, that the child couldn't possibly have been his. But—and this is the point—when the wife was medically examined before that child was born, it was found that, although she was certainly pregnant, the hymen was still unbroken, so that she was still, technically, *virgo intacta*. That's why, years later, when the old man died, still refusing to acknowledge the child as his own, the child—man, as he was by then—was able to go to court and get his rights upheld as against the son of the second marriage." He finished: "A case like that gets a lot of publicity, and so people single it out. But if it happened to one woman, you can bet your boots it's happened to others."

"Yes," said Philip Cass. "One of them's standing on a pedestal down at the Shrine."

"That's as may be," the detective returned stolidly. "Coming on top of everything else, I can understand it's a bit of a shock."

"Yes," said Philip again. Then: "Does it get us any nearer to finding out who killed Rachel?"

"Anything that tells us something about her we didn't know before gets us nearer. For one thing, it means she wasn't raped. Violence could never have left her in that state. Whoever got her in the family way, she was a consenting party."

"I could have told you that." Joanna sat bolt upright, twisting her handkerchief in her hands. "No one took her against her will. She was too happy. You've no idea how happy she was." She looked down at her writhing fingers as if they did not belong to her. "No idea."

"That must be your comfort. That, and that she probably never knew what hit her. To die that way, that's something."

"Yes," said Joanna Cass. "That's something."

## 12

Detective Sergeant Ellers stood at the side of the pond feeding cake to the swans. Jurnet, crossing the road from Forge Cottage, suddenly remembered he had had nothing to eat since breakfast.

"Hey!" he called. "Save a bit for me!"

"Sorry, sir. That's the last of it." Jack Ellers looked rosy and replete. He brushed his hands together to get rid of the crumbs. The swans, understanding the implications of the gesture, turned their backs on him simultaneously and took to the water. "Ungrateful buggers. Only proper place for them's on a box of matches."

Jurnet's whole being cried out for a cup of tea. And everything that ought to go with it in the country. Fruitcake, scones with home-made jam—

"Wonderful woman," Ellers was saying reverently. "I haven't had a tea like that since I was a boy. There was a kind of almond tart with bits of orange—" His eyes closed in blissful recollection.

"That stuff you were throwing away. What d'you do? Nick it for afters?"

Sergeant Ellers looked hurt.

"It was spice cake, see, just like my old mother used to make. Trouble was, after the teacakes and the tart and the fruit trifle I hadn't an inch left to tuck it into. So Mrs. Woodgate insisted I take a piece along with me for later, to see how it compared."

"And you had to chuck it away on a couple of birds!"

"Peckish, are you?" The Welshman directed a shrewd glance in the direction of Forge Cottage. "People bringing your kind of news can't expect to get entertained."

True enough, Jurnet conceded. What, he wondered, were the Casses doing, now that he had left them, devastated, in their pretty living-room? Had Philip Cass gone to put the kettle on? More likely, from what he had seen of them—and now his envy of owners of second homes submerged itself in a jealousy with deeper roots—they hadn't bothered with tea. To comfort themselves and each other they had gone upstairs, and there on the bed they were at that old, old thing that had nothing to do with gracious living.

The detective sat down at the edge of the pond where the white swans were mirrored in the water, itself a mirror of the sky. What a lovely place Mauthen Barbary was! He hated it, as he hated every place where he was called to a murder. Death tainted it. And besides, he wanted his tea.

"When I get back to Norwich," Jurnet said, "I'm going to treat myself to a bang-up dinner. The Nelson, or Marco's. Two portions of everything." Even as he spoke he saw himself, the real, not the fantasy Ben Jurnet, opening a tin of beans, alone in his dismal kitchen. What the hell was keeping Miriam in London? "Now can we get away from the cookery column and discuss a few other aspects of your visit with the Woodgates?"

"Yes, sir!" The Welshman was transformed instantly into a caricature of the keen police officer. "They live in a very nice house just outside the village on the coast road—you must have passed it on your way in this morning. Small estate, very select, every one with a double garage."

"What does Woodgate senior do for a living?"

"Bank manager, over at Cromer. All the managing he does. Didn't get two words in the whole time I was there. My guess his missus told him to keep his mouth shut. She'd do the talking."

"Bossy type, is she, then?"

"Majestic. Fine figure of a woman, as they used to say. In private, probably chews her old man up every night after supper and spits out the pieces, but in company she's very dignified—and a marvellous cook."

"We're not back to that. What about the son?"

"Apple of her eye. Could knock off the whole ruddy village and she'd cover up for him."

"Thing is, is there anything to cover up?"

"I spoke to the lad. He was upstairs, lying down, but he came down when his ma called him. Like death he looked. Wouldn't touch a bite of his tea."

"Must've been bad. What did he say?"

"Said he went over to the Shrine a little before ten-thirty. Mrs. Chitty and the Maidens were in the forecourt, all except Rachel Cass, and nobody seemed to know where she was, only just then Barnabas came out of the Shrine and said she was staying behind with the Lady. Neil—that's his name—offered to do the same, but Barnabas wouldn't have none of it. Sent him off to the Rond to check that the gates into the Manor grounds were open. So that's what he did—fastened back the gates and then came home again. Said he didn't fancy hanging about, if Rachel wasn't going to be there."

"Mother saw him come in, I suppose?"

"Matter of fact, she didn't. She was out at the back, spraying the roses. Not an insect in that garden without a pass. They wouldn't dare. Pa didn't see him either. He'd gone off early to Sheringham for a round of golf. The boy says he went up to his room and did some studying till he reckoned the procession would be over. He was hoping that, then, Rachel'd have a bit of time for him. He was going to suggest going over to Blackney. There's a hotel there with a pool open to non-residents."

"What did he do when he thought it was time for them to be back?"

"Left the house and went back to the Shrine. Just in time to hear the girl'd been murdered."

"And then?"

"Fainted clean away. Next thing he knew was some black women from Brixton screeching round him like banshees. Maybe you heard 'em yourself?"

Jurnet shook his head. He remembered only a girl's scream that had somehow intensified a terrible quiet.

Ellers continued: "He thinks one of the women went to fetch the doctor. All of a sudden, he says, he couldn't stand no more of it; broke away, ran as fast as he could, all the way home."

"Did he let his mum know he was back?"

"Says he just ran upstairs and threw himself on the bed. Didn't feel he could talk to anyone, not even Mummy. Wasn't till lunchtime when she came upstairs to see if he'd come in that she found out what had happened. She says she found him incoherent and for a long time she couldn't make head or tail of it. When she finally got it out of him she went downstairs, poured out half a tumbler of Scotch, took it up and made him drink it down."

"Half a tumbler?"

"I'd say it was a good measure of the emergency. I'd be surprised if Sonny Boy ordinarily gets offered anything stronger than a Babycham. Anyway, it worked. In ten minutes he was dead to the world and they had to wake him up to speak to me. The poor kid looked like he wished to God they'd let him lie."

"Poor kid, eh? Do I gather you've crossed Master Woodgate off your lists of suspects?"

"Oh, he could have killed her all right. I've known choirboys with the faces of angels who've kicked their old grannies down the stairs for a matter of tuppence ha'penny, let alone a girl with an unwanted pregnancy. He'd know about that side door, and for all we know the girl may have told him last night she wasn't going on the procession. He could have knocked her off before he even spoke to Barnabas, or alternatively, he could have nipped back to the Shrine soon as he'd fixed the gates, and done it then. With all those humps and bumps sticking out of the grass it wouldn't be difficult, even with people about, to get into the Shrine unnoticed—and away again, even with blood on your clothes."

Ellers smiled, pleased with his own perspicacity. "I asked him what he'd had on. He looked a little blank, then said, 'Same as I have now,' but I could hear the washing-machine going out in the kitchen, and Mrs. Woodgate didn't strike me as one to do her laundry on the Lord's Day. The lad also said he'd been carrying a jacket. Too hot to put on, he said, but he'd brought it along in case Rachel thought it too informal to march in a religious procession in your shirt sleeves. He could easily have slipped it on, after, to cover up any stains."

Jurnet teased: "Wonder you didn't think of having the washing out on the kitchen floor on the chance there was some blood not yet washed out."

"Thought of it all right." The little Welshman was unabashed. "But you haven't met Mrs. Woodgate. Much as my life was worth, boyo. You should have seen her bristle when I started questioning the boy about his clothes. *She* understood what I was getting at, if he didn't. If I hadn't had my tea already I'd have been lucky to be offered a drop of water out of the lavatory pan."

"Any chance she knocked the girl off herself? Strong woman taking measures to rescue her chick from designing female."

"Nothing like that. She seemed genuinely upset. Rather to my surprise, I must say, she was all for the Maidens and that stuff. Said she was glad to know her son was going about with a good girl, though in her young days you didn't have to put on a uniform to show you were respectable. Still, if that was what Mr. Griffin wanted—" The little Welshman grinned. "That was the key, really. Bit of a social climber is Mrs. Woodgate. If the Lord of the Manor wanted Maidens, then Maidens were OK by her."

Jurnet squinted up into the sun.

"Do *you* think Neil Woodgate could have made Rachel Cass pregnant?"

"I assume he has the apparatus, sir." The sergeant spoke in his most official tone. Then his eyes twinkled. "But I'm pretty sure she'd have had to show him how to use it."

"Excuse me—"

A shadow fell across Jurnet's face. Lydia Massingham interposed herself between the detective and the sun.

He scrambled to his feet, feeling less sure of himself than his years and experience warranted. Damn that shirt and slacks!

"Excuse me—" Lydia Massingham began again. Out of that unshapely bulk came a voice surprisingly high-pitched. Not so much a dyke, thought Jurnet, as a eunuch. And not so much ugly as unfortunate. Ugliness was at least a positive quality. Lydia Massingham was just a mess.

Jurnet, not an especially compassionate man, was pierced through with a sudden pang for the awful, unloved child she must once have been. Joanna Cass's hostility was explained. It would have flourished had there never been any little sister-in-law in danger of being corrupted.

"Police, are you?"

Sergeant Ellers, oppressed by the size of the creature, rose up on his toes importantly.

"I didn't like to disturb them—intrude. I just wanted to know how they were—"

*How the hell did you think they were?* In a neutral tone Jurnet responded: "Upset, naturally."

The woman sensed his anger nevertheless, but had no idea

how to counter it. Probably it was an emotion she was resigned to arousing, simply by being what she was. Tears trickled down either side of her stubby nose. She cried hopelessly, as if aware that tears would never get Lydia Massingham anywhere. And indeed, even as he recognised the injustice of his own reaction, they only made the detective angrier.

In a dry, official voice he asked: "Was Miss Cass a friend of yours?"

"Friend?" Lydia Massingham repeated the word as if she were unsure of its meaning.

"You live next door. You must have seen a lot of each other."

"We had coffee together. Or sometimes, in the evenings, she'd pop in for a mug of chocolate." She looked at the detective with a pathos he found completely resistible. "She said I made it better than anyone else she knew."

"Did you see her this morning?"

"Just for an instant. I happened to look out of the window—"

"Did you yourself go down to the Shrine?"

"You'll never catch *me* there! We had a demo—"

"Before that."

"We all went over to The Pirate. Our posters and stuff were parked there, in a shooting-brake."

"We?"

"Me and the girls who were here for the demo."

"Did you all go off to The Barbary Pirate together?"

"Except that I stayed behind to wash up the mugs. It only took a minute."

"And you never went near the Shrine?"

"I told you. I only saw that hideous object once, when Charlie first found it, and that was more than enough."

Jurnet produced the little gold cross from his pocket.

"You didn't give this to Rachel Cass, by any chance?"

Lydia Massingham shrank from the shining symbol like the Devil in a medieval morality. "I'm a humanist. I don't give crosses. And if I did, and that's gold, I couldn't afford it anyway."

"Did Rachel ever show it to you?"

The woman shook her head. A look of malice came over her face, making it, if possible, even more uncomely.

"Why don't you ask Lionel Persimmer? He was mad about her. And crosses, after all, are his business."

# 13

The High Street was deserted. Wattle-and-daub notwithstanding, it reminded Jurnet of nothing so much as those empty, clapboarded streets along which, in Westerns, the hero, hands dangling within reach of his guns, moves like fate to meet the bad man: Fun Shirt Jurnet and his sidekick Tiptoes Ellers moving in for the final shootout. The detective chuckled, and his companion commented unexpectedly: "He is a bit of a laugh, isn't he? Swap the Lady of Promise for 'im any day of the week."

Jurnet followed the direction of Sergeant Ellers' gaze, and discovered it fixed in admiration upon the plaster pig in the window of Mr. Beslow's butcher shop.

"That's what I call sculpture! Realistic. Looks like it could open its mouth any minute and tell you the price of sausages."

"Realistic, eh? How many pigs you seen in three-piece suits?"

"How many pigs can afford 'em, the poor buggers?" Jack Ellers looked about him and stopped joking. "Creepy kind of place, sir, wouldn't you say?"

"All villages are the same. There's never a soul about."

But all villages were not the same as Mauthen Barbary. The fear that had emptied the streets had turned the place in upon itself. With murder abroad, only home was safe.

Presently, as Jurnet well knew, would come the sightseers. Provided Mr. Charlie Griffin had the *nous* to see no one washed the Shrine floor, he could be on to a good thing. 5p to see the bloodstains. And presently, reading about it in the papers, seeing it on telly, the natives would forget their fear and begin, even, to be proud of their very own murder.

Ellers said: "Not just the emptiness, the cleanness. Not so much as a toffee paper. Way I feel this minute, a coke tin or an empty packet of Woodbines'd make me as happy as Robinson Crusoe when he saw that footstep in the sand."

"Come back next weekend and have the time of your life."

The little Welshman looked at his watch.

"The news'll be going out in ten minutes. With all the pretty pictures. Idols and dancing virgins. Quite a sight, it ought to be."

"Don't let your imagination run away with you. That procession was about as sexy as liquorice allsorts."

The sergeant sighed.

"Norfolk was never much of a place for orgies."

A figure appeared in the distance, breasting the rise at the end of the High Street.

"There's your Man Friday."

It turned out to be the *Norfolk Mercury* man to whom Jurnet had spoken earlier in the day.

"Thought your lot had turned it in till tomorrow," the detective greeted him.

"I decided to hang on for a bit. Knowing who was on the case I reckoned it could all be sewn up by dark."

"Flattery will get you nowhere."

"You wouldn't consider giving me a statement on account of my beautiful blue eyes?"

"That's different." Jurnet cleared his throat. "Our inquiries are proceeding," he said primly.

"Gee, thanks a lot!"

"Think nothing of it," said the detective. "By the way, when you get back to base you'll find Sergeant Bowles has been on the blower. We want all the photographic stuff we can get our hands on. Have a word with your editor, will you? I don't want anything thrown away till we've had a look at it."

"Will do. Anything else?"

"I can't think of anything," said Jurnet. "Except, do me a favour and don't try on any of your celebrated foot-in-the-door technique in Mauthen Barbary. There are people here who are suffering. Leave 'em alone."

The young man flushed.

"I don't think I need any soft-hearted copper to tell me how to do my job."

"I'm telling you how not to do it," said Jurnet.

The yews on either side of the path up to the church door needed trimming. Spiky leaflets reached out for the detective inspector and his sergeant as they toiled upward in the heat.

Even in the sun it was a church which made of faith something sad and defeated. Its tower of dilapidated flints looked like a fortress whose defenders had long since fled.

"'Parish Church of St. Blaise,'" Ellers read aloud from the notice board. "And who the hell's St. Blaise when he's at home?"

"He was a bishop," said Jurnet who, as a native of what had once been a great wool county, was familiar with the name of the patron saint of the wool trade. "Got himself done in by heathens. They tore the flesh off his body with iron combs, the kind they used to card wool with in the old days."

"Lovely way to go. This where it happened, then?"

"Don't be daft. Asia Minor or somewhere."

The Welshman looked about him with distaste.

"Shouldn't be surprised it turned out to be here, whatever you say."

The church had no porch. As Ellers reached for the latch the door was opened from the inside, followed by a body moving with a thrust and determination that sent the little Welshman sprawling into one of the yews.

"Beg par'n," muttered a short, broad man with other things clearly on his mind. His face was an astonishing, not to say alarming, red.

"Bonkers!" exclaimed the man, hurtling down the path. The epithet did not appear to be addressed to either of the two police officers. As he plunged down the slope they heard his voice again. "Stark, staring bonkers!"

Sergeant Ellers stayed where he had fallen. His face held astonished disbelief.

"Did you get a look at him?"

"I did. What's so special besides his fluorescent complexion and his beautiful manners?"

"The pig! Three-piece suit and all!"

Jurnet made the connection.

"I had a thought I'd seen him before! Not such a good fit round the shoulders, though."

"I'd never've believed it if I hadn't seen it with my own eyes."

Jurnet said: "You've got a second chance to check up. He's coming back."

Ellers heaved himself out of the yew and took up an official stance, its dignity somewhat impaired by the woody detritus which had attached itself to his hair and clothes. Nevertheless it was to Ellers that the man addressed himself, ignoring the dark young man in the bright shirt and slacks.

"You police?" the man asked. "I thought I seen you in the village."

"You ought to look where you're going," returned Ellers severely, contriving an admission and a reprimand in the same form of words. "What appears to be the trouble?"

The man's little pig eyes darted suspiciously from Ellers to his companion.

Jurnet said: "I am Detective Inspector Jurnet. This is Detective Sergeant Ellers. Can we be of any assistance?"

"You can have a go. I'm Beslow, the churchwarden. Vicar's gone off his head and I want to report a burglary!"

"There's nobody here," said Jurnet.

The statement was apt in more senses than one. Within, the church was as impoverished of spiritual content as without. The butcher led the way down the centre aisle without speaking, turning at the altar rail towards a side chapel of whose existence the detectives had been unaware, and at which, given the rest of the church, they could never have guessed.

Wrought-iron tracery closed off an elegant little withdrawing-room dominated by the alabaster effigies of Sir Amyas Griffin and his wife Anne, recumbent upon a marble bed guarded at each corner by a griffin brandishing an heraldic pennon. Here the man who had destroyed the Priory and its Shrine had made his own separate peace with heaven. With hindsight one could fancy in the stone features a secret amusement. The Lady of Promise reposed safe underground, and her preserver awaited with calm self-confidence that resurrection which was his just reward.

Meanwhile, from the look of it he rested comfortably. Angels spread-eagled against the roof beams blew upon golden trumpets. Brass candlesticks adorned an altar table covered with embroidery taken from the cope of a bishop centuries dead.

The space between the candlesticks was empty.

Prostrate before the altar lay the Reverend Lionel Persimmer.

"*He's* here all right," Mr. Beslow said unnecessarily. "But *it* ain't!" He pointed a thick forefinger at the space between the candlesticks. "Four hunnerd pounds, they said, last time they was here from Norwich. An' *he* don't even want to call in the police!"

"Well, they're in now," said Jurnet. "So stuff it a minute, will you?"

One at either side, the two detectives carefully raised the distraught clergyman, cassocked and surpliced for the evening service, to his feet. Lionel Persimmer seemed quite unable to support himself, or to stem the sobs which racked his lean frame. At a jerk of the head from the sergeant, Beslow came forward with one of the rush-seated chairs that stood lined up facing the altar. Having lowered Persimmer on to it, the two men were constrained to stay close by him, lest his limp body slump sideways and down to the floor again.

How they had all loved that girl, thought Jurnet; discovering that from pity he had moved on to falling in love with her himself, a little. Love was a contagion. You couldn't move among lovers without catching a dose.

In a curt voice he ordered the churchwarden to fetch a glass of water, and when it was brought, grudgingly, the detective sluiced Persimmer's face with it.

The sobs became spasmodic, ceased. Without moving from his position of support, Jurnet turned his attention back to the churchwarden.

"Now, Mr. Beslow—what's this about a burglary and four hundred pounds?"

"That was donkey's years ago. Lord knows what it'd fetch today."

"What would *what* fetch?"

"The crucifix. What else d'you suppose I'm on about? The crucifix off that there altar which one of them scum that was here this morning has taken himself off with!"

"I see. Could you describe it?"

Sergeant Ellers fished his notebook out of his pocket.

"The crucifix." Mr. Beslow could as well have described the look of a pound of brisket. The familiar things of life spoke for themselves.

"It was silver, very heavy, about twenty inches from plinth to the top of the upright." Lionel Persimmer's voice was tremulous but under control. "Not what you would normally find in a church of our communion, but as the gift of a Griffin, made specifically for the adornment of the Griffin chapel, we had a faculty for its use. The figure of Our Lord was in parcel-gilt— German, I believe, eighteenth century. There was a certain exaggeration that jarred a little: but fine workmanship, very fine—"

"I see. And when did you first notice it was missing?"

Persimmer shook his head helplessly. Tiny beads of red

showed on his forehead where he had grazed the skin on the tombstones with which the chapel was paved.

"I'm the one as missed it," Beslow intervened. "Parson wouldn't miss what was under his nose even if it wasn't there."

Jurnet made no attempt to unravel that one.

"Well then," he demanded, "when did *you* miss it?"

" 'Bout half an hour ago, when I come to make sure all's in order for evensong."

"So it was here this morning?"

"Can't say, can I? Always go by the bell, don't I, mornings? Come down here the minute he starts ringing. That gives me plenty of time to look round before service, specially now we got no verger. Only this partic'lar morning—" the churchwarden threw an angry look at his priest—"bell was late, weren't it? Time I got here, didn't have time to do nothing but find the place in the hymn book."

"Mr. Persimmer," said Jurnet, "is it true, as Mr. Beslow here says, that you didn't want to call in the police?"

Lionel Persimmer shut his eyes, as if the effort of assembling his motives was too much for him.

"I felt—after what happened this morning I felt it didn't matter." There was a long pause before he added: "And then, too—a crucifix, a figure of Our Saviour. I felt it demeaning to Him to turn the symbol of His sacrifice into a case for a police court. I shall, of course, report it to the diocesan office and they, no doubt, will take any action they see fit. It was just that I myself did not feel it a matter for the police."

"Do you always leave a valuable object like that out here in the open, unprotected?"

"We're not as naïve as that, officer. Mostly, we keep it in the vestry, in the safe with the communion plate. We only bring it out on special occasions."

"And you decided today was one of them?"

"I felt one must make a gesture. I hoped some of those self-styled pilgrims might find their way here and see it, and, perhaps, reflect on the Passion of Our Lord—"

"They came in and saw all right!" The butcher's voice was heavy with sarcasm. "Came an' saw an' took!"

"Have you a photo?" the detective asked, ignoring the interruption.

"There's bound to be one at Norwich."

"That should be helpful." Jurnet looked at the clergyman

and decided he was recovered enough to take stronger treatment.

"You understand," he began, "we have to pursue our inquiries into this theft further, in view of what happened at the Shrine today. There could be a connection."

"Our Lord on the cross!" Lionel Persimmer cried. "What possible—"

"I only said *could*. We shall have to see how we go on." Turning to the churchwarden, Jurnet continued: "Thank you for your help, Mr. Beslow. We needn't detain you any longer."

"You're not detaining me. It's nearly time for evensong."

"Then I suggest you go outside and head off anyone who shows up. Mr. Persimmer's in no state to conduct a service."

The vicar got shakily to his feet.

"I'm all right." His voice strengthened with his determination. "There's a fresh surplice in the vestry. Of course I shall take the service."

"In that case, Mr. Beslow," Jurnet's suggestion carried the unmistakable force of an order, "perhaps you'd be good enough to fetch the surplice, and another glass of water." When the churchwarden had departed, unwillingly, the detective asked quietly: "Just one more thing, Mr. Persimmer. Why *was* the bell rung late this morning?"

"I—I went for a walk down by the river."

"Do you often do that before a service?"

"Occasionally. On a Sunday when we have no early Communion."

"And are you often late getting back to ring the bell?"

"I needed to pray. I was upset. About the pilgrimage. About that black devil, the Lady of Promise."

"And about Rachel?"

Lionel Persimmer began to cry again. "Oh God!"

"You'll have to pull yourself together if you really mean to take that service." The words, for all their brutal directness, were spoken kindly. "I'll report the loss of the crucifix and let you know what turns up. As I say, it may have nothing to do with the murder. But—" and he brought out the gold cross with the little balls at the end of the arms—"here's something that certainly does. Did *you* give it to the dead girl?"

"A cross! She'd never let me give her a cross." Persimmer's hand went out unconsciously towards the gleaming little object, a gesture of love. "It's very beautiful. I can't believe it was Rachel's."

"I can't say for certain it was. All we know is, we found her clutching it."

The clergyman looked at the detective as if he had just been presented with a gift of infinite price.

"Thank you, Inspector. It's a great comfort to know she died with the symbol of eternal life in her hand."

His voice was firm. He took the water from Beslow, who had returned; sipped a little, and set the glass down on Sir Amyas's tomb. Without fumbling, he exchanged his creased surplice for the one the churchwarden had brought him.

He straightened his back and said: "I must go and ring the bell."

## 14

"Well?" Jurnet asked. "What do you think?"

He had chosen the route through the Manor grounds rather than return from the church by way of Church Lane and the High Street. Mr. Griffin's parkland was exquisite in the evening sun, a landscape that made it hard to keep one's mind on murder.

Sergeant Ellers said: "He had the time to do it." Even as he spoke, the bell clanged from the church tower, late again. "Prayer by the river—very proper for a parson, I'm sure, but not when he's supposed to be minding the shop. So, murdered her maybe. Shouldn't think for a moment, though, he was the one that laid her."

The Sergeant's choice of word sent a wave of irritation coursing through Jurnet. Recognising the injustice of taking umbrage, he commented, mildly: "Oh, I don't know. He's not a bad-looking chap, in a Christian martyr kind of way."

"Celibates the lot of 'em, weren't they? My brother the sun and my sister the moon, but never my sweetheart the bird. No, my money's on Falkener, from what I saw of him. Artistic. Women go for that in a big way."

"You never heard the way he spoke about her."

"Maybe it was just some fellow she picked up in the bushes."

"No!"

"Not promiscuous," the Sergeant, startled to find he had given offence, hastened to explain. "More out of pity. Maybe, way she looked at it, giving it away was the biggest sacrifice she could offer to that Lady of hers. Like giving everything you have to the poor. Very religious, actually."

"Load of codswallop! And what man would even want a woman to go to bed with him out of pity?"

"Don't know about that. Often think it's the only reason they put up with us. Take my Rosie—"

Jurnet thought of Rosie Ellers, dimpled as a well-buttoned armchair.

"Don't be daft. Anyone can see she's crazy about you."

"Go on! Every morning, I tell you, she wakes up, takes a look at me and thinks 'the poor bastard!' Recipe for a very happy marriage, sir." The Sergeant beamed at his superior, all wide-eyed innocence. "Can't all be tall, dark and handsome."

Refusing to rise to the bait, Jurnet merely remarked: "Another reason against Falkener—it has to be somebody gentle, and Falkener looks like he takes his sex on the boisterous side. Incomplete intercourse, Colton said. Anything rollicking and the hymen would've been broken."

"That puts young Woodgate back in the picture. But I don't know, sir—" Ellers was plainly averse to abandoning his favourable opinion of "young Woodgate"—"those virile-looking blokes, shirts open to the belly button—Always suspect what's below the belt, that's my experience."

"There are two crimes here," said Jurnet, "and a third thing—pregnancy—that, in other circumstances, would be none of our damn business. Provided it's nothing to do with the case, I couldn't care less who knocked off the vicar's crucifix, and similarly, so long as it has nothing to do with her death, I don't even want to know who made Rachel Cass pregnant."

Poor kid. As if a violent end were not enough, there had to be the monstrous intrusion of post-mortems, police inquiries, newspapers and telly. The corpse as showbiz.

Murder should be a private affair.

They had come into the copse, drawn by the magnet of shade. They came upon the grotto unawares.

"What's this then?" demanded Jurnet, all his professional suspicions aroused by the spectacle of an open grave.

"Must be where Mr. Griffin dug up the statue. The village bobby was telling me about it. Grotto, the old man calls it. Grotty, more like it."

As he spoke, Chloe leaped from the undergrowth. It took some minutes for the detectives to realise that the dog was bent on welcoming, not devouring them.

"Chloe! Chloe!" called a voice with an American intonation, nearer with each repetition. And finally: "Down, Chloe! Get down!"

"It's all right." Sticky with tokens of canine affection Jurnet found himself confronting a handsome, lean-shanked woman as tall as himself.

"Are you OK?" Alice Diefenhaus inquired anxiously. "I guess she doesn't know me well enough to obey my orders."

"She doesn't know me at all," said Jurnet, feeling dirty and at a disadvantage. "I hate to think what she's like with old friends."

Mrs. Diefenhaus laughed.

"She does tend to regard this spot as her special domain. After all, she was the one who really found the Lady—" information which did nothing to endear the dog to the detectives. "I'm Alice Diefenhaus. My husband and I are Mr. Griffin's house guests."

Jurnet passed a hand over his ruffled hair. The Sergeant, he noticed, was well up on his toes.

"We're police officers. As it happens, we were on our way to have a word with Mr. Griffin." He introduced Ellers and himself.

"Mr. Griffin's been expecting you. He's up in the Muniment Room right now, with my husband. Anything to take his mind off what's happened. The poor man's heartbroken."

Jurnet said: "Everyone seems to have been very fond of Rachel Cass."

Alice Diefenhaus came back without equivocation: "I'm in no position to know how Mr. Griffin felt about the girl. We only got here yesterday. I meant, heartbroken about the Shrine. A place dedicated to life has been defiled by murder."

"He can always get in a bishop to reconsecrate the place."

"Exactly what we told him." She shook her head. "He says that as long as the Shrine stands, the bloodstains on the floor will cry out in affront to the Lady."

"Nothing to stop him putting in a new floor."

"Not enough, he says. He'll have to pull down the whole Shrine and build a new one. And he doesn't have the money."

\* \* \*

Alice Diefenhaus led the way up the terrace steps. They were the first of many flights up which she sprang untiring, the two police officers toiling behind. It annoyed Jurnet to find himself so out of condition. Ellers, overweight and used to panting, climbed with greater stoicism. He even found breath to comment on the barley-sugar banisters and the griffins on the newel-posts; the tapestries, sportive with gods and goddesses diverting themselves in various ways, most of them improper, that hung from ceiling to floor.

On the third floor landing their progress was halted by Anguish, the manservant, who, told that the two were police officers, stared at Jurnet unbelievingly, and let them pass only upon production of their credentials. Even then he would have had them wait while he went to inquire whether his master was of a mind to receive them.

"Mr. Griffin prefers not to be disturbed when he's in the Muniment Room."

"Just as we prefer not to be disturbed by a murder," said Jurnet, setting foot firmly on the first step of the next and, as it turned out mercifully, the last flight up to the turret where Charles Griffin hoarded his family history.

The Muniment Room was bright with sun but musty with the smell of the past. Every window was tight shut, and guarded on the outside by a stone griffin whose back, presented to the room, effectively discouraged any addict of fresh air.

The two men who sat at a large table among the bookshelves and the filing cabinets appeared to be in no need of any; but Alice Diefenhaus, stepping over the threshold, exclaimed: "Eliot! Your allergy!" Whereupon, predictably, Professor Diefenhaus began to sneeze.

Jurnet liked Charles Griffin at once. Of all the people he had come into contact with that day, he was the only one who disregarded the way he was dressed without managing to convey, even ever so little, the fact that he *was* disregarding it.

"You must forgive me for not rising to greet you," the old man said, when Mrs. Diefenhaus had made the introductions. "Transporting my bulk to these rarefied altitudes depletes my physical resources. If my financial ones were not even more depleted I should put in a lift. I suppose you've come about the Shrine?"

"About the murder, actually."

"That is what I meant. A very sad business. We shall have to move the Lady of Promise as soon as your people permit it. She mustn't be left where she is a moment longer than can be helped."

Jurnet said stiffly, modifying his good opinion of a moment earlier: "I'll check with Norwich and let you know."

"Now you're out of temper with me," Griffin said, "because I seem more concerned for the Lady than for poor Rachel. I admit it freely. One represents life, the other is dead. How can formal affirmations of outrage help that poor child now?"

Mollified, Jurnet responded: "I hope you'll be able to help us find out who killed her."

"It's my hope the Lady will do that." Adding courteously: "Not that I would wish to disparage the contribution of the Police Force. It doesn't do, does it, to sit with one's hands in one's lap waiting for heaven to do all the work."

"I doubt the Chief Constable would think much of it."

"I can see you think I'm a foolish old man. Let me make myself clear. I don't expect the Lady to step down from her pedestal like the Commendatore in *Don Giovanni* and drag the miscreant down to hell. Neither do I expect her to loose a shaft of lightning, or kill the murderer with a glance."

"What exactly do you expect, sir?"

"Simply that somehow, in some manner of which I have no inkling, she will reveal the murderer."

From the other side of the table, Professor Diefenhaus put in: "If it's of any interest to you, Inspector, while I can't myself share Mr. Griffin's optimism, I can understand how he can make the statement he has just made. May I ask, sir, if you have taken time out to take a good look at the Lady of Promise?"

"I have."

"Didn't she strike you as being quite extraordinary?"

"Extraordinary, yes," said Jurnet. "But not a particularly good private eye."

Charles Griffin burst out laughing.

"Bravo!" he exclaimed. "Private eye! What a phrase for 'the Eternal Eye that sees it whole!' I can tell you're not a married man, Inspector. Like all bachelors, you don't like the Lady. Embodying as she does fertility, birth, and therefore responsibility, she represents a threat to that freedom you seldom enjoy but feel it obligatory to extol."

Because he often thought about the children he and Miriam would some day make together, Jurnet retorted, a shade uncouthly: "I understood you to be a bachelor yourself, Mr. Griffin."

"You may be forgiven for thinking me one. My wife died many years ago in childbirth with our stillborn child. And now," the old man said with unfailing kindness, "are there any other questions you would care to ask me?"

There were many, and Jurnet asked them. The two police officers were told of the party the night before, the walk to the grotto, the excursion to the Shrine. On the procession, viewed from the terrace in the company of the Professor and his wife, the old man had nothing new to add. He had noticed that the church bell had sounded late.

"How many people have keys to the cloister door?"

"Any number. Myself. Barnabas, Mrs. Chitty, the Maidens, Falkener. Anguish, I imagine, and various workmen. During the day it's almost always left unlocked anyway."

"Did people in Mauthen Barbary know that?"

"I have no idea. In a village, one's neighbours soon get the hang of the way things are run." Charles Griffin looked at his interlocutor and sighed. "You don't believe the murderer's an outsider. You think it's one of us."

"One doesn't base a murder investigation on what one thinks, sir."

"On what else?" The old man opened his rheumy eyes wide.

"On a basis of evidence, sir," said Jurnet, feeling like the archetypal dumb copper.

"To be sure," Griffin conceded. "Ratiocination is not enough when dealing with the irrational. And that can only mean you have evidence."

"Call it a pointer or two. Too early to draw conclusions. When did you yourself last see the dead girl?"

"It must have been Friday afternoon. She had some bills for food supplied to the Hospice. She came to see Anguish really—he deals with matters of that kind—but when she heard I was having tea, she joined me in the library. She seemed very happy about the impending festivities."

"Happier than usual?"

Charles Griffin said simply: "Rachel was always happier than usual."

"What I mean is—well, for instance—do you think she could have been in love?"

"Is that your pointer to unusual happiness? How young of you! But yes, decidedly, Rachel was in love."

"Who with? Do you know?" Jurnet demanded, only to be crestfallen by the reply.

"With herself, of course. Like all the Maidens. The worship of her own body, youthful and inviolate."

"If that's really what you think, sir, I wonder you started this Maiden lark at all."

"Lark," Griffin returned, not at all put out, "is an excellent word for it. An innocent frolic, in affectionate commemoration of those poor nuns who attended the Lady in the old days, padlocked in their virginity by vows taken at an age when no young woman should commit herself for a period longer than half an hour."

"You make virginity itself sound like a perversion."

"Why, so it is," said the surprising old man, "except for those who have been visited by the Angel of the Lord."

"Can't be many of those," Jurnet muttered. Aloud, he said: "When you saw Rachel, what else did you talk about?"

"I remember that when she arrived I was reading some epigrams of Agathias Scholasticus—I don't know whether you are familiar with the author of *The Reign of Justinian?*—and I translated a few for her amusement. Otherwise, it was all about the arrangements for today."

Jurnet changed direction.

"Tell me something about Barney Smithers."

"If you know that is his name," Charles Griffin replied, "I doubt if I can tell you anything you don't already know."

"He has confessed to killing the girl."

"Has he, indeed?"

"You don't seem surprised."

"We are all of us capable of the worst, as of the best. Besides, you only say he has confessed to the murder, not that he committed it."

"That's not for me to say. That's for a court of justice."

"Oh admirable sleuth!" exclaimed Charles Griffin, with a smile which took away all offence. "No thinking, no judgment! Nevertheless, you don't really think he killed Rachel, do you? If you did, you wouldn't still be seeking her murderer."

"Let's say, I'm keeping an open mind."

"That's good," said Griffin. "Very good, seeing you obviously know Barnabas's history."

"Did you know it, when you took him on?"

"I did."

"Bit risky, wasn't it, with young girls about?"

"A bit irresponsible, is that what you mean, Inspector? I don't think so. During his first weeks here, while he was still in bed, I came to know Barnabas as well as one individual can hope to know another."

"In bed? What was the matter with him?"

"Oh—I assumed he had told you. I found him dying in the grounds. The way I found the Lady." Griffin looked at the detective whimsically. "You will think I have a special gift for finding things. He was in that same bit of woodland, as a matter of fact, and, just as with the Lady, it was Chloe who led me to him. He was lying on the ground, deeply unconscious. Another hour, Dr. Teago said, and it would have been too late to save him."

"Had he taken something?"

"Nothing like that. Starvation. Quite deliberate. He had made up his mind, after what happened at Yarmouth, that he was unfit to live. He had simply wandered aimlessly until his strength gave out. That is, he believed it was aimlessly. It's possible as he comes from Lynn originally, that he was, unconsciously, directing his steps homeward. Then again," said Charles Griffin, "it's possible that, far from directing his steps, his steps were directed."

"I see, sir," said Jurnet, who did not see. "And Mr. Falkener—did you find him in the grounds too?"

"Alas, no! If I had, I might have discovered someone of greater gifts. I found Paul in a gallery in Cork Street, on one of my infrequent visits to London. My taxi was held up outside, and there was this statuette in the window, quite small but matchless. It was a nude, a young woman in, I should guess, the fifth or sixth month of her pregnancy, the contours of the body just beginning to change, and the young woman— scarcely more than a child herself—still to come to terms with her new configuration. I do not think that, the Lady herself apart, I have ever been so moved by a work of art. I paid the cab off and went inside, to buy the figurine and to inquire for its creator. To my lasting regret, the first was not for sale, and I acquired the second. You've seen the panels in the Shrine?"

"Yes," said Jurnet. "Nothing to write home about."

"Not even a postcard." The old man sighed. "A great disappointment. Still, for Paul, a greater one."

"What will happen to him now the Shrine's finished?"

"The Shrine is indeed finished," Griffin repeated calmly. "I intend to have it demolished as soon as is practicable. As for

Paul, I told him a fortnight ago there was nothing more for him to do here. I said he could stay on rent-free at The Barn until the end of the year, but after that I should be obliged to let it for profit."

"How did he take it?"

"Very well. Had our positions been reversed, he said, he'd have kicked me out a year ago. I am quoting his exact words. He did suggest staying on as estate handyman, but I didn't take the suggestion seriously. Paul remains an artist, albeit a failed one."

Griffin twisted in his chair, towards a bundle of papers lying on the table. Jurnet saw that they were cobbled together down one side with a coarse thread whose ends dangled untidily. The old man produced a pair of spectacles from his breast pocket, hooked them into place, and then proceeded to leaf through the makeshift book, scanning the pages with a speed that had Jurnet, an admirer of expertise in any field, impressed and respectful.

"Ah, here we are." Griffin pointed, the back of his hand remarkably akin to the aged paper. "*Item to Henry Pock-thorpe, for his day labour at carpenters craft between Lady Day and Michaelmas, as well as two great posts, a framed stile with all timber thereto belonging, four pounds, nine shillings, four pence*"—That's what it cost my ancestor Sir Amyas Griffin for six months' work, plus the raw materials. Ah, those were the days for hiring handymen!"

"Come now, Mr. Griffin," the Professor was moved to protest, "you aren't comparing the value of money in Henry the Eighth's time with what it is today?"

"Not really. Just a bit of wishful thinking. In all likelihood Sir Amyas complained as bitterly as I of the cost of carpenters and everything else. You can see by these accounts how carefully every item of expenditure was overseen. Every now and again there's a note in another hand—" he flipped through the pages. "Here's one, against a note of payment to a Thomas Wakefield and a Clement Crow for '*their expenses and of their horses for the bringing from Lynn of salt and fish, onions and a firkin of ale.*' They charged two and tenpence for that job, and someone—I can't help feeling it was Sir Amyas himself—has written in the margin, '*It needed not two men, and with two shillings were they well requited.*' My forbear, you see, was quite the opposite of myself. He had all the money in the world for big things, like this house, and none for the little;

whereas I have all I need for the little things, and none for the large."

Jurnet, staring at the faded script, said: "It doesn't even look like English to me."

"It's English, a little more antique than you're accustomed to. It's only a matter of getting your eye in." Griffin heaved himself out of his chair. "I shall make you a copy of these documents to peruse at your leisure. Even a policeman must rest at times from tracking his prey."

"It's very kind—" Jurnet watched the old man teeter across the room, and wondered whether he were being side-tracked deliberately.

"Not at all. You've given me an excuse to play with my favourite toy. The Professor will confirm I've been plaguing him ever since he got here to let me use my copying machine on his behalf."

He patted an imposing apparatus ranged along a wall. "One of my little things. Well, not really mine. I lease it from an organisation which is kind enough to charge me a derisory rent provided only that I use a thousand sheets of their special paper each month to make my copies on."

"A thousand a month!" Professor Diefenhaus exclaimed.

"Now you know why I've been pestering you, and why I'm about to foist these accounts on the Inspector. It's to help me feel virtuous instead of extravagant."

Alice Diefenhaus, who had remained near the door which she had left open in the interests of her husband's allergy, crossed the room to where the old man was fiddling rather helplessly with the thread which bound the account book.

"Do you want it undone? I'm a wizard with knots."

"Would you?" Griffin handed over the papers gratefully. "Ordinarily I wouldn't want to tamper with it, but it has to lie flat or you can't take a satisfactory copy."

The American woman unlaced the thread deftly.

"I bought a sewing kit in Norwich with the cutest little bodkin I've been dying to find a use for. Let me know when you're through and I'll put it back together again so you'll never know it's been apart."

"Would you really? In that case I'll take the opportunity to make a copy of every page. Two copies," Griffin amended, hugely pleased, "in case the first ones go astray. And that's apart from the Inspector's set. For once, I might even use up my quota."

"I'll have to pick mine up later," Jurnet interposed. "I have to get on."

A little thing like a murder to solve.

Griffin placed the loose accounts carefully on top of the copying machine.

"I'll send Anguish over with them. To P.C. White's. Would that be right?"

"I'm at the Hospice, actually. I think, if you don't mind, hang on to them for a moment. I doubt I'll have time to look at them for a bit."

The old man shook hands cordially. "That means we'll meet again, which will be pleasant. Your colleague too." He smiled at Ellers. "I hope, Sergeant, that just as these accounts have been preserved for posterity you will preserve your notes on this sad affair. You've no idea how illuminating they may turn out to be in four hundred years' time."

"Not my property, sir," the Welshman answered. "I dare say the police authority will treat them with the respect they deserve."

"I'll walk Inspector Jurnet and the Sergeant to the end of the drive," said Alice Diefenhaus. "And, Eliot, I think you should go and take your antihistamine."

The Professor sneezed and rose obediently.

"Jurnet!" Griffin cried. "I didn't get the name when—How do you spell it?"

Jurnet, on the threshold, paused and obliged.

"Jurnet!" Griffin exclaimed, discarding the final consonant and pronouncing the name as if it were French. "But that's marvellous! You're Jewish, of course!"

Startled, and with Miriam immediately in his mind, the detective reddened. The thought that the blush might be interpreted as shame almost made him answer yes. He'd like to have seen Jack Ellers' face if he'd actually said it.

Instead he replied curtly: "Unitarian."

"Of course! The perfect compromise! Is it possible," the old man demanded, as if he did not really believe it was possible, "that you don't know about Jurnet of Norwich, the Rothschild of the Middle Ages; the man whose money built abbeys, cathedrals, financed crusades?"

Jurnet shook his head.

"Never heard of the gentleman. Sounds like a funny line of business for a Jew to be in."

"He had little choice, poor fellow, life for a Jew in Christian

England being what it was in the twelfth century. But a man of parts, I assure you. An ancestor to be proud of!"

"I thought I read somewhere that some king—Edward, was it?—kicked the Jews out of England altogether."

"Edward the First. So he did, nearly seven hundred years ago. But it isn't difficult, is it, to conjecture there were some who, in order to circumvent that brutal decree, submitted to conversion and, like the Maranos of Spain, while outwardly subscribing to the Christian sacraments, privately kept faith with the covenant made on Mount Sinai?"

"Not difficult. A bit fantastic, that's all, after all this time."

"Time has nothing to do with it. One way or another, we are all survivors."

Brought back to the present, Jurnet said: "Except for Rachel. She never made it."

Abreast of the lodge, Alice Diefenhaus said goodbye.

"You must think I misled you. Mr. Griffin really did seem broken-hearted, the way I said. You never saw such a change in such a short space of time."

Jurnet asked: "What do you put it down to?"

The American woman hesitated. Then: "I'm not really competent to say. Eliot and Mr. Griffin have corresponded for years, but this is the first time we've actually visited with him. Maybe it's just that old people simply can't sustain prolonged grief—the heart defending itself against shocks it's no longer strong enough to absorb."

Jurnet nodded. He had taken a liking to the tall, bony woman, the directness of her gaze, her air of austere elegance.

She went on: "I heard what you said about Barnabas. I spoke to him last night. For what it's worth, not, I should have thought, a human being to kill another human being."

"What Abel thought of Cain, I shouldn't be surprised. No one is the kind of person to commit a murder till he's actually committed one."

"How awful you make us sound. The whole human race."

"At the moment I'm only interested in that portion of it which lives in Mauthen Barbary."

He looked about him, up and down the village street, at the picture postcard prettiness which disguised the rum kind of place it was.

Alice Diefenhaus, guessing his thought, regarded him with amusement.

"You ought to see California. We've got more nutty sects per square mile than Mauthen Barbary has cabbages per acre. Not that there's anything nutty about the Lady of Promise."

Jurnet said: "I'm not much of a one for graven images." He smiled.

"It must be the Jew in me."

# 15

The Hospice had not improved during Jurnet's absence. The waning day merely intensified its graceless melancholy. Waiting for Ellers to appear, and perched uncomfortably on a chair conceived with malice towards the sacroiliac, the detective felt his spirits fall. The Welshman, who had stayed behind at the Manor to have a word with Mr. Griffin's manservant, came in breezily. After one look at his superior, he tactfully rearranged his features.

"What a morgue!"

Jurnet cheered up, as the Sergeant had known he would. Criticism was an executive privilege.

"Could be worse. Well—what did the butler see?"

"Blow-all. Says he spent the morning polishing silver. Doubt it, myself. More likely lining up his bets for the week's racing. What with form books and racing calendars, his pantry looks like the back room of Ladbroke's. He wasn't best pleased when I barged in, I can tell you. Seems it's holy ground where the boss himself's not allowed to tread."

"What did he have to say?"

"Doesn't use a chopper, for a start. They've got an electric saw. Seems wood-burning fires hereabouts are strictly a second home thing. The weekenders buy it by the cord from over Swaffham way, and chop it up to fit their individual grates."

"Many of 'em?"

"Nine, not counting the Manor. I've got a list. Forge Cottage is on it, and Maypole Cottage next door. Falkener burns wood too, only he doesn't buy it. Scrounges around for what he can pick up in the Manor grounds."

"Anything else?"

"Nothing you could put a finger on. It seems Mr. Anguish

has been working for Griffin since the year dot, and it shows.
You heard the way the old gentleman kept harping on money,
or rather, the lack of it? Well, it's my guess he'd have a whole
lot more if his man was a little less fond of the gee-gees. Griffin
leaves all the household finances to him, and I'd say he's been
milking the treasury for years, and it shouldn't be hard to
prove it."

Jurnet groaned.

"Don't tell me! If it's nothing to do with the death of Rachel
Cass I don't want to know."

"That's just it, sir, isn't it? If."

Benjamin Jurnet drove off towards Norwich, towards a shower
and a change of clothing. The prospect of at last achieving
these goals imbued him with an elation which contrived to co-
exist with a feeling of deepest depression. He still did not
know who had killed the girl.

The village High Street was as empty as he and Ellers had
found it earlier; looking more than ever, thought Jurnet, like a
film set where shooting was over for the day. Even the litter
bins, the last visible reminders of the pilgrims and their
pilgrimage, had gone. The detective found their disappearance disturbing. Who, in this untenanted No Man's Land, had
sneaked out and taken them away when his back was turned?

Jurnet could not have known that Willie and Jack Gamlin,
wanting to do something and unable to think of anything
better, had removed them, as a last act of homage to Rachel
Cass.

He was glad to get out of Mauthen Barbary, into the Norfolk
countryside which, farmed from time immemorial, spoke
comfortingly of man's mastery over nature. He was glad to be
alone.

He had thought of taking Barney Smithers in with him, and
then, in the face of Sergeant Bowles' ill-concealed misgiving,
had decided against it. There was more chance of getting the
truth out of Barnabas, the Guardian of the Shrine, in Mauthen
Barbary, than out of Barney Smithers in Norwich nick.

The detective had a full evening ahead. It would take a bit of
luck to be back in the village by midnight.

Not that there was any mad hurry. Rachel Cass tomorrow
would be no more dead than she was today, and no less. Jurnet
would undoubtedly have chosen to sleep in his own bed if
Miriam had been there to share it with him. Sergeant Bowles,

a widower who often had to be reminded to go home at the end of a duty, had volunteered to put up at the Hospice for the duration. Ellers too had offered to stay, but Jurnet had said no, he hadn't the heart to deprive Rosie of her early-morning look at her poor bastard: besides which, Ellers could give Hinchley and the other two constables a lift back to town.

That way, Jurnet could enjoy the luxury of having his car to himself. Reminded of the empty rear seat, he took a quick glance over his shoulder to make sure the chopper, carefully wrapped, was lying there. He felt in his pocket for the little gold cross.

"You never showed it to the old fellow," Ellers had reminded him. He must remember to take it with him next time he called at the Manor. Not that he expected anything to come of it. It was Griffin, after all, who had started the whole phobia against crosses among the Shrine people.

Jurnet drove without haste. He was almost in Norwich before he switched on the car's lights, in a dusk that touched even the sprawling suburbs with magic. Past them and into the old city the car seemed to find its own way, like a horse homing to its stable. Through the winding streets Jurnet drove, and out to the further side, where, a little before the road spilled over a hill down towards Police Headquarters, he turned off down an undistinguished street, and pulled into the forecourt of the brick box he called home.

The familiar smell of slow-simmered underwear greeted him on the stairs. The air inside his flat was stale and discouraged. Pausing only to throw open every window, Jurnet made for the bathroom, stripped and stepped under the shower. Only then, with the water prickling his skin, did the image of Rachel Cass leave him. Alone with his naked, uncircumcised self, he allowed himself to think about Jurnet, the medieval Jew.

Swain, at the lab, was noticeably unamused at being presented with a bloodstained implement at that hour of night, a Sunday and all: and he was careful, just short of impertinence, to let the detective know what he thought of police officers who had one fetched screaming from the telly at their whim.

"I know exactly how you feel," Jurnet apologised, with the diffidence which often gained him co-operation in unpromising circumstances. "I'd have left it till tomorrow if I didn't need to take the bloody thing back with me to Mauthen Barbary tonight."

The delicate reminder that some people never got home at all had its intended effect. Swain ran a professional eye over the blade. "The hair looks the same, but we'll see. There's no suggestion this is the murder weapon?"

"You've seen Dr. Colton's report, then?" Swain nodded. "This was found nearby. Extra insurance, maybe, in case the hammer wasn't enough."

"How long have I got?"

"I'm seeing the Superintendent, and then I've a couple of things to do I'll take me, say, best part of an hour and a half. Leave the chopper and your report with the duty sergeant, will you? If he hasn't got it when I get back I'll go and get myself a cup of tea." Jurnet took his leave. "Take as long as you need."

Swain, cradling the chopper as if it were a piece of Ming, watched him go out of the door. Had Jurnet, newly shaven, in his grey suit, white shirt and plain tie, been able to read the man's thoughts, he would have been disappointed.

"Not so bad for a bleeding dago."

Mention of a cup of tea had reminded Jurnet that he was both thirsty and hungry. He had the habit, when preoccupied, of forgetting about food altogether, and then, reminded, of feeling suddenly famished. He set off, therefore, for the canteen but, being Jurnet, checked, changed direction and went upstairs, to where the Superintendent awaited him.

The latter's greeting was not one to make him feel better. "I've been having a word with the Chief," he began urbanely. "He says you'll have to have help. What do you think?" At sight of Jurnet's face he broke into a chuckle. "Don't answer that question! Trouble is, he's read Colton's report, and after that no one can tell him it's a run-of-the-mill case. Bit of a shocker, wasn't it? A pregnant virgin! What a meal the papers are going to make of that!"

"I can't see, sir, why it has to come out at all, if it turns out— as it easily could—to have nothing to do with the girl's death. Nobody dreamed she was in that condition. It doesn't even follow that the chap who put her in the family way knows about it. She may have had her own reasons for not telling him before she had to."

"You're not suggesting we can censor the medical evidence

to be given in open court?" The Superintendent shook his
head with a smile that in no way concealed a serious purpose.
"Watch it, Ben. You're getting chivalrous again. Never knew
such a one for protecting his corpses."

"They can't protect themselves, that's for sure."

"They're past needing it. The dead have no reputations to
preserve. People who kid themselves they're doing it for them
are only trying to salvage either their family pride or their own
illusions. And now," the Superintendent finished with great
friendliness, "I think you'd better put me in the picture."

At Anglia Television, as earlier at the BBC, they were very
civil; gratified at being involved, however peripherally, in the
process of detection. Jurnet, over-estimating the effect of his
quiet clothes, was sure that, compared with the shamuses they
were familiar with on the box, they must find the reality
disappointing: but in this he was mistaken. His dark, exotic
looks made a great impression, and only confirmed their quite
erroneous view of what detectives were like.

The young men who, eager to be of service, hovered about
him—news editors, studio technicians and the like—pleased
him with that evident professionalism which always earned his
respect. There was, too, a tinge of envy. Shaggy, dressed any
way they pleased, they seemed to inhabit a lovely world as far
removed from the police as the earth from the moon. Nobody
there, he'd take a bet on it, called anyone sir, not even if he
was the blooming managing director.

Just the same, trained observer that he was, he began, after
a little, to detect a kind of pecking order, and signs of
bitchiness rising like scum to dull the surface of the chromium-
bright conversation. Life, the detective reflected, was probably much of a muchness wherever your path took you.

The young men made him as comfortable as they could
while they ran their film for him. Anglia offered him Scotch,
the BBC a sherry. He refused both, wishing with all his heart
they had made it a ham sandwich.

They showed him, first, the edited version which had gone
out with the news, and then the clips they had discarded. They
ran them again and again, wondering what he was looking for;
stopped when he wanted to examine a particular frame closely.

The film, which is to say the procession, astonished him.
Arriving in Mauthen Barbary at its very end, he had, he
discovered, gathered only the slightest idea of its joyful
innocence. More than once he caught himself smiling.

There were the ladies from Brixton, shining white satin against shining black skin. There were the Maidens, all but Rachel. He watched Barnabas/Barney emerge from the Shrine, joke with the crowd, supervise the passage of Falkener's fake Madonna. Was it possible that, only minutes before, those strong, seaman's hands had smashed the life out of the girl who, beyond reach of the probing cameras, lay sprawled below the Lady of Promise like some obscene sacrifice? Jurnet watched him speaking to a personable young man whom he guessed to be Neil Woodgate. Another suspect, another face devoid of guile.

Or was it?

The women demonstrating at the Market Cross came in for Jurnet's close scrutiny. As disguise for a murderer those robes and hoods took a lot of beating.

It hadn't been much of a demonstration. Strange how Lydia Massingham, easily distinguished by her size and ungainliness, had called it off, hardly begun. Why had she done that? Could it be that the whole exercise had been designed as a cover-up for murder?

Mesmerised by the pendulum swing of the Massingham breasts, jiggling the skeleton on her robe in an unceasing *danse macabre*, it was by the merest chance that, out of the corner of his eye, Jurnet at last spied what he was looking for: evidence that any of the people he had interviewed had not, earlier in the day, been where they said they had been.

"Could I have that bit again?"

He had it twice before he was sure. Some of the shots of the demo—those taken from the Green—had included parts of The Barbary Pirate. Facing north, the courtyard of the inn lay in deep shadow, so that it took concentration and a quick eye to catch, in the instant before the camera swung away in search of matter more exciting, the figure hurrying towards the door at the far end.

Charles Griffin's manservant, Anguish.

Harry Bronstein, the antique dealer, lived in one of the big houses in Newmarket Road, among the jardinières and the stuffed birds which were part of his stock-in-trade. How Harry, who was a large man, found room to exist in the chinks left between these objects Jurnet had never been able to fathom, especially as the dealer seemed continually to be adding to his merchandise without, so far as the detective could judge, ever letting anything go.

This amiable eccentric, he knew, could well afford to indulge his idiosyncrasy. The articles he *did* business in—and very good business it was—took up hardly any room at all, being disposed, for the most part, in various pockets about his ample person. What Harry Bronstein didn't know about gem stones was not worth knowing.

He took the cross into his fat fingers with unexpected delicacy.

"Lovely! Something to do with a case?"

Jurnet nodded. He had more than once had occasion to make use of the other's expert knowledge.

"I'd like to know anything you can tell me about it. I suppose it *is* gold?"

The dealer sat stroking the cross as if enlightenment could enter by his fingertips.

"Oh, it's that, all right. Gold, and old. Jacobean at least. Could be French. No hallmark, but that doesn't mean anything—a lot of stuff in those days never went through the Assay Offices. Funny there's not so much as a scratch on it. Couldn't have been used much."

He looked inquiringly at the detective, who did not commit himself.

"Twenty-two carat," Bronstein resumed. "Could even be twenty-three. Not exactly soft, but the next thing to it. Certainly wouldn't have stood up to wear." He took out a jeweller's loupe and examined the chain link by link. "Heavy, but honest. Yes, an honest piece." It was obviously the highest compliment he could pay it. "Want me to weigh it for you?"

"That's all right. Just give me an idea how much it'd cost to buy."

The dealer's eyes twinkled.

"From Asprey's or Harry Bronstein? There's a good bit of gold there—none of your stamped-out bits of tissue paper." He chewed his lower lip, pondering. "I can't see anyone coming by it retail for less than four hundred and fifty."

"Much as that?"

"At least." Bronstein smiled at the younger man. "Have I made it any easier for you?"

"No."

"What I can't figure out is what it's meant to be. This tiddly bit of chain—it's neither one thing nor the other."

"To slip on a belt, maybe?" Jurnet tried out Paul Falkener's suggestion.

"Mm." Harry Bronstein did not sound convinced. He grinned. "Not that I'm the best expert on crosses."

"Thanks for the help, anyway."

"Happy to oblige. Anything else I can do for you?"

Jurnet took a long time returning the cross to his pocket. "You could tell me what you know about Jurnet. The medieval one."

Harry Bronstein, who was Miriam's uncle, said: "I was wondering when you were going to get round to that."

By the time Jurnet got back to Headquarters he was beyond hunger. He gave the canteen a miss and made straight for the duty sergeant. The sergeant saw him coming and had the package ready. Colton, too, had left his report.

Swain had enclosed his in a separate envelope taped to the parcel. Tearing it open Jurnet read confirmation of what he had expected. The hair and blood on the chopper were those of the murdered girl. The handle had been coated with a film of tallow probably applied with the object of removing fingerprints. There were no fingerprints.

"This came for you too, sir."

The sergeant held out a large, stiff envelope.

"Thanks," said Jurnet, taking it and, after a glance at the name printed in one corner, awarding a mental good mark to the reporter who had organised such prompt action on his request for photographs.

He spread the pictures out on the counter, and examined them one by one. Mostly, the photographer had chosen the same camera angles as the television people. The photographs could have been stills from the films.

One was different.

It had been taken early on, when the photographer, presumably seeking subject matter to beguile the time of waiting, had caught sight of Oscar and Nellie coming over the Green. The man must have crossed the High Street and aimed his camera upward, so that the birds, snapped against the sky, might, to anyone who didn't know better, have been standing on a mountain top. In fact, artfully trimmed, the picture that appeared in next day's *Norfolk Mercury* looked exactly like that.

The unedited version in front of Jurnet, while less satisfactory as a composition, had other things to recommend it. In the foreground, and by their inclusion giving away the secret that the Green was no Jungfrau, was a press of people, every face but one turned towards the Shrine. Swimming against the tide of humanity, Joanna Cass was caught by the camera as she struggled, laughingly, to extricate herself.

The woman's beauty was enough to take your breath away. She had lied to him. Jurnet knew that now, seeing she had stated that she had only gone out to the pond to feed the swans and no further: yet he felt grateful for the glimpse of that lovely face undistorted by grief. Even in black-and-white you could tell the skin was aglow, the eyes mirroring an exaltation too strong to be suppressed.

What was the cause of that joy with which she positively pulsated? Barney Smithers, confessing, had said he came out of the Shrine feeling wonderful. It was all too evident that the Joanna Cass of the photograph was feeling wonderful.

Was wonderful what it felt like to snuff out a life?

Jurnet scuffed the photographs into a pile and returned them to the envelope. The duty sergeant, who had been inspecting them as best he could wrong way round, volunteered: "Swan took a bite out of my leg once, you could've put a mutton chop in it."

"Good for you," replied Jurnet, his mind on other things.

After he had gone, the duty sergeant made excuses.

"Couldn't've heard what I said."

Funny how they all liked Ben Jurnet, in spite of his looks.

# 16

The way back to Mauthen Barbary, like all return journeys, seemed shorter than the way there. The fields lay bright in moonlight, the road a ribbon between.

The church of St. Blaise on its knoll, seen across the moonlit fields, looked, in contrast to its daytime melancholy, bright and beautiful. As the road wound towards the village, there came a point from which Jurnet could see the double line of yews that lined the path up to the church door like giant pawns facing each other across a chessboard. The continual changes of perspective made it impossible for the detective to decide if there were the regulation eight a side—a whimsicality which, on one chevronned bend, nearly sent the car into a ditch.

"Watch it!" Jurnet growled, dismissing his fancies. He applied himself to his driving; yet even as he did so, in the instant before he swivelled his eyes, it seemed to him that something, a shadowy figure, flitted between the pawns, the yews.

"Knight to Queen's Three," he mocked himself, and refused to look again.

The village, as he entered the High Street, seemed sunk in slumber so deep Jurnet had to resist an impulse to put his hand down on the car horn and keep it there. Somebody else had no such scruples about disturbing Mauthen Barbary's dreams. Driving up the incline towards the Market Cross, the detective became aware of someone singing, or shouting: a noise loud enough to be heard above the car engine.

A second later, over the rise, his lights picked out its source: a young man staggering along the street, singing as he came.

> "Life is love and love is life.
> Man takes woman, husband wife.
> Lady surely do agree
> It's child what makes the family—"

Having seen him on television, Jurnet had no difficulty in recognising Neil Woodgate.

The detective stopped the car and got out. To left and right he could hear the sound of windows being opened, and felt unexpectedly relieved that, after all, Mauthen Barbary was not as sound asleep as all that.

Taking the young man's arm, Jurnet demanded with police-manly severity: "What's all this about, then?"

The young man's arm was burdened. When Jurnet realised the nature of the load he stopped play-acting.

He wrenched the petrol can out of Neil Woodgate's hand with a strength that nearly sent the boy headlong. Woodgate clutched at Jurnet, his breath sour on the detective's face, and sang:

> "Lady's Shrine is burning down,
> Burning down, burning down.
> Lady's Shrine is burning down.
> Goodbye, Lady!"

As Jurnet, can in hand, ran back to the car, the boy, bereft of support, made it to the bonnet where he sprawled, smiling cherubically at Jurnet through the windscreen.

"Not yet. Got to get ol' Lionel first." He experimented with standing upright and failed. "Why'nt you gi' me a lift ol' Lionel? Won't take but a minute."

Jurnet put the can down carefully on the floor in the back of the car; came back to the bonnet and, locking his arms round Woodgate's chest, lifted him bodily into the front passenger's seat.

"Which Lionel's that, then?"

"Vicar. Man o' God. Our Father which art and so forth. Ol' Lionel an' God—" Woodgate crossed the first two fingers of each hand, and waved them vaguely in front of him—"like that!"

"And is Lionel expecting you at this hour of night? What's so important it can't wait till morning?"

"If you must know," Neil Woodgate said with crystal clarity, "I'm going to burn down the Shrine. If I wait till morning some blasted copper's bound to stop me. First, Shrine. Second, Mr. Charlie Griffin."

He leaned back against the headrest. The drunken voice resumed: "Know what? I could've kicked myself. I forgot the matches!"

"Is that why you want to go to Lionel's? To borrow some?" The boy nodded. "You don't have to wake him up just for that. Easier to pop back home and pick up a box."

"Had enough of a job getting out. My mum can hear the grass grow. 'Sides, ol' Lionel's got something better'n matches. Lighter Rachel gave him. Shoots out a flame long as a fish finger." He considered a moment. "A *small* fish finger. Rachel would've given me one too, she said, only I don't smoke. Gi' me a penknife instead. Four blades, an' my initials. Solid silver. Show you—" The boy fumbled in his pockets. "Can't have lost it—"

Jurnet switched on the ignition and set the car in motion. The boy looked up.

"Other way! You're going the wrong way!"

"Can't turn here," Jurnet lied smoothly. "Have to go on a bit. Pipe down or you'll wake up the whole village. You won't get far then with playing Guy Fawkes and the Houses of Parliament."

The boy slumped in the seat and closed his eyes. Jurnet

drove swiftly past the Green and the Hospice, the Shrine and the Rond, over the bridge to the select housing estate of which Ellers had told him. Finding the Woodgate ménage was no problem. In one house all the lights were on. Mum had heard something and it wasn't the grass growing.

Jurnet left the boy in her formidable hands, not entirely satisfied he had done the best thing for him, and drove back over the river to the Hospice, to find Sergeant Bowles waiting up for him with a jug of cocoa and a plate of ham sandwiches. As he sat munching and drinking the detective reflected there was something to be said for Mums after all, so long as they came in uniform and size-twelve shoes.

Not until he found himself tossing uncomfortably on a lumpy mattress in the Hospice dormitory did he feel a pang of guilt. Knowing now the stock from which he sprang, he should have said no to the ham.

When Sergeant Bowles awakened him with tea and Osbornes it seemed he had only that moment fallen asleep.

"Eight o'clock!" the Sergeant proclaimed heartily. "Thought you'd be wanting to make an early start."

Jurnet sat up in bed.

"Treat me like this, I'll be hoping for a homicide every day." He took a sip and smiled up at the hovering figure. "First-rate cuppa." Then, seeing the second cup on the tray: "Have your own. It'll get cold."

Sergeant Bowles actually blushed.

"Made it for Barney. Wouldn't eat a bite all day yesterday. I thought a cup of tea—" He broke off, embarrassed. "Took a look at him twenty minutes ago, before I put the kettle on. Didn't seem any point getting him up. Sleeping like a baby."

"Let's hope it's a clear conscience." Jurnet handed back the cup and swung his legs out of bed. "Time to think about taking him into Norwich. Take him his tea and let him know I'll be wanting another word after breakfast. I take it there'll be breakfast?"

"Shouldn't be surprised, sir. There's a female in the kitchen, and a nice smell of bacon—"

Jurnet was not going to be caught twice.

"Tell her just toast and coffee for me."

He had got his trousers on and was brushing his teeth in the washroom when the Sergeant came pounding along the passage.

"Mr. Jurnet! Mr. Jurnet, sir!"

The unexpected appearance of his superior from the washroom instead of from the dormitory where he had left him, threw Sergeant Bowles off balance. Before he could explain the cause of his haste, Jurnet, the taste of toothpaste thick in his mouth, was off down the corridor to Barnabas's room.

As Sergeant Bowles had reported, the Guardian of the Shrine was asleep—altogether too damn much asleep. The man's face was grey, the lips empurpled; the breathing ludicrously inadequate to the needs of the broad body outlined by the bedclothes. On a bedside table stood an uncapped pill bottle, empty.

There was also a slip of paper which Jurnet did not stop to read.

"Doctor—ambulance—"

The Sergeant was already on his way. Jurnet glanced swiftly round the mean little room, ran to a bookshelf and grabbed a handful of books. Dividing them more or less evenly, he shoved them under the front legs of the white-painted iron bedstead; then rolled the body on to its side and began kiss-of-life resuscitation.

Not until Dr. Teago arrived with his stomach pump did Jurnet have time to read the message Barney Smithers had left for him.

"'I'm not fit to live.'"

"Either he'll live or he'll die," the doctor snapped, before joining his patient in the ambulance. In the morning sunlight the old man looked bedraggled. He had not had time to put on a tie. Perhaps he was put out at missing his breakfast.

Perhaps, thought Jurnet, who understood very well there was no perhaps about it, he blames me. But what the hell for? For not timing my suicides to take place in visiting hours?

"I simply don't understand what's got into the place!" Dr. Teago exclaimed, stumping up the ambulance steps.

The attendant closed the doors, and in a moment the vehicle moved off, down the Hospice drive and out into the village street. The wail of its siren affronted the quiet air.

"That'll give an extra spice to their cornflakes." Blinking in the strong light Jurnet turned to Sergeant Bowles beside him. "The old bugger's right to have it in for me. There'd have been no barbiturates if we'd locked him up properly in a cell."

The Sergeant said consolingly: "He never looked the sleeping pill type to me."

"I should've known better. If your name's Barney Smithers you've got plenty to keep you awake at night."

The Sergeant clucked and went indoors to make the Inspector another cup of tea. It was all the comfort he could think of.

Jurnet remained outside a little longer, reluctant to face the grim business that awaited within. *I simply don't understand what's got into the place!* How well he understood the old doctor's angry bewilderment! Murder, if it belonged anywhere, belonged in squalid streets, patches of derelict land where rats hunted among the rubbish. Not in this lovely country scene.

Even as he framed the thought he rejected it for the arrant sentimentality it was. Death was no respecter of either persons or places.

As if to bear him out, Joanna Cass, wild-eyed, black hair hanging loose about her shoulders, appeared on the summit of the Green, and ran headlong down the slope towards where the detective stood, as if by prior arrangement, awaiting her.

"Oh, come!" she cried. "Come quickly! He's dead!"

## 17

There was blood at the edge of the pond; and a bundle of feathers that had once been Oscar.

"I came out to feed them, and I found—"

Joanna Cass was weeping noisily, as Jurnet had not heard her weeping for Rachel. He saw no incongruity in this. Murder had its own monstrous logic. The wanton slaughter of a dumb animal was a mindless malevolence that froze the blood.

Just the same, Jurnet's heart leapt with relief. He had feared—he could not say what he had feared. Only that, compared with it, a dead swan was not all that much.

He knelt down, turned the bird over, and, from the base of its throat, extracted the instrument of its undoing. He held the penknife gingerly along its edges. It was very elegant, the engraved initials delicately entwined with tendrils of woodbine.

Elegant but lethal.

The damn drunk kid!

Joanna must have glimpsed something in his face, for she stopped crying, and exclaimed sharply: "You know who it was!"

Jurnet shook his head.

"I know whose knife this is. Not the same thing." He held it up for her to see. "Neil Woodgate's. Rachel gave it to him."

"She never told me." She put a hand to her throat. "If he could kill Oscar, he could kill Rachel."

"Good God!"

Unperceived by either, Philip Cass had come out of Forge Cottage. He crossed the road and stood for a moment looking down at the dead bird. Then he transferred all his attention to his wife. Oscar's death, it was obvious, was less important than its effect on Joanna. For that matter, it was plain that Philip Cass judged the universe and all its works by their effect on Joanna.

The two embraced with an intensity that aroused in Jurnet an envy he found difficult to conceal.

"Poor Nellie," the woman murmured. Comforted, she disengaged herself, picked up a bowl from the grass and, moving round the pond to where Nellie floated motionless, proffered her largesse of bread and bacon.

The bird rejected her overtures; moved a little towards the centre of the pond. Joanna came back to her husband's side.

"Did you know Rachel gave Neil a silver penknife? It's what killed Oscar."

"Are you saying Neil did it?"

Jurnet interposed: "I'm not accusing anyone at this stage."

"May I see it?"

The detective held up the knife, still balanced between forefinger and thumb.

"Don't touch."

With his free hand he fished a small polythene bag out of a pocket, teased the upper edges apart, and dropped the knife in.

Returning it to his pocket: "It'll be gone over for prints. Which reminds me—there'll be a fellow along to look at Rachel's bedroom, and to fingerprint anybody in the village who's been in the Shrine lately. Purposes of elimination. I'm sure we can rely on your and Mrs. Cass's co-operation."

"Of course." Philip Cass spoke absently. His mind was still on the penknife. "That must have set her back a bit."

"I understand she gave Mr. Persimmer a cigarette lighter about the same time."

"Did she, indeed!"

Joanna said bitterly: "Anything you want to know about Rachel, darling, ask the Inspector. He knows it all. Except who killed her."

"Give me time," Jurnet said stolidly. "Time and the truth, that's all I ask."

"Time—" Philip Cass commented—"I suppose your superiors will give you as much of that as you need, within reason. But truth? You can hardly expect whoever killed Rachel to come out with that, just for your convenience."

"I don't, sir. But—"the detective's voice hardening— "I expect it—demand it, you might say, from everyone else concerned."

"And what the hell is that supposed to mean?"

"I imagine Mrs. Cass knows what to make of it."

In a voice little more than a whisper Joanna Cass asked: "What exactly are you accusing me of?"

"Yesterday you stated that, while waiting for your husband to return from his walk, you went and fed the swans—"

"So I did."

"And that was all. You returned to your front garden and were about to go indoors when Mr. Cass returned."

"Yes."

"Then perhaps you can explain how a photographer from the *Norfolk Mercury* came to take a picture of you on the High Street side of the Green."

Joanna said: "I can explain it. But I choose not to."

"Joanna—" her husband began.

"Be quiet, darling," she said lovingly. "This is my show. I'm the one the Inspector wants to run in for telling lies. He's the one who ferrets out all the secrets, who's killing Rachel all over again by turning her into a stranger and a freak!" She confronted Jurnet with a contempt that shamed him, little as it was deserved. "Well, this is one secret that's going to stay safe from his filthy probing!"

She drew away as from something unclean, and called out across the water: "Don't tell him a thing, Nellie! Not a bloody thing!"

\* \* \*

"Sorry about that."

Having escorted his wife indoors, Philip Cass returned to the pond to find Jurnet still standing there.

The detective nodded. Looking down at the dead swan, he asked: "Know who it belongs to?"

"Charlie, I suppose. Or is it the Queen? Do swans have to belong to anyone?"

"P. C. White'll know. I'll send him over to get rid of it."

"I'd be glad to have it out of my wife's sight. Poor girl, coming and finding it, on top of everything—"

Jurnet said forthrightly: "She shouldn't have lied."

Cass blushed to the roots of his sandy hair, for all the world as if he, a naughty schoolboy, were the one being ticked off.

"Lying's putting it a bit strong. She'd never keep back anything important."

"Mrs. Cass is in no position to judge what's important and what isn't. Maybe *you'll* tell me what she was doing yesterday morning near the Shrine?"

"I'm sorry, Inspector! If my wife chooses to tell you off her own bat, well and good. But to ask me to go sneaking behind her back—!" He not only looks like a schoolboy, Jurnet thought: he sounds like one. "It's something purely personal and completely private."

"If I may say so, a lot of what's come to light about your sister is purely personal and completely private."

"That's just it!" Cass's voice was agonised. "Joanna's had all she can take. I can't blame her for refusing to answer questions which have absolutely no bearing on Rachel's death." He turned away. "I must go in to her—"

"There was one other thing, sir. I should like to see your wood chopper. You have one, I take it?"

Halfway across the road, Philip stopped in surprise.

"But she wasn't—"

"Quite. Not the weapon. It's just that we've found one in circumstances which call for some explanation."

"Let me have a look at it. I'll know ours when I see it."

"It's down at the Hospice. I just thought, seeing I'm here— It'll be one off my list."

"Sure." Cass led the way into the front garden and along a gravelled path that edged itself between the cottage and the fence. "The shed's at the back."

There was no chopper among the logs of oak and beech, and the bundles of kindling.

Jurnet observed: "You've been busy."

"Bert, not me." Cass looked about him, patently not at home. "I wonder where he could have put it."

"You'd better come and take a look at the one we've got."

"All right. I'll just let Joanna know."

"I'll be out front," Jurnet said. "While I'm here I'll pop in next door and ask Miss Massingham to let me have a look at hers."

Cass laughed.

"Lydia? She hasn't got a tin-tack to call her own. Bert's always beefing about the way she's forever on the borrow. I shouldn't be surprised that's where our chopper's got to." He strode over to the fence and shouted: "Lydia! Are you in?"

The back door of Maypole Cottage opened, and Lydia Massingham emerged. Jurnet had a strong sense that the woman had been behind the door all the time, waiting.

God, he thought, distaste once again swamping his reluctant compassion, what a cow.

The cow was clothed in a djellaba patterned with what looked like manic bananas. While it was hard to imagine any garment which might do something for Lydia Massingham, it was harder to think of one which might do less. Had she been cleverer one might have guessed she had selected the hideous stuff deliberately, as a gesture of contempt for a world conditioned to judge by appearances. As it was, Jurnet suspected that, if asked, she would have confessed to having chosen it because it was "cheerful".

She trod heavily over to the fence, and said in her incongruously high voice: "Philip! I've been wanting so much—Is there anything at all I can do?"

Tears filled her eyes. There was no doubt she was grieving. And no doubt that her grief exasperated the two men who witnessed it almost beyond endurance.

"Sweet of you to offer," Philip Cass managed. "Have you met Inspector Jurnet? He's here to—"

"We've spoken. Did you speak to Lionel Persimmer, Inspector?"

"I've spoken to a great many people," Jurnet said. "And now I'd like to speak to you for a minute. Mr. Cass here can't find his chopper."

Was there the merest hesitation before she repeated:

"Chopper? I haven't seen it for ages. I'm afraid I can't help you."

Jurnet remarked in an offhand way: "I didn't notice any padlock on the shed door."

"Oh, nobody locks anything up in Mauthen Barbary, do they, Philip? We all trust each other implicitly."

"That's what I was afraid of," said Jurnet.

A telephone bell, sounding loudly from a box mounted on the outside rear wall of Forge Cottage, brought an end to an awkward pause.

"Blast!" Philip exclaimed gratefully. "I thought I'd turned the bloody thing off."

The ringing stopped. A second later Joanna came out of the french windows.

"It's for you," she said to Jurnet, no friendliness in her voice. The presence of her neighbour she ignored completely. "Your sergeant."

"Joanna, my dear!" Lydia Massingham bent over the fence. Her breasts, overhanging the barrier, were admittedly objects to avert the eye from. Yet Joanna Cass was cruel, thought Jurnet, to turn away without a glance. As the detective followed her into the house he could hear behind him the high, breathless voice stumbling on of it own momentum: "I want you to know how sorry—"

"There," said Joanna briefly, indicating the phone. She started up the stairs, pausing to look down over the white-painted banisters. "Please tell him about taking Oscar away. I shouldn't like the village dogs to get at him."

Sergeant Ellers was full of righteous annoyance imperfectly suppressed.

"Been looking all over, sir. Sergeant Bowles said you lit out without saying."

"So I did." Considering the Sergeant's act overdone, Jurnet added: "I was called away to a murder, actually."

The gasps at the other end of the wire recalled him to a sense of what was proper.

"Keep your hair on. Oscar the swan. Somebody did for it last night."

Ellers whistled.

"Sounds more than ever like a nut. And what about Barney?"

"Yes," said Jurnet. "Barney. I'll be back directly, and we'll talk about it. Meantime tell Bowles, will you, to get hold of White to collect the corpse. It's by the pond."

"What do you want done with it?"

"Tell him to take it along to the butcher's. Beslow can stick it in his fridge for the time being."

"Will do. Anything else? Ferguson's here for the prints."

"Have him take a look at Barney's room first, just to be sure."

"Yes, sir. About Barney," said Sergeant Ellers. "The hospital phoned to say he was dead on arrival." The silence that followed was so protracted the Sergeant at last ventured a tentative "Sir?"

"I'm here."

Highly impolitic to let a subordinate know you had just been transfixed with a pang of guilt more painful than heartburn.

"Sir—Could Barney have got out last night, d'you think, and killed that swan?"

"Am I to gather from that you've found another key to his room?"

"Yes, sir. In the bedside table, sir."

Smug little bastard, Jurnet thought. But right. He had wanted Barney Smithers down at the station nice and formal, "helping the police with their inquiries."

"Don't forget that bird," Jurnet said, and hung up.

Philip Cass and Lydia Massingham were standing where he had left them, frozen in a rictus of embarrassment.

"Ready, sir?"

"Let me just tell Joanna."

"She went upstairs."

"Oh, darling!" Philip called, face upraised; and when his wife appeared at a bedroom window: "I'm just going across to the Hospice. Will you be all right? I shan't be long."

"Shut the doors," Joanna replied, loudly enough to be heard over the fence. "I don't want any visitors."

Before the two men left the garden Philip went back to the shed and found a sack. Nellie watched unmoving as he draped it, not without tenderness, over the body of her mate.

Nothing was said as the two skirted the pond, climbed the Green and dropped down to the High Street. At the Hospice the two sergeants greeted the return of their commanding officer with an air of muted condolence. A murder, a theft, a suicide and an act of vandalism, all in twenty-four hours; what would their man make of it? Without a word spoken, and in the most delicate way possible, they let him know they were on his side.

Jurnet brought out the bag containing the penknife and handed it to Bowles.

"Mr. Ferguson upstairs?"

"Yes, sir."

"Ask him to give this a going over." Of Ellers he inquired: "Did you get hold of White?"

"Spoke to his missus. He had to stand in for the lollipop lady. Expected back any minute."

"Fine. When he's seen to the bird, have him in here to check we've got the name of everyone in Mauthen Barbary who's been in the Shrine for any reason whatever. From Mr. Griffin down to whoever scrubs the floor. Then take him along when you and Ferguson do the rounds. People feel better if they see a familiar face. Ferguson can start with Mr. Cass here."

Jurnet went over to the sideboard and brought the chopper back to the table.

"It's ours all right," Phillip said at once, then drew in his breath at sight of the blade. "Are you going to tell me what it means?"

"I was hoping you'd tell me—explain how it came to be in the Shrine in the first place."

"The Shrine!" Philip shook his head hopelessly. "What was it doing there, for Christ's sake? Unless Rachel took it herself, for some reason I can't fathom."

"A possibility," Jurnet conceded. "Except that she couldn't have hidden it, in this condition, behind the statue of the Lady."

"Behind the—!" Phillip Cass's freckled face turned a dark red. "One thing I can promise you—If ever I find myself alone there with a chopper in *my* hands, I'll know what to do with it. Chop the blasted thing up for firewood!"

"I understand you're under nervous strain, sir. I have to stick to facts, not feelings."

"What the hell's the good of facts you can't account for?"

Jurnet said pacifically: "Like I told you, it takes time. You know those kaleidoscope things kids play with? Well, you keep shaking the facts like those little bits of glass till eventually they fall into a pattern."

"Fat lot of use that is. Shake 'em again and the pattern changes."

Jurnet nodded.

"Not the best metaphor. It's a very special kaleidoscope, the one I mean. Get enough facts, jiggle them up enough, and sooner or later, if you're lucky, you get a pattern that doesn't change however much you go on shaking."

"If you're lucky," Phillip repeated, his voice heavy with disbelief.

"That's right," said the detective, and looked, of a sudden, severe and unfriendly. "If you're lucky, and if people who ought to know better don't deliberately withhold information."

Philip Cass made no reply.

A door in the outer room opened noisily, and a voice, resonantly transatlantic, called out: "Police! Are the police here? I'm looking for the police!"

Professor Diefenhaus accepted the chair Sergeant Ellers offered him, extracted a handkerchief from the breast pocket of his cardigan, and mopped his brow: re-folded the handkerchief and returned it to its place. Removing the visible traces of unease restored to him that air of portentous authority which is the mark of the American academic.

"When we discovered, Inspector, that Mr. Griffin wasn't in his room, and that his bed hadn't been slept in, I told Anguish to go through the house from top to bottom while I went over to the Shrine on the chance he might have felt some sudden impulse to commune with the Lady, and then been taken suddenly sick. As you have seen for yourself he was not a strong man."

"Why the past tense?"

"Good Lord!" Out came the handkerchief again; this time, after use, stuffed unceremoniously into a sleeve. "Did I say 'was?' I guess it shows you what I've been thinking."

"I guess it does," said Jurnet.

"It was difficult to know what to do for the best. Alice—Mrs. Diefenhaus—was all for calling in the police right away, but Anguish, shaken as he was, was against it. Mr. Griffin would not approve, he said; and, assuming there to be some reasonable explanation for the disappearance, my wife and I were not anxious to cast ourselves in the role of hysterical foreigners, deplorably lacking in your celebrated British phlegm. Mrs. Diefenhaus went to look around the garden and the grounds, while I went over to the Shrine. If Mr. Griffin *had* gone out, we figured he couldn't have gone far."

"You didn't find him?"

"We did not." The Professor's fine-chiselled face was disfigured for a moment by a grimace which had the effect of rendering him more human, even down to his language. "In the Shrine it was real spooky. The bloodstains still on the floor, and the Lady so triumphant, so full of power. It was enough to scare the pants off you." He spoke with a certain diffidence, unsure of his listener.

"I know exactly what you mean."

Reassured, the Professor continued: "So when I saw he wasn't there I thought, hell, this English cool is all very well in its way, but when a host vanishes into thin air his house guests can't just sit quietly by in the hope he'll show up for lunch. You get professional help."

"Very proper." Jurnet stood up. "We'll give you a lift back to the house with us." To Bowles, who had just come in: "We'll be at the Manor. Mr. Ferguson nearly through?"

"Coming down directly, sir."

"Tell him I'll be wanting a word with him later." Jurnet turned to Philip Cass. "You won't mind hanging on a few minutes to get those prints done?"

Cass nodded.

"But poor old Charlie! What d'you suppose could have happened to him?"

"Let's hope we'll soon find out."

He had barely completed the sentence when the telephone rang.

Ellers answered it, listened for a moment, and then passed over the receiver without comment.

"Detective Inspector Jurnet speaking."

Jurnet listened in silence. At the end of what seemed a long time he said: "Don't touch anything. We'll be over right away."

Replacing the receiver on its cradle, he looked from one to another of the intent faces ranged on the opposite side of the table.

Jurnet said: "Chloe found him."

"Found him—how?" Professor Diefenhaus asked the question as if he would prefer not to have an answer.

"Found him—dead."

## 18

Charles Griffin lay on his back in the hole where his ancestor Sir Amyas had buried the Lady of Promise, and whence he himself had resurrected her. His had not been a dignified death. The face with its popped eyes and lolling tongue was unrecognisable. The tiny feet in their shoes of soft kid, the paunch sticking up ridiculously, were what most readily identified the late Lord of the Manor of Mauthen Barbary.

"I got as far the edge of the copse when Chloe came out." Alice Diefenhaus was white-faced but composed. "I knew at once something was wrong. She didn't frisk about the way she usually does—just made sure she had my attention, then turned quietly and went back the way she'd come. I imagined Mr. Griffin must have walked over to the grotto and then had a heart attack. When I found him—"she faltered momentarily— "Chloe was licking his face."

Jack Ellers, down on his haunches among the pebbles, looked up from the corpse.

"No sign of the ligature," he reported. "Not rope, nor wire. Something softer. A towel, bit of cloth, something like that."

Jurnet nodded. He was thinking that a man's death was a poor way of having one's hunch confirmed. Took all the pleasure out of it.

As if he read the detective's thoughts, Professor Diefenhaus commented: "I take it that as the pilgrims have long since departed, this has to mean the murderer is somebody local."

"Could be."

Jurnet circled the grave morosely. Anguish finished retching under the trees and drew shakily nearer; but, even at such a moment, not so near as to overstep the invisible barrier dividing the servant from the served.

"Nothing we can do here for the moment." Jurnet carefully kept out of his voice the anger violent death always provoked in him. "Ground's hard as iron, and these stones—"He broke off and bent to pick up a pebble, sea-smoothed and gleaming save for a dull brown stain no bigger than a penny piece.

Alice Diefenhaus asked: "What have you found?"

"Oil. Just a spot."

"A lot of pebbles from the shore have oil on them."

"Thick, tarry stuff out of a ship's tanks. This is much lighter. More like bicycle oil."

"You mean someone cycled here to meet Mr. Griffin and then killed him?"

Jurnet frowned.

"I can't think Mr. Griffin would arrange to meet anybody this far from the house. He'd never be sure he could make it.

There must be a dozen places nearer home he could have chosen."

"The bathchair!" Mrs. Diefenhaus exclaimed. "He could have been pushed in the bathchair."

"Had one of those, had he?"

"A marvellous one that was made for the Prince Regent. Mr. Cass had it modernised with ball bearings."

"Mm. Sergeant Ellers—"the little Welshman scrambled to his feet. "Remain here till P. C. White arrives, and then join me in the house. Tell the constable he's to stay until the lot from Norwich get here. And now—" turning to Anguish— "suppose for a start you show me where this chair's kept, and then you and me'll have a little chat."

There had been nothing visible to the naked eye to suggest that, alive or dead, Charles Griffin had ridden to his last resting place in the bathchair which had once had the honour of conveying Prinny. Back in the house, Jurnet left the pebble on the hall table. Old-fashioned about technical evidence which, in his experience, usually raised as many questions as it answered, he entertained no hopes of it.

At the detective's request, Anguish conducted him to his master's bedroom, a spacious apartment on the first floor, with windows affording views to the river. Given the size of it, the furnishings were surprisingly sparse, though what there was of them—a four-poster bed, a bureau, a small table or two—were evidently antiques of the highest quality. Dark on the faded wallpaper were the outlines of other pieces which once had stood with their backs to the walls; one of them, to judge by its height and width and the classical pediment reproduced in ghostly silhouette, a breakfront bookcase of substance and dignity.

As it was, the room had a strangely impoverished air.

"What time did Mr. Griffin go to bed last night?"

Jurnet had to repeat the question before Anguish appeared to take it in. Looking at the lined face, Jurnet realised for the first time that he was dealing with an old man. Fewer people would grieve for Charles Griffin than grieved for Rachel Cass, but here was one who grieved for him. Or did butlers and valets always fall into the sere and yellow when their bosses kicked the bucket?

"I'd like you to begin by telling me when you last saw Mr. Griffin alive."

"When I brought him his cocoa." The manservant nodded towards a bedside table where, next to a telephone, a thermos stood on a tray with a clean cup and saucer beside it. "Ten-fifteen, like I always do, 'cept when he's playing bridge."

Jurnet went over to the table and unscrewed the top of the flask. It was full to the brim, the liquid still warm. The sweet, milky smell rose into the surrounding air.

Jurnet, who was not really a cocoa fan, screwed the top on again.

"Did he always drink it?"

"Sometimes did, sometimes didn't." Anguish sounded hostile, averse to divulging his master's secrets, however insignificant. "It was all according."

"According to what?"

"According to how he slept or didn't sleep. He never drunk it straightaway. That's why the thermos—so's if he had a bad night he could take some at two, three in the morning and still find it hot."

"It's obvious last night he didn't even try to go to sleep. The bed's untouched. When you brought the cocoa, did you stay and help him undress?"

Anguish shook his head.

"Never cared for anyone fussing round. Left his clothes all over the floor for me to pick up in the morning." The affectionate grumble ended in something not far from a sob. "Jest his shoe-laces, that's all. On account of the bending down. Always untied his shoe-laces."

Envisaging the corpse, its little feet pointing upward, shoes neatly laced, Jurnet asked: "Did you unlace them last night?"

"Said so, didn't I?"

"When you came up, did you find him already undressed?"

"Wasn't undressed at all. Had his dressing-gown on over his clothes, all but the jacket."

"Was that unusual?"

"Not this time o' the year, with no fires. It can get parky of a night, even at midsummer."

"When you brought the cocoa," Jurnet persisted, "did you notice anything out of the ordinary? Anything at all out of the way? Try to think."

Anguish hesitated. Then, as if the recollection surprised him: "He seemed to be happy."

"What was so unusual about that?"

"Considering what'd happened—"

"Considering Miss Cass had been murdered, the Shrine desecrated, you thought it odd—"

"Not odd." The old man retreated, stubbornly on the defensive. "I on'y mentioned it 'cause you asked."

"Did you have any further conversation?"

"Just good night."

"Mornings, were your instructions to wake Mr. Griffin up at any particular time?"

"Not him! Sleeping so bad no one was never to disturb him once he did get off. No matter what time it was. Sometimes he'd ring at seven, sometimes it was past nine. Made breakfast difficult, I can tell you."

"I can understand that."

"Once it was near ha' past and I went up anyway thinking he might've been took bad, and he didn't half bite my head off."

"And today?"

"It was gone ten. I didn't hardly know what to do. In the end I spoke to Mrs. Diefenhaus—sensible woman she seems—and she said I ought to make sure he was all right even if I did get bawled out for it. Better'n letting him lie there if he needed help. So I come up—"Anguish lifted his head and looked at the undimpled pillow as if he still could not believe what he saw.

"Yes," said Jurnet. Then: "Did anyone phone Mr. Griffin last night?"

"Not last night nor all day yesterday, 'cept Dr. Teago just after breakfast about a bridge game, and all them bloody reporters about Miss Rachel."

"What about after he went to his room?"

"No one who knew Mr. Griffin'd phone him after ten. They knew him better'n that. Or should have."

Something in the tone of the final observation made Jurnet interject: "You mean somebody *did* phone?"

The old man shook his head.

"Phone *or* come knocking at the door. Should've known better, that time of night."

"Who should have known better? Did somebody come to see Mr. Griffin late last night?"

"Fine hope he had of seeing him that hour!"

"Him? Who came? Who are you talking about?"

"Him—" reluctantly. "The vicar. Should'a known weren't no earthly use to come knocking and banging after ten."

"Did you let your master know that Mr. Persimmer wanted to see him?"

"That pipsqueak! Didn't so much as let him into the hall. Told him to calm down and come back after breakfast."

"Calm down? Was Mr. Persimmer excited then?"

Anguish reflected.

"Het up," he pronounced at last. "Not excited. Het up."

"Isn't it the same thing?"

"Not to me."

"OK," said Jurnet, conceding defeat. "Have you ever known Mr. Griffin to go out after he had officially retired for the night?"

"What he want to do that for, he weren't daft!" After a moment Anguish added: "Number o' doors in this house, the bleeding Household Cavalry could come in and out and nobody know the difference."

"Supposing he *had* gone out, while you were still up. How about getting back in? Don't you go round last thing shooting the bolts?"

"What bolts? Half the door ain't had bolts since the Diamond Jubilee. If I told him once I told him a hundred times—" the man stopped abruptly.

"Yes. Well," said Jurnet. "That covers it for the time being." He looked at the manservant in a friendly way. "And now, suppose you tell me what you were doing at The Barbary Pirate yesterday morning while the procession was going on?"

"I weren't never—"

"Look," said the detective, "let's not muck about. They got you on television, so there's no point arguing."

The old man's hand twitched. But he said nothing.

"Shall I take a guess?" Jurnet prompted. "Where are they running this week? Plumpton? Newmarket? I'm not a racing man myself. Somebody at The Pirate running a book, is he, and you popped over to get your bet on?"

Still there was no answer, and the detective's voice hardened.

"On the other hand, could be you've run up a bit of a debt with that bookie behind the bar and he's dunning you for payment. Which was difficult, seeing that only the day before, Rachel Cass had been to see you about the accounts for the Hospice. There was something funny about them, wasn't there, and she'd found it out and wanted an explanation. Otherwise she was going to go to Mr. Griffin and tell him you'd been cooking the books. All of which makes it downright providential that a couple of days later she's murdered. And now, Mr. Griffin too—"

In a voice of biting sarcasm Anguish interrupted: "And am I supposed to've done him in like I did Rachel?"

"Depends how much you've landed yourself in for. More than you can make up this time, eh, by fiddling the housekeeping. I bet there's a nice little legacy coming your way in Mr. Griffin's will, so why not anticipate your inheritance? Or maybe Rachel tipped Mr. Griffin the wink after all, and he tackled you with it last night when you brought him his nightcap. And somehow, not exactly intending it maybe, it ended up in murder."

"And then I suppose I carried the body pick-a-back out to the grotto, an' left it there for Chloe to find in the morning?"

"Or wheeled it in the bathchair."

Strangely, the accusation seemed to have a revivifying effect on the manservant.

"Know what?" he said. "For a smart young feller, you're a bloody fool. Pick up a crumb of the truth an' before you can say Jack Robinson you've blown it up to a three-tier wedding cake, white icing and all."

Jurnet said: "What was the crumb?"

"The accounts. You had an inkling. But on'y an inkling."

"Rachel found you out."

"She found me out." The old man moved his head in rueful admiration. "But if you think she was the kind to give a pal away you got another think coming."

"What did she do?"

"Gi' me the money to pay it off, that's what. Long as I promised never to bet again."

"How much was it?"

"Four hundred and twenty pounds. She had it in a building society—money from her pa and ma. Wouldn't hear of me paying it back either—said if I simply exchanged one debt for another I'd still be tempted to gamble to pay it off. She come by with it Friday afternoon, an' I took it over to Joe yesterday morning." The man looked at Jurnet sorrowfully. "Know something? I took that cash by false pretences. I never meant to give up the horses. But now she's dead I couldn't lay another bet if my life depended on it."

"Too high a price to pay for the reform of one old punter."

"I never killed either of 'em. The on'y two people in the world I give a brass farthing for."

"One of whom you systematically swindled over a period of years."

"A quid here, a quid there. Shouldn't mind betting Mr. Griffin knew about it all the time and decided it weren't worth making a song-and-dance over." Anguish pointed to the marks on the bedroom wall. "Weren't my fiddles made those. Chippendale that was; and over there, low down, that was what they call a cassone. In a museum in America now. Went for a pile of dollars. The Lady of Promise got it all. That's where the big money went. She got the lot."

He moved across the room and pulled aside a curtain which concealed an alcove. A prie-dieu filled the narrow space, beneath a bracket on which stood another small representation of the statue in the Shrine.

Touching nothing, Jurnet examined the little piece with a lively interest. It was made of the same dark wood as the statuette he had seen in Rachel's room; but again there were subtle differences. Recognisably the Lady, and at first identical in all but size with the statue in the Shrine—the same negroid features, heavy belly, big breasts—its promise was nevertheless of a very different kind from that of the original. The emphasis, in some way the detective was unable to pin down, had shifted from the imminent birth to the blessed rest which would surely follow the pangs of parturition.

That bugger Falkener was a ruddy genius once he got the scale right. Why didn't somebody tell him?

Rest. That was the promise of the lovely little piece of wood. What better hope could the Mother of Heaven hold out to a sick old man?

But not in an open grave, strangled.

# 19

Professor and Mrs. Diefenhaus were waiting for him in the Muniment Room, as he had requested.

"Sorry about this," Jurnet began without preamble, taking in the American woman's pale face, the marks like bruises under the blue eyes, "but I'm sure you both understand why it can't wait."

"You meant there may be some more killing?" The Professor's Californian tan seemed to float on a pallor only a little less intense than his wife's.

"Two murders in two days are two too many, whichever way you look at it."

Alice Diefenhaus said: "Tell us how we can help."

"You can tell me if anything—anything at all—about this room today is different from the way it was when you left it last night."

"Eliot's the one to give you the details of that," Mrs. Diefenhaus replied. "I only looked in for a minute to see whether he needed his antihistamine."

Her husband got out his handkerchief in haste. Jurnet waited until the seizure had spent itself.

"Well?"

The query was addressed to the Professor; but Alice Diefenhaus had not finished.

"The great difference last night, of course, was the moon. There was only those little reading lamps on, but the room was full of that great white light. White light and black shadow." A shiver agitated her thin shoulders. "It may be hindsight, but it looked exaggerated, unreal. Like something by Caravaggio, you know? Or De La Tour—"

"Now, Alice," the Professor protested, "I can't imagine an excursus into art history is what Inspector Jurnet is looking for at this precise moment."

"How can we establish if anything's changed if we don't first establish what it was like before? That's right, isn't it?" The woman looked at Jurnet, who nodded in reply. "Mr. Griffin, of course. That's the biggest difference. The way Mr. Griffin was. That was the most unreal, exaggerated thing of all."

"The way Mr. Griffin was?" the Professor echoed. "I never noticed anything—"

Alice Diefenhaus regarded her husband affectionately.

"No, dear, I'm sure you didn't." She returned her attention to Jurnet. "You remember, yesterday, we were trying to decide why he stopped being upset so soon? Well, it was the same last night, only more so. He seemed, the best way I can put it is, positively exhilarated."

"I never noticed anything," Professor Diefenhaus repeated. "I wouldn't say we had the pleasure of Mr. Griffin's acquaintance long enough to form any firm judgment as to his state of mind at any particular moment in time. My guess would be that he was always happy up here among the family memorabilia. A truly cultured English gentleman of the old school."

He looked about the room with an air of humorous forbearance.

"An amateur, however. I hope, Inspector, you won't take it as the sign of a pedantic academic that I find the want of scholarly method displayed in the keeping of this archive a little shocking."

"Not at all," Jurnet answered politely. "I can well understand how all these piles of papers must offend a professional. Has anything been moved, so far as you can tell?"

The Professor responded with a certain caution.

"I can only speak as to general impression. It looks the same. I can't go further than that."

"I quite understand," said Jurnet. He turned back to the wife. "What I'd like to know from you, Mrs. Diefenhaus, is, did you pick up any clue as to the cause of this exhilaration which struck you so forcibly?"

"I can't say I did. As I said, I was only in the room for a brief spell. I just remember looking at Mr. Griffin and thinking, 'He's happy. That's fine!' the way one might feel pleased a child has got over a little upset and was back having fun again playing with his toys."

"That," her husband supplemented with feeling, "is more than a metaphor. Playing with his toys is exactly what Mr. Griffin was doing last night, a large part of the time." He jerked his head towards the copying machine along the wall. "You recall, Inspector, he promised to run off those household accounts for you? Well, he started off on those, and after that he began to take copies for himself and heaven knows who else, just for the hell of it, so far as I could judge. Once he got going with that gadget, he just hated to stop."

The Professor shook his head. The lack of order was getting him down. Moving to the copier, he thrust an exploratory hand into the aperture at its base.

"What do you know? There are still some in here. And here—" back at the vast table which filled most of the room— "will you look at this!" He pounced on a yellowed sheet sticking out from a tumble of photocopies, and shook his head again, at his wife this time. "You never should have taken those pages apart for him. Originals and copies all mixed up higgledy-piggledy. Amateurs!"

A blush suffused the Professor's face as he came back to a

recollection of the fate which had overtaken this particular amateur.

"God rest his soul!" he pronounced reverently.

"Mrs. Diefenhaus," Jurnet asked, "while you were here last night, did you have any conversation with Mr. Griffin?"

The American woman knit her brows.

"Nothing you could call conversation. I've been well trained not to be chatty when there's an invisible sign up: men working. I just quietly placed Eliot's antihistamine at his elbow—"the Professor sneezed in acknowledgment—"and was all set to creep out of the room again when Mr. Griffin looked up and said a few words. He was sitting at the table then, going through some of those sheets I'd undone for him. I suppose he started in on making all those copies later."

"That's right," her husband confirmed with some severity. "As soon as you left the room. I expect you broke his train of thought."

"A few words," Jurnet quoted. "Yet enough for you to decide he was 'exhilarated'. What *were* they, as closely as you can remember?"

"Oh," returned Alice Diefenhaus, "they had nothing to do with it. The exhilaration was simply there to be seen, like the moonlight. As I recall, I merely said I was going downstairs to find a book to take up to bed with me, and Mr. Griffin recommended something in Greek—I'm afraid I didn't get the name—that he'd been reading, and which he said I'd find on the sofa table in the drawing-room. I said I didn't understand Ancient Greek and it didn't sound like bedside reading anyway, but he said I was quite mistaken, and if I cared to look on the library shelves among the Loeb Classics I'd find some of the same material in translation. I didn't like to admit that what I really fancied was an Agatha Christie, so I just said good night and left them to it."

The Professor added: "I must have left about forty minutes later. It was still pretty early for me—not yet ten—and I'd found some quite remarkable stuff—" the Professor sighed. "I could have gone on happily until the small hours, only that darned machine kept buzzing away, and, not to put too fine a point on it, it began to get on my nerves. Naturally, Mr. Griffin being my host, I didn't feel I could ask him, for Pete's sake, turn that thing off. So I did the next best thing. Called it a day, told Mr. Griffin good night, and came down to bed."

"Did Mr. Griffin say anything to make you think he had plans to meet anybody later on?"

"Nothing at all. All told, I'd say we exchanged even fewer than Alice's few words. He brought a page or two to the table from time to time, to have me admire the quality of reproduction. But otherwise the only sound in the room was that infernal buzz."

"I suppose there's no possibility Mr. Griffin was working the machine deliberately, in the hope of driving you to pack it in?"

Professor Diefenhaus looked startled.

"I can't think that for a moment!" It was clearly not the behaviour to be expected of a truly cultured English gentleman of the old school. But the sentence which had begun so positively petered out to an indecisive close. "Why in the world would he want to do a thing like that?"

"He could have had an appointment. One he didn't want you, or anyone else, to know about."

"At that hour of night!"

"He certainly met someone," said Jurnet. "His murderer."

After a silence Mrs. Diefenhaus said in a small voice: "Know something? I'm beginning to feel awful homesick. I suppose you wouldn't let us pack our bags and get the hell out of here?"

"I've no powers to compel you to remain in Mauthen Barbary any longer than you choose."

"But you'd rather we stayed."

"I'd be grateful if you could see your way to doing so."

"It *would* look a bit fishy if we lit out before you solved the crime. The crimes. You've been so polite, but I guess, just the same, we're suspects too, aren't we? I can't quite see how we could have murdered the girl but I shouldn't be surprised, in real life, it's the easiest thing to slip away and kill someone, and come back into the room without anyone even noticing you've been away. And Eliot and I are certainly the two people who could most easily have killed Mr. Griffin."

"Alice!" the Professor cried. "You let your sense of humour run away with you! We barely knew him."

"In the flesh," she conceded. "But don't forget you and he were in correspondence for years. How's the Inspector not to know he didn't write you a letter telling you he possessed some document or other you wouldn't stop at murder to get your hands on?"

"Alice, for heaven's sake!"

"All I say," she concluded reasonably, "is, how's the Inspector to know?"

"I don't know." At Jurnet's tone, amiable and disarming, the Professor's anxieties visibly subsided. "Let me simply repeat that I'd appreciate it if you could hang on here for a bit. In an investigation it naturally helps to have all the relevant pieces, and people, to hand."

"We are quite prepared to do so," Professor Diefenhaus said stiffly. "Though not for the reasons my wife puts forward."

"Ought we to stay on here, though?" his wife inquired. "At the Manor? You, Mr. Jurnet, will know the etiquette better than we do. Is it OK to stay on as a house guest in an English country house when your host's been murdered?"

"Put like that—" Jurnet smiled—"the question's not one I'm qualified to answer. Mr. Griffin must have had a solicitor who'll know who the executors are. Officially, they're the ones to say stay or go. But I'm sure they'd be only too pleased." He added: "You might consider doing it for Anguish's sake. In his present state I shouldn't like to think of him left in this great place on his own."

"We should have thought of that! Of course we'll stay!" Alice Diefenhaus beamed an approval which the detective was conscious he did not deserve. He did not, however, feel it necessary to explain that he did not fancy a second suicide on his hands.

In the little wood, outside the rectangle of canvas screens which fenced in the grotto, P. C. White sat on a tree-stump and moodily munched the sandwich Sergeant Bowles, that kindly man, had had sent out to him. It was not a bad sandwich as sandwiches went, but P. C. White would have enjoyed it better had he not known that, at that very moment, the air of his police cottage was deliciously perfumed with the aroma of what he called stew and Sandra, his wife, *bœuf* something or other.

She had a way of putting wine in: P. C. White's heart swelled with pride. He'd lay a bet the Superintendent himself didn't sit down to a better dinner than Stan White, the village constable.

Except that today, by the look of it, he wasn't going to sit down to anything. What was he supposed to be guarding, for Christ's sake? They'd measured and photographed, they'd taken away the body. What was he stuck here for, to make sure nobody made off with the ruddy screens?

The constable sighed; shifted his buttocks in a vain attempt to find a more comfortable resting place for them, and took another bite out of his sandwich.

A flash of grey among the trees all but brought him to his feet. P. C. White relaxed. Only that dog again.

"Chloe!" he called encouragingly. "Here, old girl, then. Here!"

The dog took no heed. It loped noisily through the undergrowth in a wide circle with the grotto at its centre. Round and round it ran, unceasingly.

Poor old tyke!

Poor old Mauthen Barbary, for that matter.

P. C. White felt anger rise in his gorge, mingled with the taste of the sandwich. For all her high connections the Lady of Promise didn't seem capable of looking after her people the way they ought to be looked after. An instant later he blushed, remorseful. They were his people too, and he had failed them equally.

He jumped up just in time to catch the screens as they keeled over. Chloe, as silent as a moment before she had been noisy, had squirmed her way under one, dislodging its legs and caving in the other three sides.

"Fuck you!" cried P. C. White, trying vainly to restore the fragile structure to their former stability, and, in the process, quite losing his compassion for bereaved pets. "Get out of it!"

Chloe's response was to jump into the shallow grave which had held her master's body. Powerful and purposeful, she went to work, scrabbling beneath the pine boughs, flinging earth and pebbles up behind her.

"Fuck you, I said!" P. C. White repeated, abandoning the screens and advancing upon the furiously digging animal. "Get me the push you will, you stupid bitch!"

Impervious alike to obscenity and obloquy, Chloe dug on like one possessed. The policeman found a stick and raised it to strike.

And lowered it.

Something had appeared among the pebbles. Something gleaming. A shaft of silver and a golden Christ, eyes up-rolled in a theatrical agony.

P. C. White threw away his weapon and went back to the tree-stump to retrieve the remnant of his sandwich. Chloe had earned it.

When he turned back to the grave, the dog had vanished.

## 20

"This case," the Superintendent remarked after P. C. White had departed, glowing with commendation and released after all in time for his *bœuf,* "seems, if I may so put it, to be positively bedevilled with crosses."

He frowned with a civilised distaste at the crucifix on the Hospice table.

"Valuable, I'm quite sure, but not likeable. Those eyeballs, that pouter-pigeon chest. Too melodramatic by half."

Jurnet, who found the crucifix utterly repulsive, never-theless found himself obliged in fairness to observe: "Being crucified's a pretty melodramatic experience, I shouldn't be surprised."

"Which is why reducing it to caricature is a kind of blasphemy. But that's neither here nor there. What I find hard to understand—" the Superintendent went on, with a disap-proval he clearly intended to accompany him back to Head-quarters—"is how it came to be overlooked. I shouldn't have said P. C. White was all that lynx-eyed."

"They'd no call to go digging," said Jurnet the peace-maker. "And I fancy the dog had more to do with the finding than the constable let on." Looking at the shining object as if he would rather not: "I suppose someone just *could* have stolen it, and picked on the grave as a hiding place."

"You don't sound exactly convinced."

"I'm not."

"Keep an open mind," advised the Superintendent, who did not sound exactly convinced himself. "At any rate the vicar will be glad to get it back."

"That remains to be seen."

"Yes," the Superintendent agreed thoughtfully. "It does, doesn't it?" Then: "The Chief's right, you know. You've got to have help."

"I was hoping you'd decide Jack and I could manage between us."

"Speaking for myself, I'm sure you can. But two murders. The Chief will insist."

Jurnet sighed.

"I thought he might. Especially when he hears about Oscar."

"Who?"

"The swan. Great animal lover, the Chief. Will you be taking over yourself, sir?"

"I said help, not a takeover. I was thinking of Hale and Batterby."

Jurnet, face carefully composed into an expression of polite indifference, made no comment. The older man watched him closely, then said: "Let's see—today's Monday. They've one or two things to clear up first. Suppose I send them along, say, on Thursday? Unless, of course, you've got things straightened out by then—"

"Not much hope of that."

"Hope for the best." A smile ridged the skin at the corners of the Superintendent's eyes into creases as impeccable as those of his pale grey worsted trousers. "Well—time being of the essence, I'll shove off. I mustn't delay you."

"I've already sent Jack over to the vicarage to fetch Persimmer."

"Good."

"I think first, though, I'll pop down to the Shrine. Time I took another look."

"I'll go with you," said the Superintendent.

The Shrine was dusty. The sky seen through the skylight looked shop-soiled. Rachel Cass's blood on the floor could have been any stain: beer, baked beans.

Jurnet went towards the cloister and folded back the doors to let in the freshness of the Priory garden. He returned to find that the Superintendent had moved down the length of the long hall to the inner room at the far end. There, the air was rancid with the smell of tallow. Half-burnt candles were still impaled on the spikes along the walls: stalactites of wax hung from the iron rungs. Paul Falkener's panels looked grubby and commonplace.

Out of the ill-kempt place the Lady of Promise rose imperturbable; so freshly astonishing that Jurnet, who had believed his recollection quite uncomfortably precise, felt he was seeing her for the first time. Had those breasts really been so heavy, that belly so enormous? He certainly did not recall that tip of pointed tongue, caught in the act of moistening the thick upper lip.

"What exactly are we looking for?" the Superintendent asked presently.

"Just looking. Trying to understand." Jurnet was a brave man. The only thing he feared was to appear ridiculous.

He swallowed and took the chance.

"Trying to understand how it is that every damn thing that's happened seems one way or another to lead back to *her*." He glowered up at the great black figure. "Makes you feel she's the only thing round here really alive, and the rest of us just ticking over."

"I'd say you've just given a good definition of a great work of art."

Jurnet plunged in at the deep end.

"Don't know about art, sir. If you want to know what I think, I think she's evil. I don't believe she's the Mother of God or ever was. I think old Griffin dug up some heathen idol and hadn't the eyes to see what he'd got."

The Superintendent shook his head decisively.

"You're wrong there. I've been looking it up. This is unquestionably the same image that brought kings and commoners to Mauthen Barbary right up to the Reformation."

"Could be they got it wrong too."

"Could be," the Superintendent agreed readily. "Could be five hundred years of prayer are all you need to transform an earth goddess into a Virgin Mother. But you're *wrong*, Ben, about her being evil." He turned his gaze back to the statue. "She's beautiful. As the father of three children I can tell you unequivocally that no woman is ever more beautiful than in her last month of pregnancy, bearing your child."

"*Your* child. That's different." Thrusting away an instant fantasy of Miriam nine months gone, Jurnet said coarsely, reckless of giving offence: "God knows whose brat that one's supposed to be carrying."

But the Superintendent, a clever man, merely replied with unruffled humour: "He does, Ben. He does."

With a last appreciative look, he turned and sauntered, an abashed Jurnet following, back along the hall towards the cloister.

"All this talk about evil," he proffered over his shoulder. "Not a copper's business. His job's to investigate, not pass moral judgments."

"Yes, sir."

"You don't agree," said the Superintendent, interpreting

Jurnet's answer correctly. "As if you didn't know how seldom you can parcel things up into black and white. Nothing, for example, makes people kill other people so much as love and money, both very agreeable in their way."

"I started out thinking Rachel Cass was killed for love. But now I'm pretty sure she wasn't."

"What makes you say that?"

"The way she was killed, for one thing. A man who kills a woman for love wants to see her die. He doesn't creep up behind and bash her brains in."

Jurnet's superior looked distinctly disapproving.

"That's a sweeping generalisation! Am I to gather, then, that you think it's money?"

"Not that either. Anyone who wanted to get money out of Rachel Cass had only to ask. I suppose her brother'll come into what's left. A few thousand, he said. I have to check on that."

The Superintendent nodded.

"Even a few thousand can come in uncommonly handy if you're in a tight spot. Could Cass have done it?"

"They *all* could! The Casses, that big cow who lives next door, the boy friends, Barney Smithers, Anguish. Even those Americans staying at the Manor. Nowhere in this bloody village is more than ten minutes away from anywhere else. Very handy for a brisk homicide."

"I take it we're agreed the second death arises out of the first?"

"Unless you think murder's catching, or we've got a nutter out to pick off the Lady's followers one at a time."

"Not impossible, of course. Have we done anything about warning people not to open their doors to strangers?"

"It's not a stranger we're up against, but someone they'd think nothing of asking into the house."

"Just the same—"

"P. C. White's having a word with the Maidens. And Mrs. Chitty, their matron, or whatever she calls herself, has got a sister in Thetford. We're suggesting a visit, till this thing's settled. Short of providing protection for each of them individually there's not much else we can do."

"Except catch the villain responsible. Do you think Griffin was killed because he found out who killed the girl?"

Jurnet shook his head.

"Unlikely. If he had, he'd have lifted the phone and given us a ring. But he knew something, that's for sure. Mrs. Diefenhaus said he was 'exhilarated'. I can't see him jumping for joy at learning who'd done Rachel in."

"Unless he had a spot of blackmail in view. From what you've told me, he wasn't over-flush."

"Far from it. He'd been flogging the family heirlooms. I wouldn't put blackmail past him. I believe he'd have cheerfully sold his old mum down the river to keep the Lady of Promise in the style to which she was accustomed. But the old chap was no fool. If he *had* made a date with the murderer, he'd never have kept such a dangerous appointment without covering himself: a note for Anguish, instructions to go to the police, something of the sort. I think it more likely that, whatever it was he'd found out, he didn't himself realise its significance— its significance to the murderer, I mean. Something that gave the game away without him knowing it."

"That opens up other possibilities. I gather Griffin spent most of his last weekend in the company of the American professor."

"Professor Diefenhaus, yes. And his wife."

"What do we know of the Professor?"

"I had him looked up. Very eminent academic gentleman." Jurnet added: "Pleasant wife."

"The fact remains that if Griffin unwittingly gave the show away, the Diefenhauses were the people most likely to hear it. They were right on the spot."

"So was Anguish."

"Quite right. That makes three of them."

"Except that, if it was any of those three, he needn't have gone to the trouble of lacing up his shoes."

From among the Priory ruins a figure appeared, making its way towards the Shrine. The sun, lighting the shoulder-length hair and the thick beard, made the face radiant and awesome. There was something so compelling about the tall, ragged man moving barefoot over the grass that the Superintendent's shoulders twitched with annoyance when Jurnet, at his side, volunteered: "Falkener, sir."

Close to, the Superintendent had to admit, the artist was less striking. The tattered shirt would have been more picturesque had it been cleaner, the wonderful hair the better for a shampoo. For the sour smell of wine and sweat the fastidious Superintendent could find no excuse whatsoever.

Falkener said: "I saw the door open." He came in uninvited,

yet reluctant, his eyes sliding away from the stain on the floor. He had the look of someone who had not slept for a long time.

Jurnet asked in a business-like voice: "What can we do for you, sir?"

"Who the hell wants you to do anything? I told you, I saw the door open. Mounties get their man yet?"

"Our inquiries are proceeding." This time it was the Superintendent.

"Your inquiries are —oh God! You actually talk like that! I thought it was only on telly."

Jurnet said: "They get it right sometimes. Our inquiries are proceeding, and, in the course of them, I'd be glad of a further word with you, sir."

"Better make it snappy then," the man said, "or I shan't be here to have a word with."

"How's that?"

"There's no law against it, is there? I'm not expected to hang about here, am I, waiting for you boys in blue to decide who done it?"

"You're free to leave Mauthen Barbary at any time, so long as you let us know where we can contact you should the need arise."

"More'n I know myself." Falkener half-closed his eyes and squinted out at the sun baking the ancient stones. "Asia's what I fancy. The Golden Road to Samarkand and all that crap." He shut his eyes completely. Lines of suffering etched themselves in his face. "Christ, I need to get away from here!"

The two police officers, trained to listen to others speaking, said nothing, waited. After a little, the man opened his eyes and protested angrily: "I am *not* running away."

"No, sir."

"I'm willing to help all I can—answer your damnfool questions, send you picture postcards so you'll know where to put Interpol on my tail. It's in your best interests really, my going," he continued, calmer. "Because if I'm here much longer and you still haven't found out who killed Rachel I'll be forced to bump off every man or woman in Mauthen Barbary I personally feel might have done it, so's to be sure of getting the right one. And if you *do* find out, I'll kill him. However carefully you lock him up, I'll kill him! All said and done," he ended, "it'll save you a lot of hassle to have me safely out of the way."

Jurnet, with no appearance of being moved by what he had

just heard, said: "Mr. Falkener, if you're set on leaving
Mauthen Barbary, I'll keep you company back to your home.
We could have that chat right away."

"Why not here?" Then, low: "No. Not here."

"I must be getting along," the Superintendent said. "Good
day, Mr. Falkener. Ben—"

"Good day, sir."

The two left behind in the Shrine watched the spare figure
move with an easy stride among the ruins, bearing away
towards the High Street. Once or twice the Superintendent
stopped and put his hand on a segment of sun-warmed wall;
and Paul Falkener smiled, unaware he was doing so. He too
understood the need to touch, to experience reality through
the fingertips.

"Let's go, shall we?"

"Half a mo'," the artist said. "I remember now. I saw the
door open and I remembered the spots. I promised Len."

"Come again?"

"Spotlights. Len Foulcher borrowed a couple from the
people he works for. They'll be wanting them back."

"I never saw any spotlights—"

"Too busy muck-raking. Look up, man—look up! There!"
He pointed, first, to a flex dangling behind the candle-racks,
and then at the ceiling.

Jurnet, raising his head to see a fitment, previously unnoticed, lodged there unobtrusively, inquired: "Where's the
bulbs?"

"Decided not to use them in the end. I took them home for
safekeeping."

The detective lowered his gaze to the Lady of Promise.

"Pity. I'd have liked to have got a look at her in a proper
light."

"You wouldn't. Takes away all the mystery."

"That's what I mean."

"I thought a copper's job was solving secular mysteries, not
religious ones."

"Sometimes the two go together."

Jurnet watched as the artist padded away down the hall and
disappeared through the doors of the vestibule. He heard
another door open and shut; the one to the storeroom
presumably, for soon the man was back, carrying an aluminium
ladder which he set carelessly alongside the candle-holders.

Apprehensive of the spikes, the detective came forward to

hold it steady. Too late. Falkener sprang up the rungs nimble as a monkey, to the very top.

"Look!" he called down, flapping his arms in derision. "No hands! Look—one leg!"

"Break your own bleeding neck," said Jurnet, taking his foot off the bottom rung.

His words had their effect. Falkener stopped play-acting, reached into the hip pocket of his jeans for a screwdriver, and with deft and economical movements removed the crossbar and its attached holders.

By contrast, his descent down the ladder was slow and clumsy. He seemed to have grown suddenly tired. He moved with a perceptible limp.

The chap swings to and fro like a ruddy pendulum, Jurnet thought, coming forward to relieve him of his burden.

"Ta." Back on the floor, Falkener looked round vacantly. "That's it, then."

"I'm ready, if you are."

The man's wavering gaze had been caught by the panels on either side of the Lady.

"I carved those, did they tell you? Alone I did it."

"I know."

"Dreck. Shit of the highest quality."

"I've seen a couple of small things of yours I liked a lot. The little statuette in Rachel's room, and the one in Mr. Griffin's."

"Charlie showed you that? He *must* have taken to you. He won't let me anywhere near it." Falkener jerked his head towards the ladder. "Want me to take that back?"

"Leave it."

"I shan't be coming back."

"I said, leave it."

"Charlie wants the Lady shifted back to the Manor. Says he can't leave her here after what's happened. But he'll have to find somebody else."

Falkener looked up at the broad black face of the Lady of Promise. It was to her that his words were addressed.

"I shan't be coming back here, ever again."

That was when Jurnet said: "Mr. Griffin won't be coming back either."

## 21

Paul Falkener sat in a wicker chair which creaked with every movement of his body, and shed tears for the death of Oscar the swan. His reaction to the news of the violent end of Charles Griffin was more equivocal.

At first, when Jurnet had told him Griffin was dead, the artist had taken it for granted that the old man's heart had given out at last. Poor old Charlie, he had lamented; a regret, the detective fancied, not unmixed with that imperfectly suppressed relief with which, often, the relatives and friends of a sick man received the news of his demise.

Mixed with something besides. What it was Jurnet only discovered when, arrived at The Barn, he deemed the time had come to reveal how Charlie Griffin had met his fate.

Falkener wiped his eyes on a corner of his red cotton neckerchief, poured himself a beaker of wine from a bottle standing uncorked on the paint-stained table. He grimaced as the vinegary stuff coursed down his gullet, and announced: "Of course he had it coming to him, the old sod."

"What makes you say that?"

"Shocked you, have I?" Falkener pushed the bottle across the table. "Help yourself. There's a mug somewhere." He half-rose from the chair, then collapsed back into it.

"I don't want a drink," Jurnet said. "I want to know what you had against Mr. Griffin."

"Little man playing God, that's what. What fucking right has anyone except God to play God?" He broke off to replenish the beaker. "Mauthen Barbary." He flung out an arm in a gesture that encompassed the village. "Quaint little place. Haven of rural peace. Or was until Charlie-boy got busy with his bucket and spade."

"Funny. I thought you were all for the Lady."

"So I am, mate. Heart and soul, liver and lights. Question is, is she all for me?" Falkener heaved himself out of the chair, this time successfully. "Know what the Bishop of Norwich said when Charlie got him down here to have a look at her when she was first dug up? 'Put her in the Castle Museum, Mr. Griffin.' That was His Lordship's advice: put her in the

Museum. And when Charlie said he didn't think it right to stick her away in a glass case, d'you know what His Beatitude replied? 'Actually, Mr. Griffin, I wasn't thinking of a glass case. I was thinking of the Castle dungeons. That's the proper place for her. Behind bars. Like any other dangerous animal.'" Bracing himself against the table, Falkener thrust his face towards the detective's. "What d'you say to that?"

"I'm inclined to think the Bishop had something. Though, after all, it *is* only a statue."

"Tha's what they said about the Trojan Horse." Falkener let out a loud belch. "Pardon!" he said. "Manners!" He reached vaguely for a knapsack lying on the table. "Well, I wish you joy of her. I'm leaving. Got to phone the bugger Minchin, where the hell's my last cheque. Then I'm off."

"Minchin?"

"Mr. Minchin of Minchin, Fylow and Apthorpe, Charlie's solicitors in Fakenham. So mean he can't bear to pay money out even when it's out of somebody else's pocket."

"What's the hurry to leave? Afraid you're next on the list?"

Paul Falkener said in a voice of complete sobriety: "No, Inspector. Not afraid. Bored. Bored with failure. Bored with grief—"

Jurnet remarked brutally: "Failure I can understand. But grief? I'd have thought Rachel hadn't been dead long enough for you to be bored with it already."

The knapsack lay nearer Falkener than Jurnet, but the detective made no move to push it towards the artist's questing hand. Instead, he moved away from the table, and paced deliberately round the long, bare room that, roughly plastered and open to the roof beams, spoke plainly of its former incarnation as a storehouse for grain. Save for a recess at one end housing a sink and a battered stove, the room appeared to comprise the entire living accommodation.

Not a bad pad for a woodcarver, the detective decided, skirting wood sliced like giant swiss rolls, and slabs with the sheen of honey. Sweet-smelling shavings crisped beneath his feet. Drawings were heaped perilously in an armchair that teetered drunkenly on three legs. A great lump of clay squatted atop a chest of drawers like some creature of the primeval ooze. The divan bed was covered with a horse-blanket no decently bred horse would have allowed within a mile of the stable-door.

Pretty basic. No bathroom, no loo that Jurnet could see.

What the estate agents called ripe for further development. Over-ripe! Still, Charlie Griffin could have made a packet if he'd lain out the money for a proper conversion.

"You've been having a bonfire," Jurnet observed, looking at the ashes in the mean little grate.

"Only bills, income-tax demands, and vital evidence," Paul Falkener replied. "Next question."

"Last night. Did you go out, or receive any visitors?"

"I never receive visitors. I am a taker of hospitality, Inspector, not a dispenser of it. I scrounge. As for going out, I went down to the bog at the bottom of the garden, and twice I didn't bother to go all the way. Nitrogenous waste. Return unto the earth what thou hast taken therefrom."

"Yes, sir. Were there any messages, then? Anybody phone?"

"No messages. And no one phoned. Not surprising, as there isn't any phone. When I need to make a call, I use the box in the pub yard along with the rest of the proles."

"Were there never occasions when Mr. Griffin needed to be in touch?"

"He'd send over Anguish. Or if it was after opening time he'd have him try The Pirate."

"What about Barnabas? Did he never need to get hold of you outside working hours?"

"Barnabas!" Falkener chuckled. "Barnabas won't touch me with a barge pole. You know how it is—reformed alcoholic, afraid of catching a dose all over again."

"I see." Jurnet looked thoughtfully at the divan, and then transferred his gaze to its owner.

"And what about female company?"

Self-disgust disfigured the handsome face.

"What kind of a tramp would let herself be bedded down on *that*? You do me an injustice, Inspector. I'm not a seducer. I get invited in."

*Conceited bastard!* Jurnet got his own back by asking: "Did Rachel never come here?"

The man looked up sharply.

"I don't care for the juxtaposition."

"Did she?"

"Rachel was different."

"So I'm told. Did she come here often?"

"If she'd made a casserole. Or if she hadn't seen me around and was afraid I might be choking in my own vomit." Falkener covered his eyes with a hand. "Oh my God!"

"When was the last time she came?"

Falkener let the hand drop, and said wearily: "Wednesday, Thursday, Friday—I don't know. One day last week."

"Was it a casserole, or had you been drinking?"

"If you must know, she came to give me some money."

"Why should she do that?"

"For months I'd been going on about getting away from here. Talk, that's all it was. You may have noticed, Inspector, I'm a talker the way some people have loose bowels. Well, Rachel must have thought I meant it, because she turned up with three hundred pounds."

Remembering the bundle of notes in the girl's dressing-table, and knowing the answer beforehand, Jurnet asked: "How come you're still here?"

"What do you take me for?"

"You said yourself you were a scrounger."

"But not from Rachel!" Falkener exclaimed. "You still haven't a clue."

"In that case you mustn't hold it against me if I ask stupid questions. Here's another. Why do you think Rachel wanted you to have all that money?"

Paul Falkener said, in a kind of hushed wonder: "I think she must have loved me."

"Loved you how? Sexually?"

"You ought to have your mouth washed out."

"Even if I tell you she was four months pregnant?"

At that, Falkener aimed a great flailing blow at the detective; lost his balance, and fell sprawling across the table.

"She was a Maiden!" he shouted. "A virgin!"

"That's right. It happens like that occasionally."

Somehow the man found his feet, somehow found his way back to his chair. Its protest, as he sat down, seemed to echo his own.

"You're out of your mind!"

"The medical evidence will bear me out."

"You know where you can stick your medical evidence!"

Paul Falkener shook his head, shook his whole body like a dog shedding water after a swim.

"I've had too much to drink. I'm not hearing you properly."

"You heard. Rachel Cass was four months pregnant. She was still, technically, a virgin."

The detective was not prepared for Falkener's next remark, which was a long time coming.

"So that's another murder," he said at last. "Whoever killed Rachel killed her child as well." There was a pause. Then Falkener said: "You've certainly got your work cut out, Inspector."

He got up from the chair again and went towards the chest-of-drawers. Halfway there he checked, and Jurnet heard a sharp intake of breath. The man resumed his barefoot way, only now he was limping again.

"Done something to your foot?"

"Splinter. Occupational hazard."

At the chest-of-drawers he bent over and, grasping its wooden knobs, levered out the bottom drawer. Inside was an object swathed in rags, which he lifted out tenderly and brought to the table.

"Funny to think I showed this to Rachel just that night of all nights." Falkener looked across at Jurnet. "You said I was good at small things." He undid the wrappings. "I don't show this to many people. Rachel had never seen it. I couldn't take her money. But I needed to show her I wasn't completely hopeless."

Jurnet looked at the little wooden figure revealed on the table. It was carved out of some wood he did not recognise, and "carved" was a mis-description. The wood seemed to flow of its own volition, and to have congealed into curves as uncontrived as they were inevitable. The detective had no doubt he was looking at the statuette which, long ago in Cork Street, had cut short Charles Griffin's cab ride, and brought Paul Falkener to Mauthen Barbary.

Griffin had called the piece matchless. As well he might. The slender body rounding to pregnancy, the wistful confusion, a child bearing a child: all was as the old man had described it. But there was something Charles Griffin had missed.

Jurnet did not miss it.

"Yes," he agreed. "You weren't completely hopeless."

After which, he bade Falkener a brisk good-day, left The Barn, and crossed the Green of Forge Cottage.

Joanna Cass must have seen him coming from one of the windows, for, before he had even pushed open the gate to the front garden, the door was opened.

"I've been at The Barn," he began without ceremony to the

beautiful, haggard woman waiting on the threshold. "I've seen it."

"I'm glad," she said. "Come in."


# 22


She ushered Jurnet into the living-room and sat down on the sofa facing him. For a moment the detective stared at the undented seat cushion next to her. Joanna Cass looked incomplete without her husband beside her, their shoulders touching.

She said: "Philip's gone to get the car filled up. We're going back to town. I can't stay here any more. We'll be back for the funeral, whenever that is." When Jurnet made no comment, she burst out with: "You're not going to stop us, are you?"

This was getting monotonous.

Jurnet said, as he had said to the others: "I've no power to do that."

"Philip thinks we ought to stay."

"We should certainly appreciate it—"

"I can't breathe here any longer!" The woman put her hand to her throat. "I can't swallow. I—" She stopped helplessly.

"It's all been a great strain—"

"You said you'd seen it."

"Yes."

"Now that you know all about me," said Joanna, "it doesn't matter, does it, whether I go or not."

"I don't know all about you," Jurnet said. "I just saw the statuette, that's all."

"Didn't Paul tell you?"

"Mr. Falkener told me nothing. All he did was show it to me. He wasn't drunk enough to tell me the how or why."

"No," she considered. "I should have known that. Paul's never drunk enough. Even when he showed it to Rachel he wasn't drunk enough for that. She had to come and ask me for an explanation."

"Like me," said Jurnet.

"I have to go back a long time." Joanna Cass pushed her dark hair back from her face. "It hardly seems me I'm talking about.

Only first I want to say one thing, in case you've got the wrong idea completely. Paul Falkener wasn't the father of my child."

"I see," said Jurnet, who had got the wrong idea completely.

"I was eighteen. A year younger than Rachel. I was at art school and I was living with a boy named Alan Shand. Paul and Alan were friends. Paul admired him tremendously."

"Was he an art student as well?"

"Alan? Oh no. Alan was at the London School of Economics. He was studying political science and he was going to be prime minister. Such drive! Such ambition! A born winner. Paul saw in him everything he lacked in himself."

"And you? What did you see in him?"

"I loved him. Or thought I did. Actually, I was too young to know what love was. I was too young to know lots of things—including contraception. In those days it wasn't crammed down your throat from the minute you could walk. And so I became pregnant."

Her face had become even paler.

"Do you know one of the things I've been thinking since Rachel—since yesterday? It's that the man, whoever he was, must have been glad she was going to bear his child, or she couldn't have looked the way she did."

"If she told him."

"I hadn't thought of that." The thought plainly distressed her. "Alan was furious. It didn't fit in with his plans at all. He wanted to know how on earth I could have been so stupid. And when he told Paul, Paul got him the name of somebody who would get rid of it for me. Eleven years ago it wasn't easy, the way it is today."

Remembering the statuette, Jurnet prompted: "But you decided against it?"

"Yes. Because, whatever Alan said, I didn't feel stupid at all. Till then, I'd never given children a thought. But suddenly it seemed to me the most wonderful thing that could ever happen to a woman." She turned on Jurnet eyes that looked beyond him, into the past. "All at once I grew up. And I wasn't going to let anyone take my child away from me."

"Did your family know?"

Joanna shook her head.

"There was only my father. My mother died when I was thirteen. He taught maths in a boys' school, and he never really got used to having a young girl about the house. I think he was quite relieved when I went off to London to study art."

Jurnet asked: "And what about the child?"

"You'll have to let me tell this in my own way, because I still don't find it easy to speak about." Joanna paused, then went on, a faint pink, which gradually deepened, tingeing her cheeks. "I did exercises, drank lots of milk. I went to a doctor. As I said, I'd grown up. I looked at Alan with new eyes and saw for the first time what a ruthless person he was—that he'd used me the way he used everybody else who came his way. I thought about leaving him, only I didn't, because by then I'd become pretty ruthless myself—not for myself, but for the child I was carrying. For the child's sake I needed a roof over my head, and so I hung on, though there was nothing between us any more. I wonder sometimes he didn't pack up his things and move out."

Joanna Cass drew a deep breath.

"And then, one night, when Paul was there and I was about seven months pregnant, I miscarried—if that's the right word when you're so many months gone. I suddenly felt terrible, and I cried out to Alan to fetch the doctor, and after that I remember being on the floor, and Alan and Paul bending over me. And then, a long while after, lying on the bed, and Alan telling me, very gently, that the child had been born dead."

"I'm sorry," said Jurnet, not knowing what else to say.

"They hadn't fetched the doctor, though one or the other could have gone for him, don't you think? They never fetched the doctor. Two days later, they borrowed a car, bundled me up in blankets, and drove me down to Cornwall, to a commune run by some friends of Paul's. They never fetched a doctor there either. They didn't believe in them, they said, and it didn't matter anyway, because by then I didn't care whether I lived or died. But I lived," she went on. "After a month I walked out and thumbed a ride back to London. A girl I knew put me up until I found a job and could afford a room of my own."

She looked at the detective.

"You're wondering what all this has to do with Rachel. What I'm doing is telling you how I came to be in that newspaper photograph. I'm establishing my alibi."

"Oh?"

"Because what I haven't told you is that when I was down there on the floor, amid all the pain there was suddenly a moment of indescribable joy. A moment when I knew it was all worth while. I heard my baby cry."

"But—"

"But they said it was born dead. A boy, they said. And they

said they had got rid of it right away, so that I shouldn't be upset by the sight of a dead baby."

"Even so, they had no business—" Jurnet began: then amended what he had to say. "Perhaps you imagined it."

"That's what *they* said." She got up from the sofa. "Don't ever say that again."

"I'm sorry," Jurnet said. "You heard the child cry. You understand what you're suggesting?"

"Perfectly." She sat down again. "We lived in Chelsea, one of those slums a little way back from the Embankment. I often wonder whether they dumped my baby in a dustbin or a builders' skip, or threw him into the river."

Gritting his teeth, Jurnet demanded: "What happened to the born winner, the future prime minister? To the best of my knowledge he hasn't made it yet."

"Oh, Alan?" she returned indifferently, as if the subject were of small interest. "He was killed in an air crash a couple of years later. I never saw Paul again until he turned up here in Mauthen Barbary."

Jurnet said: "You can't have told your husband, or he'd never be on the terms he is with him."

"No, I didn't tell Philip. He knew I'd had lovers, but not about the child. He wants so much for us to have one ourselves, it would have been too cruel. The doctors I've been to since, they knew at once, of course, but I wouldn't let them let on. It's not even relevant, in medical terms. They all say there's no reason I shouldn't bear another child, no reason Philip shouldn't father one. Doctors, you see, don't believe in divine retribution."

"I can't see how He or anyone else can blame you."

"Knowing how Alan felt, I should have left him months before. Never trusted him—never trusted the pair of them! The proof is that after ten years of marriage Phillip and I are still childless, and until yesterday morning I still heard the sound of my baby crying."

"Tell me about yesterday morning."

"You were quite right," Joanna Cass went off at an apparent tangent, "to ask what happened to that note Rachel left. All the household things were there, just as I said: but at the bottom she'd written, 'I've seen Paul's carving of you, so please stay up so we can have a talk.' I stayed up, as you already know, and when she came in I told her everything, just as I've told you. And she told me I had to tell Philip."

"*Had* to? A bit holier-than-thou, wasn't it?"

"You still don't know her."

"Obviously." Jurnet did not conceal his irritation. "And did she announce her intention of telling her brother herself, if you still refused to?"

"For which reason I rushed down to the Shrine first thing next morning and killed her before she had the chance!" Joanna smiled tremulously, and clasped her hands together in her lap. "I told her I'd think it over. She kissed me very lovingly and went up to bed. And I sat there, thinking."

"Coming to what conclusion?"

"None, that night. Or rather, morning. The birds were beginning to sing when I went upstairs. I couldn't have had three hours' sleep but I woke up feeling marvellous; and knowing, the instant I opened my eyes, that Rachel was right. I had to tell Philip everything."

"And did you?"

"He was up already, and just going out for his stroll. So I thought, I'll tell him over breakfast. Getting it ready I was so happy—the relief of knowing there'd be no more secrets between us!—that I felt I had to pop down to the Shrine and let Rachel know. Thank her, thank her!"

She shook her head incredulously.

"What did Rachel say?"

"I never got there. There was such a crush in the High Street I could hardly move. I realised I'd never be able to get through, speak to Rachel, and be back in the cottage before Philip returned. And I wanted so much to be there, waiting for him."

"You could have gone round to the cloister door."

"It never occurred to me. Every time we've been there we've always gone in through the front."

"So what did you do?"

"Gave up and came home. Philip was just opening the gate. We came into the house together."

"And did you tell him the whole story over breakfast, the way you'd planned?"

"I told him before. And as a result, we didn't have any. Breakfast. We went back to bed together." Jurnet watched the tears well up and fall unheeded down the lovely cheeks. "The two people who, out of the whole world, Rachel should have been able to count on—we were in bed together and happier than we'd ever been in our lives, while she was being killed!"

\* \* \*

Philip Cass drew his car alongside the fence as Jurnet emerged from the garden gate. The car coasted to a standstill quietly, expensively: a Citroën, the detective noted, at the upper end of the price range. Still, it could have been a company perk.

The man got out quickly and demanded: "You haven't been—"

"Pestering your wife again? It's all right," said Jurnet. "She'll tell you all about it."

"Look—"congenitally unable to sustain aggression—"I know you have your job to do, Inspector. But Joanna's at the end of her tether. Did she tell you we're going back to town?"

"She did say something. Sorry about that."

Philip Cass looked discomfited, the overgrown schoolboy again.

"I'll speak to—I'll see if we can't put it off a day or two."

"Every little helps."

"Yes. Well." Cass turned towards the gate, then back; amiable again and cooperative. "One thing. Did my wife mention Charlie Griffin's phone call?"

"Mr. Griffin's name wasn't mentioned."

"After Rachel, I don't think Charlie's death really registered. Still, I said we mustn't forget to tell you."

"When did Mr. Griffin phone?"

"Last night. About nine-forty-five, I should guess. It must have been before ten, because, except when he's got something special on, he's always in bed by ten."

"What was the reason for the call?"

"A formal expression of condolence, so far as I could judge. I answered, and after he'd spoken to me he had a few words with Joanna—"

Something in his tone made Jurnet ask: "What was it about the call you found puzzling?"

Cass's sandy head came up in appreciation of the other's perspicacity.

"Hard to put one's finger on it. Everything he said was correct, as you'd expect from Charlie." He consulted his recollection, and came up with: "A certain absent-mindedness is the nearest I can get to it. After Joanna had finished she said to me: 'He's not even thinking about Rachel.' I thought it a bit odd, because she and Charlie always got on like a house on fire. He's always been very fond of her, very warm."

"Can you remember his exact words?"

Philip Cass pondered.

"Not easy. They were so much the clichés people always trot out on such occasions. Sincere condolences. Deepest sympathy. Friends must rally round. He seemed to think the whole village was crammed into our living-room helping us keep a stiff upper lip. Got it mixed up with an Irish wake, the way he spoke. When he repeated more or less the same thing to Joanna, she replied pretty sharply that we were alone, and all we wanted at the moment was each other's company." He finished: "I'm afraid that's the best I can do."

"You've both been very helpful." Jurnet added: "Mrs. Cass has just been telling me how she came to be in that photo."

"Oh, did she?" Philip Cass's face twisted, but there was relief in his voice. "I'm glad it's out. You can't be expected to do your job if people lead you up the garden path."

"No, sir. Nor if they take themselves off when they might be more use staying."

"Point taken. I'll speak to Joanna. Do you think it will be long now?"

"Till we solve the crime?" Jurnet regarded the earnest, open countenance with something not far short of affection. What was it the chap had said about Mauthen Barbary? *This was where you opted out of time, or at least had the illusion you did?* Well, all idylls came to an end, sooner or later. Time for Mr. Philip Cass, poor bugger, to get himself a clock that worked.

Aloud, Jurnet said, using one of those clichés people always trot out on such occasions: "Time will tell."

## 23

Jurnet crossed the road to the Green, and paused by the pond, where Nellie the swan floated motionless. The village lay quiescent, drugged with summer.

At the High Street, the detective turned momentarily towards the Hospice; then, changing his mind, continued downhill to the Manor. He turned into the drive as an ancient Mini shot out of it.

With a screech of brakes and a crunching of gravel the little car reversed back into the drive as speedily as it had ejected itself. Jurnet flung himself into a rhododendron and waited until he heard the engine turned off. Then he straightened up, brushed himself off, and strolled over to the offside door.

"Know what, Ferguson? One day you're going to find yourself in trouble with the police."

"Me, Inspector?" The driver was a young man with an engagingly ugly face. "And I thought you were going to congratulate me for not losing a minute getting on with the job!"

"Never mind the minute. You nearly lost an inspector." Jurnet grinned. "Find anything?"

"Only the dead man's prints, and the butler's—Lord High Everything Else, or whatever he is. Didn't take to me at all. Messing up his bedroom. *His* bedroom!"

"Butlers or whatever-they-are are trained to talk like that. No other prints at all?"

"Nary a one. If anyone visited there last night he kept his gloves on."

"Ah well." Jurnet sighed. "What did you make of that penknife?"

"Another dead loss. Someone gave it a good wipe."

"Ta anyway. I take it you're off to Forge Cottage now?"

"Correct. Other side of the Green, Sergeant Bowles said."

"That's right." As the car rattled into life again, Jurnet said: "Go easy, over there. They're pretty cut up."

"Nineteen years old, wasn't she?" Ferguson rammed the Mini into gear with unexpected ferocity. He was not all that much older himself. "Makes you want to spit!"

"You again?"

Jurnet passed into the hall, taking no offence at his welcome. The old man's appearance shocked him. In the short time since they had last spoken, Anguish's face had fallen in—or rather, the skull had obtruded until it seemed on the point of breaking through the flesh.

There were organisms, weren't there, which could only live in tandem, each needing the other for mutual support. Take away one, the other packed up. The detective delved deep and from some unsuspected reservoir brought up the word *symbiosis*. It looked as though whoever bumped off Griffin was going to get Anguish as a bonus. Which would be richly comic in a gruesome way if it was Anguish who had done the bumping off in the first place.

"You're looking a bit done up," the detective observed. "You ought to lie down for a bit."

"Pity I didn't. Nobody to let you in, then. Or that puppy with his messes."

"Mr. Ferguson," said Jurnet, correctly interpreting this last, "has his work to do. You want Mr. Griffin's killer found, don't you?"

"Won't make no difference now he'd dead, will it?"

"To his killer it will. You really ought to lie down. Mrs. Diefenhaus can answer the door for a bit."

"They're up in the Muniment Room. Knock till Doomsday, they won't hear you up there. What you want anyway?"

"It won't take but a minute. You told me about Dr. Teago phoning. I never asked you about outgoing calls."

"What about them?"

"Would you know whether Mr. Griffin made any? Any time after he heard Rachel'd been killed?"

"I'd know like I always do."

"And how's that?"

"Better see for yourself."

Anguish led the way, across the hall, to the door which led to the servants' quarters. The corridor behind the green baize was dank and cheerless, its only light that which filtered from the windows of the small rooms—some little more than cupboards—which opened off it. At one of these the manservant stopped, and motioned the detective to look inside.

The room housed a wooden chair and a small, old-fashioned switchboard.

"So you were his telephone operator as well," Jurnet said. "But did he never ask for a line and then get the number himself?"

"Him! Never knew what his own was, let alone other people's!"

"Did you get him any yesterday afternoon or evening?"

"Mr. Minchin, the solicitor, after tea. And Mr. Cass, just before he went to bed."

"I see." Looking about the little box of a room Jurnet commented: "Pretty isolated here. What happened when Mr. Griffin wanted you to get him a number and you were busy somewhere else in the house, too far away to hear him buzzing you?"

"Had to wait, hadn't he?"

"Incoming calls, at any rate, you'd be able to pick up from the nearest extension."

"Not ours, you wouldn't."

"How's that? I saw one in Mr. Griffin's bedroom—"

"Four of 'em. Bedroom, drawing-room, library, Muniment. Only thing is, they don't none of them ring. Guvner said the bells broke his concentration, and had 'em taken out."

"Seems unnecessarily inconvenient."

"Anyone who knew us knew all he had to do was keep on trying. Sooner or later I'd hear the phone going. Anyone who didn't was always about bills. Mr. Griffin weren't exactly falling over himself to hear from *them*."

"I suppose not," Jurnet agreed. And: "Thanks very much then. I needn't trouble you any more. I'll let myself out."

Anguish's expression was enough to make it plain that servants had a duty to keep strangers under their eye until they were safely off the premises. The old man shuffled ahead along the corridor, every now and again touching the flaking walls. Back in the splendour of the hall, and abreast of the open doors into the drawing-room, Jurnet stopped to gaze admiringly: and then, drawn by the beauty of the room and in disregard of Anguish's all but vocal disapproval, stepped over the threshold.

Steeped in light from the tall windows giving on to the terrace, the drawing-room looked out upon such a vista of rural peace that it was hard to say whether the view was an extension of the room, or the room of the view. So far as Charles Griffin was concerned, Jurnet reflected, heaven would have its work cut out coming up to what he had been accustomed to down below.

In the drawing-room, the detective noted, no telltale discolourations disfigured the walls. The Lord of the Manor of Mauthen Barbary had been careful not to dispose of furnishings whose absence might be remarked by the casual visitor.

One of the couch cushions was still dented, a smaller cushion creased from supporting a back. Anguish, following the direction of the detective's glance, took it as a reprimand, and crossed the room scowling to punch the upholstery back into shape.

"Was that where Mr. Griffin sat when he was in here?"

"They're all Mr. Griffin's chairs. He sat where he pleased."

Jurnet smiled as affably as if the old man had said something agreeable. He sauntered over to the sofa table and picked up a small calf-bound volume that lay there. He opened it at random. Old glue crackled drily.

Anguish rushed forward.

"Don't you know how to handle an antique book?"

"Sorry." Jurnet shut the book with more care than he had opened it. "Greek, is it? Double Dutch to me."

He looked down at the book, surprised at the pleasure his fingers communicated to him. The leather felt warm, resilient. A book that felt like that deserved to have something inside worth reading.

"Agathias Scholasticus," the manservant muttered unwillingly.

"Cor!" Exaggerated admiration. "You read this lingo?"

"Who d'you think bring him his books when he wanted 'em?" The anger, continually upthrusting, seemed itself a form of grieving. "See *him*, with *his* legs, top of them library steps?"

"This must be what he was reading to Rachel Friday teatime. Agath—what you said. That was the name." Jurnet opened the book again, turned a few pages with elaborate care. "Care to give me an idea what's it all about?"

"He taught me the letters, not to understand!" the old man glared, as if the detective had insulted him. It was obviously as much a solecism for a manservant to understand Ancient Greek as for his master to know how to polish silver.

"That's all right," Jurnet said peaceably. "Mrs. Diefenhaus doesn't understand it either. She wanted something to read in bed, and Mr. Griffin told her there was a translation in the library." Frowning in recollection: "The something classic, I think she said."

"Leob Classics," said Anguish, raising his eyes to the ceiling in weary disgust. "Greek and English on facing pages."

"That's it. Think you could find it for me?"

"Greek Anthology." Anguish's tone indicated little faith in the detective's literacy, in any language. "Five vols. You want the lot?"

Jurnet held up the leather-bound book.

"The one with this in it."

"Vol I." Anguish made no move to fulfill the errand. "Reckon I oughtn't to let any of Mr. Griffin's things out of the house."

"I'll give you a receipt." Jurnet's patience dwindled. There was always a moment when, in self-defence, other people's woes had to be shuffled off. "In Ancient Greek, if it'll make you any happier."

Back at the Hospice Sergeant Ellers greeted his superior with an ostentatious forbearance of which the latter was completely unaware. Jurnet had come in frowning, his dark, Mediterranean face set in concentration.

But concentration on what? That was the crux. Between the rhododendrons of the Manor and the laurels of the Hospice the detective had become aware of something—something that somehow, somewhere, he had failed to see; or seeing, had failed to take into his calculations. Something that buzzed about in his head like a fly you kept swiping at, and as often missed. Something somebody had said? Or ought to have said, and hadn't? Something that didn't add up.

It had nagged at him all the way back, obstinately resistant to all efforts at recall. Something. Something. He felt he knew the way an oyster felt, irritated by that crumb of grit in its shell, coating it with layer upon layer of nacre.

At least an oyster, at the end of the day, had a pearl to show for it. What did he have? *Something!*

Ellers said: "We've got the vicar." And could not resist adding: "We were wondering when you'd be back, sir."

Jurnet blinked, and exchanged his problem for the matter in hand. He caught the whiff of impertinence and ignored it.

"I don't see him."

"He fainted." The Sergeant's tone made it clear he had no great opinion of persons who so indulged their sensibilities. "Like young Woodgate, remember? Must be something in the air. I sent him to lie down in one of the dormitories till you got back. Sergeant Bowles is keeping an eye on him."

"How did it happen?"

"It was when I told him Griffin'd been done in. No—" correcting himself—"when I mentioned where he'd been found. Previous to that—" Ellers looked with curled lip at a damp patch on the linoleum—"he'd only vomited."

"And what brought that on?"

"That was when I showed him the crucifix. Sicked all over it." The Welsh chapel-goer grew shrill with a disapproval which would have done credit to a Roman. "Shocking bad taste in a reverend."

"I assume we can take that as identification." A glint of amusement showed in Jurnet's eyes despite himself. There was a point where even tragedy became comic; a serpent coiled round on itself, tail in mouth. The Reverend Lionel Persimmer might or might not be a murderer. He was a born clown.

"I had Mr. Porker Beslow fetched from his shop to make sure. Happy as a sandboy to see it back, till he saw the way it was all scratched about, what with the stones and the dog's paws. Seemed to think it was our fault. And not so happy either about that swan you wished on him. Says it's getting on his nerves to see it hanging there every time he goes to the fridge. Very sensitive lot we've got here in Mauthen Barbary, sir."

Jurnet gave a sudden chortle.

"Have young Ferguson take it back with him to Norwich. That'll slow him down a bit."

Ellers said, with genuine concern: "Know what the parson did, sir? Buried the crucifix himself!"

"Admitted it, did he? A kind of white magic, I take it, to counteract the black magic of the Lady of Promise?"

"That's what it was, exactly. You'd think we were living in the Dark Ages." The Sergeant moved his shoulders in a shiver intended to convey that sensitivity was not the exclusive property of the natives. "Intended to dig it up again after the party was over, and put it back with no one the wiser."

"It still doesn't let him off the hook. He had time to bury the crucifix *and* kill the girl. And that cross in her hand—another bit of magic, white or black? *And* Griffin's murder—what colour was that?"

"I never got that far before he passed out."

"Very convenient for avoiding awkward questions. I think you'd better ask Sergeant Bowles if his patient is sufficiently restored to answer a few now."

The Reverend Lionel Persimmer looked pale but composed. A clown, Jurnet thought again. Black-ringed eyes, hollow cheeks: a clown, even down to the make-up. Jurnet suddenly remembered that he had never, even as a child, seen what was so funny about clowns.

"Sergeant Ellers tells me you've admitted hiding the crucifix in the grotto. It seems an extraordinary thing to have done, and one that has entailed quite unnecessary trouble for the police. In view, however, of the much graver occurrences which have taken place in Mauthen Barbary, I propose to spend no further time on it than what may prove germane to our inquiries into the deaths of Miss Cass and Mr. Griffin."

"It was foolish of me." The clergyman sounded exhausted. "I

can't understand how I came to do anything so—so callow. But it has no relevance to Rachel's death, or Mr. Griffin's."

Jurnet went on as if the other had not spoken.

"I understand that last night you paid a call at the Manor?"

"Hardly a call. Anguish refused even to let Mr. Griffin know I was there."

"You knew Mr. Griffin always went to bed at ten. What was so urgent it couldn't wait till morning?"

"I wished to resign the living."

"And that couldn't have waited?"

"At the time I felt it couldn't."

"Isn't it, anyway, the sort of thing that gets done by formal letter rather than by word of mouth? That is, assuming Mr. Griffin was the right person to address in the first place, not the Bishop or the Diocesan Council, or whatever."

"The living was in Mr. Griffin's gift. I wanted to give him his gift back."

Jurnet looked keenly into the clownish face across the table.

"That sounds a mite unfriendly."

"I hated Mr. Griffin," Lionel Persimmer said with no especial show of emotion, "as I abhor any force of evil." His voice faltered a little as he added: "I hate only myself more, that for the sake of a church and a livelihood I suppressed my feelings, and did nothing to stop the harm he was doing here in Mauthen Barbary."

"You still haven't explained why your resignation couldn't wait till morning."

"I wanted to leave Mauthen Barbary without wasting a second. I wanted to tell Mr. Griffin to his face that he had killed Rachel with his idolatries, and then shake the dust of this accursed place from off my feet for ever."

"Then how is it, seeing you didn't get to Mr. Griffin last night, you weren't on his doorstep first thing this morning?"

"After I left the Manor I went to the church—" into Jurnet's mind came the memory of St. Blaise's by moonlight, and a shadowy figure flitting between the yew chessmen. "I spent the rest of the night in prayer before the altar. In the morning I went back to the vicarage to wash and tidy myself before going over again to the Manor. And then—" A look of embarrassment came over the clergyman's face.

"And then?"

"I sat down on the bed and—"

"And?" the detective prompted a second time.

Reluctantly, a clown who knew his destiny, always to muff his dramatic opportunities: "I must have fallen asleep. The next I knew, someone was banging on the front door."

"Just about to break it down I was," Sergeant Ellers put in wistfully.

Persimmer said: "You would have been fully justified, since I killed Mr. Griffin." Jurnet sat up straight in his chair. "I mean, I didn't know he was dead, or I shouldn't have been going over to the Manor to speak with him. But just the same, I killed him."

Christ, thought Jurnet, not another one! But cracked, or very, very crafty?

"You'll have to explain that in words of one syllable."

"He was found, was he not, in the grave where I buried the crucifix? It speaks for itself."

"Not to me it doesn't."

"The wrath of the Lamb!" declared the Reverend Lionel Persimmer. "*'And said to the mountains and rocks, fall on us, and hide from the face of him that sitteth on the throne, and from the wrath of the Lamb!'*"

"This is getting a bit too mystical for me," Jurnet said. "Are you saying that, somehow or other, the crucifix killed him, and you're responsible because you put it there?"

"God will not be mocked!"

"He's not the only one," said Jurnet. "I'm investigating two murders, and I don't take kindly to people who deliberately make the police's work harder for them. Now I'm going to put a question to you to which I expect a rational answer, with none of the carry-on we've had to put up with so far. It's this: did you ever have sexual intercourse with Rachel Cass?"

"You must be mad! Mad and vile. Rachel was a virgin."

"That's right. At the same time, the medical evidence shows that she was four months pregnant. So, not unnaturally, we want to know who was responsible."

Lionel Persimmer stared at Jurnet. His body froze like a lizard's. Then he was down on his knees, eyes upturned to heaven.

A thin wail emerged from his lips.

"They have murdered the Saviour of the world! They have killed the Messiah in the womb!"

## 24

Fakenham, thank heaven, was not picturesque. After two days in a village which looked like a garden escape from Disneyland, it was a relief to be back among streets of no architectural distinction, where the past did not oppress, like a ghost that would not be laid.

Sergeant Ellers parked the car behind the Crown, and the two detectives strolled companionably across the courtyard and into the bar, where they munched sandwiches and drank their pints with the air of men who had been far away and were glad to be home.

For the first time since Sunday Jurnet felt rested and relaxed. The previous night he had gone to bed early in that bleak dormitory, and, against all the odds, had enjoyed a sleep deep and dreamless.

Prepared for insomnia, he had placed Griffin's book of Greek translations on the bedside locker; and, once in bed, had looked up the index under Agathias Scholasticus and selected an entry at random.

> A. Why do you sigh? B. I am in love. A. With whom? B. A girl. A. Is she pretty? B. In my eyes. A. Where did you notice her? B. There, where I went to dinner. I saw her reclining with the rest. A. Do you hope to succeed? B. Yes, yes, my friend, but I want a secret affair and not an open one. A. Are you averse to lawful wedlock? B. I have learnt for certain she is very poorly off. A. You learnt! You lie, you are not in love! How can a heart that reckons correctly be touched with love's madness?

Big deal! Maybe Griffin knew what he was doing when he recommended old Agathias Christie to his guests. As a sedative it beat Mogadon into a cocked hat. Jurnet had intended to work his way through the index references. Instead, the next thing he knew was the burly form of Sergeant Bowles with an early-morning cuppa.

"Same again?" asked Jack Ellers.

Another pint and another sandwich later, Jurnet wiped his

mouth and announced it was time to call on Mr. Minchin at his office behind the market place. The respite was over. The detective was mischievously pleased that his sergeant had managed to demolish a whole bowlful of pickled onions. Their rich odour, he felt, would humanise the impending discussion with Charles Griffin's solicitor.

Mr. Minchin, the senior partner of Minchin, Fylow and Apthorpe, was, as it turned out, an affable elderly gentleman exuding an aroma of port more than equal to Sergeant Ellers' pickles. His sorrow at Charles Griffin's death exceeded regret for a lost client.

"We were boys together. Dreadful thing—" His faded blue eyes watered a little.

"Did he consult you often?"

"Time to time, you know. When anything cropped up. Mostly over the phone. Hadn't seen all that much of him in recent years. Used to go over to the Manor once a week for bridge. Gave that up."

Something in the way this last was said alerted Jurnet, as doubtless it was intended to.

"Why was that, sir, if I may ask?"

"Oh, because he cheated, don't you know? Cheated outrageously. Always found out, of course, he did it so badly. Some kind of joke, I dare say. Only thing, jokes of that kind grow stale after a time."

"I can understand that, sir."

"Fortunately, some woman moved into the village. Big as a bus but plays a good game of bridge. Enabled me to bow out gracefully. *Nil nisi bonum* and all that, Inspector," Mr. Minchin went on, with a sharp glance at the detective, "but, as an officer of the Court, I know my duty. Police need every scrap of information they can come by. Big things, little things—rake it all in, then sieve for what's significant and let the rest go."

"I'm very grateful. As it happens, I met Mr. Griffin myself, briefly. In connection with another killing."

"Ah yes—that poor girl. Charlie now—horrible, but in the natural course done out of a year or two at the most. But a young thing with all her life in front of her—" Mr. Minchin paused. "By my age, Inspector, one has learnt to put a proper value on youth. I hope you find her killer."

"Hope I find the person, or persons, who killed the two of them."

"Same person, or persons, in each case?"

"Rather not commit myself, at this stage."

"Quite. Though one would hardly expect to find two murderers at large in one small village at the same time. Except that Mauthen Barbary is rather in a class by itself."

"It has its unusual features. I understand, Mr. Minchin, that the Lady of Promise gets Mr. Griffin's estate."

"In effect, that is so," the solicitor concurred. "That's why you're here, I imagine—to find out how things stand. Briefly, there's a trust. I and the bank are trustees. Everything to go for the upkeep of the Shrine. The Manor House is to become the administrative centre of the cult, and the Hospice, providing always that funds are available, which is doubtful in the extreme, is to be modernised."

"I expect you heard that Rachel Cass was murdered in the Shrine. After that, Mr. Griffin didn't think it would do any more. He was going to have it pulled down and another one built nearby."

"Preposterous! He never mentioned a word of it when he telephoned on Sunday. Knew very well what I would say."

"May I know what the call was about?"

"You may. Money. As usual."

"Surely he told you what had happened at the Shrine?"

"Not a word. First I heard of the girl's death was on the six o'clock news. It was exactly the same as always. Money. Griffin, I must tell you, was a chronically bad landlord. Or a model one, depending upon whether you were his legal adviser or one of his tenants. Owned the best part of a parish, and still reduced to selling off a family treasure every so often to keep his head above water."

"How was that?"

"Most of the cottagers are still paying the rents they paid back in the twenties. Cost him more in repairs than he ever got back in income. Wouldn't hear, though, of taking anyone before the Tribunal. And with the commercial properties he was just as bad. Said he intended keeping the village alive if he bled to death doing so."

"Not a bad ambition."

"No indeed. Even if there was a large helping of vanity mixed up with it." After a moment, during which he seemed to be pondering his own words, the solicitor said: "Afraid that, in trying to tell you about Charles Griffin, I have, in fact, told you about myself."

"You didn't care for him."

"He was immensely likeable. Great charm. But a certain amorality. A true descendant of that rapscallion ancestor of his, Sir Amyas."

Jurnet remarked inadequately: "I must say I thought he was a very pleasant old gentleman."

"Oh, we're all of us pleasant once we're old," said old Mr. Minchin. "Senior citizens are, by definition, the salt of the earth. I was thinking, rather, of the young Charles Griffin who took the girl I was engaged to marry away from me. Married her and killed her."

"Killed her!"

"She died in childbirth."

"Oh, well. That's not quite the same thing, is it?"

"From your point of view, Inspector, perhaps not. From mine—" Mr. Minchin broke off and, again, smiled pleasantly. "Ancient history. You'd rather hear about the phone call. Had to fetch me in from the garden. As if it couldn't have kept till Monday."

"Any idea why it didn't?"

"I imagine because, for a change, it was good news. For once, instead of scrabbling about for money at his wits' end, he actually had it."

"Had it? How much? And from where?"

"Can't answer any of that. Just sounded tremendously pleased with himself. Implied a very large amount. Enough, he said, to go ahead with all his plans."

"Surely you asked for details?"

"We'd had a heavy shower and the delphiniums were every which way. Told him to ring in office hours. Wasn't to know, was I?"

"No, sir." Jurnet prepared to go. "One last thing. I believe, on Mr. Griffin's instructions, your firm's been sending a monthly cheque to Mr. Paul Falkener."

"Signed the last one on Friday. Money thrown away if ever I saw it."

"What I'd like to know is whether the cheque has, in fact, been despatched; and if so, by what class postage."

"Easily ascertained." Mr. Minchin's hand went to the telephone on his desk. To the voice at the other end he repeated Jurnet's inquiry, and listened to the reply.

"Too bad," he said then, replacing the receiver. "Not sure I wouldn't have held it back if I'd known it was still in the office, in view of—But there it is. It was put in the post first thing this morning. Seems Falkener rang up. The girls in the outer office think him very romantic. They stamped it first class."

## 25

It was late afternoon when Jurnet drove back to Mauthen Barbary, alone. Having taken his leave of Mr. Minchin, he had left Ellers to find his own way back to the scene of the crime. He himself had taken off for Norwich, where telephone calls to Anglia and the BBC had once more prepared the way for him.

This time the young men at the studios, though civil as before, were measurably less thrilled to see him. Enough was enough. Inquiries, even into a murder, or two murders, were, if prolonged, an impertinent interruption in the infinitely more momentous activity of ensuring that never for the briefest interlude, during the prescribed hours, should the public be exposed to that horror of horrors, a blank screen.

What was he looking for, Jurnet asked himself, sweating in a gloom lit by the flickering images. Something he had missed first time round? Or something that wasn't there to be missed, but whose absence he should have noted? How could you begin to look for something when you weren't even sure what you were looking for?

Nevertheless he scrutinised every frame with a strained attention that tried to pry out its secret, like a winkle eater wielding his pin. He was surprised to find how much the films of the procession moved him. After all, he had seen them before.

But then he had been on the outside, a detached observer. Now, he watched the young people walking hand in hand and found the way they looked at each other almost unbearably touching. He looked at the ladies from Brixton, magnificent in their white satin, and was moved by the pathos of their hosannas to a black madonna. He discovered in Lydia Massingham a forlorn dignity he had completely missed in their encounters.

Even she, the painted bones on her robe proclaimed, was mortal. All flesh was grass, even when there was enough of it to turf a football pitch.

He studied the face of Neil Woodgate, seeing in it, this time, the features of the drunken boy who had staggered singing along the village High Street; the boy whose penknife had plunged deep in the neck of Oscar the swan. Barnabas, Guardian of the Shrine, came out of the vestibule once again, and turned to face the cameras, laughing. Jurnet, watching intently, saw instead grey-faced Barney Smithers, rapist and self-accused murderer, unconscious on the ambulance stretcher.

The Maidens in their blue dresses looked sweet and foolish like something out of a musical comedy of the twenties. Just so, Jurnet was suddenly convinced, must have looked Charles Griffin's young wife, stolen from Minchin and long dead. Ancient history, like the old solicitor said.

Dead like Rachel.

When you were dead you were outside history altogether. Ancient or modern made no difference. No clocks in the grave.

Jurnet came out thankfully into the bustle of the city, and drove to his flat. He knew there would be no letter from Miriam, but he wanted to be sure. There was no letter.

Thirsty and dispirited, he drove into Mauthen Barbary just as the evening bus was pulling away from the Market Cross. Among the disembarked passengers were several of the Maidens, looking cool and fresh in their flowered cottons. Did they change into their blue frocks after working hours? Virginity as a leisure activity.

Jurnet caught sight of the broad figure of P. C. White bearing down on them from the Green, and hoped he would scare the pants off them.

Mrs. Woodgate exclaimed: "You!"

It could have been discouraging.

Jurnet who, against the odds, had harboured hopes of a cup of tea and some of that cake Ellers had made such a fuss about, managed a cheerful: "Hope I haven't chosen an inconvenient time—"

Mrs. Woodgate's expression held out little hope of any time chosen by the Inspector proving convenient.

"The Welsh one's been here twice already. I can't see what else—"

"Sergeant Ellers tells me you've been most helpful," Jurnet interrupted smoothly. "Wish we could say as much for everyone."

Unappeased, the woman did not invite him in. She stood square in the doorway, cutting off his view of the hall. Too bad from her point of view, Jurnet reflected, she wasn't wide enough to cover up the little red sports car standing in the driveway with a suitcase sticking up from its back seat.

He deliberately let his gaze wander to the case and stay there.

There was a silence, and then Mrs. Woodgate burst out with: "I hope we haven't got to a state where you have to have to ask the police permission to go and see your sister in Harrogate!"

"Harrogate, eh? Fine city. Do you good to get away for a little. You'd be surprised how many people are thinking of doing that very thing. Regular exodus."

Like a ruddy mystery play, he thought, but did not say: only with all the suspects walking off the stage and out of the theatre at the end of the first act. What would old Agathias Christie have made of that one?

In a voice unctuous with sympathy he finished: "Can't say I blame 'em."

"Well—" the wind taken out of her sails—"I've still things to do. 'Tisn't as though there's anything I can tell you." The prospect of getting rid of him rendered Mrs. Woodgate almost cordial.

"Especially as, actually, it was your son I called to see. He *is* home, I take it?" Nodding towards the car: "Sergeant Ellers was going on about that nice little runabout of his. I'm glad I caught him before he left."

"He's only driving me into Norwich. To catch the train."

"Shut up, Mum." Neil Woodgate pushed his mother aside and came out of the hall on to the porch. He was carrying a holdall and an anorak. His face was white and rigid.

"Is it OK for me to go? It was Mum's idea, but—" he spoke with no particular conviction—"I wouldn't mind getting away from here if it's all right with you."

Jurnet answered, as he had answered the others: "I can't stop you."

"So there isn't enough evidence to arrest me. Yet."

"Neil!" his mother cried.

The boy looked at Jurnet, eyes screwed up as if he had some difficulty in focussing.

"Do you think there are two murderers in Mauthen Barbary? One for Rachel and one for Mr. Griffin?"

"I'm keeping an open mind," said Jurnet, professionally non-committal.

"But not likely, is it?"

"The odds are against it, admittedly."

Neil Woodgate drew in his breath audibly.

"Because if there's only one, it couldn't have been me that killed Mr. Griffin when I was too smashed to know what I was doing. Because then I'd have had to kill Rachel too. And I didn't kill Rachel."

"Of course you didn't, dear!" Mrs. Woodgate glared at Jurnet. "Neil wouldn't hurt a fly!"

"How's he on swans?" Jurnet felt tempted to ask, but refrained. Instead, he spoke to the boy gently.

"If I were you I'd put the trip off for a couple of days."

"I couldn't stand going over it *again.*"

"Isn't that what you're doing all the time anyway, in your own mind?"

The boy put down the holdall as if it had suddenly become too heavy for him.

"Neil!" His mother put her hand on his arm. He moved away and spoke to Jurnet.

"The awful thing is, each time it's different. How do I know which one is true?"

"Could be they all are, and it's just the perspective that alters."

"Do you think so?" Eagerly: followed by a dejected shake of the head. "No. I was smashed. When I try to remember, everything whirls like a top. And, times when it isn't whirling, everything is strange and not at all the way the Green and the High Street really are. It's a jungle with shadows, and dim shapes waiting to pounce. Oh!" Neil Woodgate raised a hand and let it drop in a gesture of despair. "I'll stay, but what's the use? It's all so crazy."

"Mauthen Barbary," said Jurnet. "A jungle. Shadows, and dim shapes waiting to pounce. Not so crazy as you think."

Detective Inspector Benjamin Jurnet got his tea after all. Within minutes of his arrival back at the Hospice Sergeant Bowles came in with a loaded tray. The frowsty air was overlaid with an odour of spices.

"Cinnamon toast!" exclaimed Jurnet, unable to believe his nose.

The Sergeant reddened with pleasure and pride.

"Nothing to it. Often fix it at home. Reckoned you'd be ready for a cuppa."

"It's a banquet!"

Settled back in his seat, Jurnet ate and drank with relish. The chair was no more comfortable than the first time he had tested its horse-hair, the other furnishings no less repellent to the eye; yet over the rim of his uplifted cup he surveyed the room with something approaching affection.

Home.

He shook his head in wry deprecation. He knew the signs. He had staked out his territory, much as a robin outside in the garden might be doing at this very moment. Except that the robin had it all over its human counterpart when it came to dealing with intruders.

Thursday, the Superintendent had said. One day more to be monarch of all he surveyed. After that, enter Hale and Batterby, and instead of seeing them off with a peck up the vent he would have to trot out the old bonhomie. *Make yourself at home, chaps!* They would sit at *his* table, on *his* chairs. Goddamit, who said he needed help?

He hoped to God he didn't need help.

Jurnet punished himself for his big-headedness by being particularly kind to Sergeant Ellers who came in at that moment, going so far as to offer him the last piece of cinnamon toast. The Welshman accepting with alacrity, Jurnet felt he had done sufficient penance for one day.

"Gather you've been back to the Woodgates. Shouldn't have thought you'd have room for anything else after another of Mrs. W's teas."

"The affair is over," replied Ellers in a vibrant baritone, licking the last of the cinnamon toast off his fingers. "Seems the young master is too delicate to be badgered with questions by the horrid policeman."

"They talked as if you'd given them the third degree."

"Nothing to what they gave me. Nearly ruptured myself with aggravation. Couldn't get a straight answer to anything: what time he got to the Shrine Sunday morning, how long it took to open the gates into the Manor grounds, what time he got back home. It was like getting blood out of a stone, 'cept there wasn't any blood."

"Did you tell his mum it was his penknife did for Oscar?"

"That was when she really went to town. The thought that Sonny Boy might have assassinated that bird upset her more than if he'd confessed to doing in Charlie and the girl together."

"Understand it, in a way. Poor old Oscar! He never asked to be caught up in human quarrels."

Ellers said cheekily: "You're making me cry. That bird's been a ruddy godsend to the papers. They'll be marching to Trafalgar Square next, calling for the return of capital punishment."

"The kid had no blood on him when I picked him up."

"Don't signify. Colton told me over the phone, the way the knife went into the bird's neck, the blood would have welled up, not spurted. Lucky blow."

"Not for Oscar."

"Never mind swans." Sergeant Bowles had come in to clear away. 'Vultures. Reporters. Hanging around outside all afternoon. Waiting for the flesh that dies." After a moment: "Poetry."

"Very apt," said Jurnet. "Nobody there, though, when I came in."

"Wouldn't be, would there? Pirate's open."

"Of course! Still, can't blame 'em for wanting to know if we've nabbed anyone. Only wish we could oblige."

"Personally," said Ellers. "I don't think they care sweet Fanny Adams who done it. All they're waiting for is the next killing."

Sergeant Bowles contributed: "There's a TV man going round with a mike asking people how it feels to be living in a village of fear. I ask you!"

Jurnet said: "What answers is he getting?"

"Mostly oh ah." Sergeant Bowles smiled broadly. He was a Norfolk man himself.

"That doesn't sound as if they're all that frightened. That's something."

"Wetting their drawers, I shouldn't wonder. But they're hanged if they're going to let on to a bloody foreigner."

## 26

Later, when Sergeant Ellers had gone home to his Rosie, and the evening light had touched even the laurels outside the window with a semblance of grace, Jurnet sat at the Hospice table in front of a fresh pot of tea and a fresh mound of cinnamon toast.

He poured himself another cup and took up the little book which, at his request, Sergeant Bowles had brought down from the dormitory. He might as well have another go at seeing what Charles Griffin had found so special about Agathias Scholasticus.

But he consulted the index, turned over the pages of the anthology, with only desultory attention. The sensation that he had missed something he ought not to have missed persisted and grew stronger. Almost, it spoiled his enjoyment of the cinnamon toast.

The Greek was a queer fish, that was for sure. One minute he was dedicating himself and his works to Pan or Bacchus, the next, wallowing in a palpitating Christianity that fair turned your stomach.

"*O passion, O cross, O blood that purgeth of the passions.*" Oh Gawd.

"*On the threshold of my soul is the saving blood of the Lamb. Away, Destroyer, come not near.*"

Some people had odd ideas of what made good bedtime reading.

"*Trumpets! Lightnings! The earth trembles! But into the Virgin's womb thou didst descend with noiseless tread.*"

Well, there was no accounting for tastes. Jurnet shut the book and pushed it away. Definitely not the Book Society choice for a descendant of the Rothschild of the Middle Ages.

Out of humour that his brain was not functioning better, he ate more than his body could comfortably accommodate, and wound up heavier-witted than ever. When the telephone rang it was an effort to lift the receiver.

Professor Diefenhaus's orotund periods at the other end of the wire did nothing to relieve Jurnet's discontent with himself. What *was* that vital element which continued to elude him?

"Since your suggestion that we pinpoint anything, however apparently trivial, that was otherwise than we might have expected, Alice and I have been going through the Muniment Room literally inch by inch."

Jurnet managed a grunt which he hoped might be taken for gratitude and approbation.

"Anything to be of assistance," said the Professor, taking it so. "Well, this is to advise you that there *is* something—it may be nothing at all—" His voice, while cautious, held undertones of self-congratulation.

Jurnet pulled himself together.

"Oh?"

"I'd prefer to come over. What I have to say will be easier to clarify in a face to face conversation. I can be with you in a matter of minutes."

"Fine," said Jurnet, and went to spend those minutes with his head in a basinful of cold water. At the conclusion of the exercise he emerged damp round the collar, but refreshed. He rubbed his head with a towel, combed back the black hair that, wet and shining, gave him something of the look of a seal.

He looked at his reflection in the wash-room mirror with neither dislike nor approval. The world was the way it was, and he with it.

"You'll live," he said.

Professor Diefenhaus sat in a chair across the table from Jurnet, wincing as the horse-hair upholstery demonstrated its contempt for his transatlantic summer suiting. In front of him he carefully disposed four folders, from each of which in turn he drew forth the contents. Three of them, so far as Jurnet could make out, contained photocopies: the fourth, a pile of yellowed papers which the detective recognised as the accounts whose binding thong he had last seen Alice Diefenhaus unlacing in the Muniment Room on the afternoon of Rachel's murder.

"You'll recall these, of course," said the Professor. "Mr. Griffin intended one of these sets of photocopies for you. What I've done is sort out the copies and collate them, and put the originals back in their proper order—a simple task as the entries are all dated. And—" the complacency now patent— "that was when I made my little discovery."

"Which is?"

"That one sheet of the original book is missing."

"Missing in the state in which Mr. Griffin discovered it, or since? Do you have copies of the missing bit?"

"Indeed I do. That's how I know of its existence." The Professor carefully removed a page from one of the piles of photocopies. "Here it is. Page four. I've numbered the copies for ease of reference."

Jurnet took the proffered paper and saw at a glance that he was able to decipher no more than a word here and there. Containing a certain irritation, he inquired mildly: "Couldn't it be you just haven't managed to put your hands on it? You said yourself Mr. Griffin's papers were in a mess."

"True. But this collection, as you know, was whole and complete only hours before Mr. Griffin died. Alice and I have looked everywhere. We even moved the photocopier away from the wall on the chance it had slipped down the back. In addition, with Anguish's help, we searched Mr. Griffin's bedroom. To no avail."

The Professor smiled.

"I can see you think I'm wasting your time. It must hardly appear feasible that, present or missing, statements of account jotted down nearly four hundred and fifty years ago can have anything to do with a murder, or murders, committed in the last quarter of the twentieth century."

"I asked you to let me know if there was anything at all—"

"What I was going to say," Professor Diefenhaus continued, "was this. While I can't imagine that Sir Amyas Griffin's petty cash book can tell you who killed his last descendant, the particular page that has gone astray does, I believe, explain why Mr. Griffin was in such a state of euphoria on Sunday afternoon."

Jurnet pushed the photocopy back across the table.

"You'd better translate, sir."

The Professor adjusted his bifocals and pointed.

"Here's what I believe to be the relevant entry." He read out: "*'Item to John Gastard in the matter of my lady, nine pounds, five shillings.'*"

Jurnet frowned.

"Does it have to be something to do with the Lady of Promise? Didn't this Sir Amyas have a wife, or a girl friend?"

"The entry is dated October, 1538. Sir Amyas's wife died in 1535. He never remarried." Professor Diefenhaus settled down pleasurably to his exposition. "While 'my lady' could, admittedly, refer to a female with whom he enjoyed a, shall we say, less formal relationship, I hope to convince you that this is unlikely. However, for the moment my purpose is not to acquaint you with what I personally think about this particular entry in the account book, but with how, upon reflection, I believe Mr. Griffin interpreted it."

"Go ahead."

"I don't know, Inspector, how much you yourself know of the early history of the Lady of Promise?"

"Assume I know nothing and you'll be about right."

"Well then, I must tell you briefly what I myself had from Mr. Griffin: that in 1538, at the time of the dissolution of the monasteries by King Henry the Eighth, Sir Amyas Griffin was sent to Mauthen Barbary with instructions to shut down the Priory, sequestrate its possessions, and, in particular, to take possession of the celebrated statue of the Virgin known as the Lady of Promise. Sir Amyas's orders were to bring the statue back to London where it was to be burned in full view of the populace, in order to dispel once and for all the myths and superstitions which had gathered about it."

"I knew people used to come here on pilgrimages in the Middle Ages."

"After Canterbury and Walsingham it was the most famous shrine in the kingdom. Barren women flocked here in their thousands. In 1536 King Henry himself came with Queen Jane Seymour, in the hope that the Lady would bless them with a male heir."

"Yet only a couple of years later he says chuck her on the fire!"

"Ah, but by then Jane had borne him a son. He no longer needed the Lady's good offices, and he did need money. The shrine was a veritable treasure house. Why, the King himself, on the occasion of his own visit, had donated a life-size Infant Christ in solid gold."

"But the Lady wasn't burnt—"

"Exactly! Here we come to the core of the matter. What Sir Amyas said was that he arrived in Mauthen Barbary to find the local people had already set fire to her, and he was too late to retrieve her for a more spectacular *auto-da-fé*. And when Chloe and Mr. Griffin between them rediscovered the statue it was assumed by most historians that it had, in fact, been buried for safekeeping by the monks of the Priory before the royal commission arrived, and that Sir Amyas had made up the story of its destruction to save his own skin. Mr. Griffin had a different explanation. He had a great affection for his ancestor and, I think, wanted to represent him in a better character than history has so far accorded him. According to Mr. Griffin, it was Sir Amyas himself, who, for his own good reasons, had preserved the Lady from the flames."

"Did he have any evidence?"

"Of a sort, including an early item in this very account book, relating to some lead off the roof of 'the Virgin's house.'"

"I can't see how this bit about 'item to John What's-his-name' makes it any more proven."

"As I say, I'm trying to look at it through Mr. Griffin's eyes. First, I have to tell you that John Gastard appears to have been a carpenter. There are earlier payments to him for a door and for wooden yokes for the dairymaids—work for which he was paid in shillings rather than pounds. Nine pounds five shillings was a princely sum in the sixteenth century, and I'm quite sure an amount like that would have caught Mr. Griffin's eye. Especially coupled with the later payments."

"Later? I thought you said earlier."

The Professor positively twinkled.

"Oh, not the door and the yokes. I mean the blackmail."

"Blackmail!"

"Pages seven and eleven; and again, on page seventeen—" Pleased with his *coup de théâtre,* Professor Diefenhaus pushed a pile of photocopies towards the detective's side of the table. "If you'll look at them you'll see—"

"I'll take your word for it."

"Ah. Well. If you look, as I say, you'll find the same entry, three times repeated. 'Item to John Gastard his dues £5.' Again, in the context of the time, a large sum. The only difference between the three entries is that in the last one the word *dues* has been crossed out and the word *demands* written above it in a different hand. Demands! What can that mean except that money was paid to keep John Gastard's mouth shut? Sir Amyas couldn't possibly have buried the statue unaided. Gastard must have organised the burial for him, and he wasn't going to let his boss forget it. If it had come out, it would have been as much as Sir Amyas's life was worth."

"Or Gastard's. Whether it came out or not. Three payments, you say. Only three?"

The Professor looked at the detective admiringly.

"It must be your training. Yes, I looked Gastard up in the parish records. He died in 1540, I calculate just about the time another payment was due. The entry in the register reads 'waylaid and slain by miscreants unknown.'"

"Hm!" Jurnet sat back and regarded the Professor thoughtfully. "That's quite a story."

"You don't have to accept it. I guess we're never going to know exactly what happened in Mauthen Barbary in the Year of Our Lord 1538. But I believe you'll be able to go along with me that it's what put Mr. Griffin in such high spirits that last afternoon of his life. At last he had found what must have seemed to him conclusive proof that his ancestor had indeed been the preserver of the Lady of Promise."

"As it happens," Jurnet said, "information from another source would seem to indicate something more practical, like filthy lucre. It seems some was coming Mr. Griffin's way unexpectedly. But please—" he rallied the crestfallen academic—"don't think what you've told me isn't of the greatest interest. I'm sure it was a factor. Only, what you haven't explained is why Mr. Griffin kept the good news to himself."

Professor Diefenhaus looked startled.

"It's true, isn't it?" the detective insisted. "If he'd found out all that about Gastard and come to the same conclusion as you, he'd have been bursting with it, wouldn't he?"

"You're right! I can't understand why he didn't—"

"And now you can't even find the original. All that evening, when you were working together in that turret, he said nothing."

"Not a word. Most of the time he was fooling about with that damn copier!"

"And before that, when you were both working at the table?"

"Nothing. The only time he spoke was when Alice came up with my antihistamine—" the Professor sneezed his ritual sneeze—"and he told her about the Greek book. In our room later Alice and I had quite a laugh over his idea of a book to read in bed."

The Professor rose.

"You're right," he said. "It doesn't make sense. I guess I've wasted your valuable time."

"On the contrary!" declared Jurnet, suddenly re-animated. The last of the lethargy which had clogged his mental processes lifted from his brain like morning mist rising to meet the sun. If he looked up, he felt, he would see it there, the last

grey tatters losing themselves in the plaster curlicues of the
ceiling. "You've been the greatest possible help. It's me. I've
been looking at things the wrong way round."

"I don't follow you."

"*Why* didn't Mr. Griffin tell you what he'd found out? Why
did he keep it a secret?"

"I'm afraid I don't see—"

"That's all right," said Jurnet, as, at last, he remembered
what he should never have forgotten and it all fell into place. "I
do."

He ushered the bewildered Professor out of the door: then
picked up the phone, got through to Headquarters, and, in
tones urgent and precise, made the necessary arrangements.

## 27

They drove into Mauthen Barbary as darkness was falling,
arriving by a circuitous route that avoided the High Street
altogether. They came in as if from the coast, past the outlying
farmhouses and the executive homes, to the piece of wasteland
at the side of the Wesleyan chapel, where they found Jurnet
awaiting them.

There were two cars: one containing four police constables;
the other, Sergeant Ellers and the Superintendent. Their
drivers coasted to a halt and switched off their lights. There
was no exaggerated pretence of caution, merely a disinclina-
tion to advertise.

Jurnet was glad to see them. It had seemed, alone with the
answers, a lonely time awaiting the arrival of his companions.

The weather had changed: for the better, so far as Jurnet was
concerned. Tonight there would be no moon to reveal a trap to
the quarry for whom it was set. Clouds scudded across the
darkening sky while, below, the air lay heavy and foreboding.
The willows along the river rustled uneasily with intimations of
the coming storm.

The Superintendent's greeting was a model of its kind;
delicately waiving command, yet, by the simple use of
Christian name, making it clear where power lay.

"Well, Ben! All your instructions have been duly noted, and
acted on. What do you want us to do?"

The constables—who, Jurnet was pleased to note, were, as specified, men who had already been on duty in Mauthen Barbary—were sent to take up their positions.

"Just make sure you've got cover front *and* back. No blue behinds sticking up in the balmy night air. OK?"

A murmur signified all had understood.

"Soon as you cross the bridge, get off the road. Follow the Shrine boundary and you'll come to a ditch that ends in a bit of the Priory wall. Don't hole up a mile from the cloister door. It's on the cards you'll be needed in a hurry."

"I take it there are enough of us?" the Superintendent murmured deferentially, as the men moved off with the sprung gait of children playing adventure games. "We don't want to leave any loopholes."

"No, sir," agreed Jurnet, taking no offence. The brass you had was the brass you pulled: it was a law of nature. "P. C. White'll be joining them. He had a couple of jobs to do for me." Jurnet stepped quickly out on to the road, looked towards the High Street, and came back again. "That's one of them done. The lights are out."

"Mayn't that arouse suspicion?"

"I don't think so. They were only temporary, put up for the celebrations."

"You're quite sure tonight's the night?"

"Quite sure."

"With respect, Mr. Jurnet," said Ellers, rising up on his toes—he looked rested and fulfilled, Jurnet thought. Rosie had made good use of the time at her disposal—"where have you got picked out for the three of us to go to ground? There isn't enough cover inside the Shrine to hide an undernourished flea."

"There's the further wall of that inner room." This from the Superintendent.

"Too risky," Jurnet declared. "We'll have to wait outside in the vestibule. I tried it out before you came. You can open the doors a crack and get a view down the whole length of the hall."

"Fine," said Ellers. "So long as no one comes barging in to spend a penny."

"That's a chance we have to take." A sudden flash of lightning lit up the sky. "We'd better get going. That's one plug I can't disconnect."

* * *

Night closed in. To Jurnet, the back of his neck prickling with the tension of concentrating on the crack in the vestibule doors, it seemed that the blackness had compressed itself into an essence, and that this essence had crammed itself, like a quart into a pint pot, into the Shrine of the Lady of Promise.

He felt it pressing on his ears, forcing itself up his nose and down his throat. He felt stifled by blackness.

Black night for a black Virgin.

Outside, the cloud cover had thickened to a pall which made it impossible even to locate the skylight in the Shrine ceiling, let alone distinguish the sky. Every now and again there was a rumble of distant thunder. Behind him, Jurnet could hear the Superintendent wrestling with the little cough which took him in moments of stress. Jack Ellers had had garlic for supper. It was oozing out of his breath and his sweat. Garlic-flavoured blackness—it was too much!

Jurnet pressed his face harder against the door, willing himself to see the Lady of Promise in her alcove at the end of the long hall. Black as the night was, she must be blacker. He strained every nerve, and was at last rewarded with a sight of her, enormous, sublime.

He blinked and she was gone, leaving him unsure whether he had seen her indeed, or only imagined it.

Thus preoccupied, he missed the sound at the cloister door. What he caught was the stiffened attention of the two at his back. Now he registered the muffled click of the latch, and saw, a moment later, with a thrill of exultation, a pencil of torchlight discovering that the blackness had a floor.

The torchlight moved through the blackness like a living thing, seeking. At last it found what it was looking for. It ran up the Lady of Promise quick as a mouse, and down again. There was a fleeting glimpse of draperies, breast, thigh. Then the light swerved to a wall of the inner room, and caught, silver, the rungs of the aluminium ladder which still leaned there.

The Superintendent was trying to see over Jurnet's head. Jurnet hunched himself submissively, but was not displeased when the light went out, returning all to blackness once more.

Not a thick blackness any longer. It was tenanted, which made all the difference. Someone was moving the ladder. The rungs creaked a little.

Now the torchlight was on again, close to the Lady's body,

but obscured by a mass which bulked between it and the watchers. Jurnet held his breath and strained his eyes and ears.

Not long now.

He dared to open the doors wide enough to get an arm through. Feeling the light switches under his hand gave him the illusion of having taken the initiative. He had to control his impatient fingers.

Not yet.

Not quite yet.

From the far end of the hall came little squeaks and moans of wood beneath an instrument. The sound grew louder, became a grating protest. Something, someone, was being hurt.

A voice uttered an unintelligible cry.

Jurnet switched on the lights.

In the soft light which illumined the Shrine the entire lower half of the Lady of Promise stood open ("like a bloody cocktail cabinet," was how Sergeant Ellers was later to describe it to his Rosie), great belly swung back to reveal the precious fruit she carried in her womb. An Infant Jesus the size of a two-year-old child, in solid gold.

It was in truth a birth like no other. A circle of emeralds nodded on golden wires above the Baby's head. Diamonds shone among the golden curls and in the folds of the plump little neck. Set in the baby breast was a heart made of rubies that pulsated in the light.

In His left hand the Child held a bird made of precious stones that, winking and flashing, seemed to quiver with life. The right hand was raised in blessing, each chubby finger loaded with rings of price.

It was incredibly beautiful.

It was the ultimate obscenity: the Hope of the World not eternal salvation, but gold.

For a second, the three men who had rushed into the room stayed frozen in their tracks. The figure on the ladder remained equally immobile. Then, the first to move, it reached over towards the golden effigy and, from the crook of its right arm, plucked the one thing which had not been placed there by order of King Henry the Eighth—a stubby hammer stained with what looked like, but was not, rust. There was gold, too, on the hammer; but a different gold from that of a king's offering. Hairs from the golden head of Rachel Cass.

"Look out!" cried the Superintendent.

The hammer came whizzing through the hall and struck the candelabrum squarely. The three detectives covered their heads with their arms as the lights went out and glass showered down. Jurnet felt a piercing sting, followed by a warm drip of blood down the left side of his face.

Only the light in the inner room, the dim bulbs placed below the Lady's pedestal, and angled upward to illuminate her, remained on. The broad black face appeared in no way discommoded by the revelation of her secret. The figure on the ladder lumbered to the floor and was lost in the shadows.

"The cloisters!" the Superintendent shouted, unnecessarily.

As he spoke, the torches came on, police torches that sent their powerful beams into the Shrine. From their hiding places among the ruins, P. C. White and his helpers from Norwich advanced on the cloister door.

The figure caught in their criss-crossing beams stood still: spread its arms wide like a crucified Christ, and turned to face Jurnet and his companions.

Paul Falkener screamed: "Do you think I wanted to kill her?"

## 28

"I'd have lain down my life for Rachel Cass, and I killed her. Can you begin to understand that? Not that it matters a pig's ear whether you can or you can't.

"I realised the Lady was made to open when Len Foulcher fixed up his spotlights Saturday evening. Up to then I'd only seen her in poor lighting. It was the way the shadows fell in the folds of her skirt put me on to it. Otherwise you'd never have guessed, even in broad daylight. Bloody ingenious and most beautifully done. Of course I took the spots out at once and told Charlie they were too vulgar for words.

"I guessed at once what was inside. It didn't take much to put two and two together. Every time Charlie had some new people round he'd go into his vaudeville routine about his precious Sir Amyas and the glories of the ancient Shrine. He never missed dragging in Henry the Eighth and his Infant Christ in solid gold. He must have noticed the way people reacted to those two words. They salivated like dogs at the very sound.

"I'm a fine one to be talking!

"No one needed that gold more than I did. Why I needed it is my business. You wouldn't understand. It wasn't stealing. How can you steal from someone who's been dead four hundred years, or from a monastery that's nothing but lumps of rubble sticking out of the grass?

"The only problem was how to get hold of it. Barnabas was at the Shrine all day, and there were people who took it in turns to come in at night: it didn't take much thinking to see my only chance was Sunday, while the procession was on. Everyone would be out, doing the round of the village, and the Shrine would be locked and empty. I had my own key to the cloister door, and a lot of my stuff was still in the storeroom. Even if somebody saw me lugging a bundle away I could always say it was some of my gear.

"On Sunday morning I kept out of sight behind a bit of Priory wall till I heard the procession move off. Then I ran down to the cloister door. It wasn't locked, and the key was in it, which surprised me a bit, but I just thought in all the excitement someone had forgotten it. Anyway, the Shrine was empty, which was all that mattered.

"I'd brought along a chisel and a small hammer, which I reckoned would be all I needed to get the Lady open, should I have any difficulty finding the spring, or pivot. I didn't bother getting the ladder from the storeroom. I stood on a chair and got on to the pedestal that way, and found I could easily reach up as far as I needed to.

"There was absolutely no problem at all. The wood moved stiffly, but it moved; and in a couple of minutes that great big belly swung open and Baby Jesus was staring me in the eye.

"Well, you've seen him. You can guess how I felt when I first set eyes on him. But you'd be wrong, dead wrong. Oh, I felt greed all right. 'Solid gold!' I kept muttering to myself, just like Charlie. But that was only part of it. Mostly, what I felt was jealousy. Because whoever made that Child knew things about the human form I'd never even dreamed of. Or, even if I had, could never carry out with the little gob of talent that's all I've been favoured with. I hated his guts and I hated the thing he'd made. That bloody Infant looked at me with those sapphire eyes and mocked me for the failure I'd always been and always would be. It was all I could do not to smash his smug little face in then and there.

"Funny thing, I've never felt like that about the Lady. You can't be jealous of a miracle. But the bastard who made that holy doll, I tell you every curve and plane was an insult directed at me personally.

"OK, I thought. You're the genius. I'm the dud; but I'm the dud who's going to gouge out those sapphire eyes and flog them, and the emerald halo and the ruby heart, and all that lovely solid gold. I'm going to take your fucking masterpiece home and cut it up into little pieces that are going to keep me in comfort for the rest of my natural!

"I jumped down to the floor and went to the storeroom, where I'd left some large cloths I'd used to protect my carvings. They'd do fine for a wrapping. I think I was a little haywire. I wanted to smash up the kiddo but even more I wanted to smash up the guy who'd made it. It didn't register I was gunning for someone who'd been dead four hundred years. He was right there in the Shrine, taking the mickey out of me.

"When I came out of the storeroom with the cloths Rachel was standing in front of the Lady with her back to me. She had a big bowl of irises and columbines in her hands, so I suppose she must have been in the washroom all the time, arranging them.

"I watched as she put down the bowl among the other flowers at the base of the pedestal, and then she climbed on to the chair I'd left in position. For a long time she just stood there, looking up at the golden Child; then she reached out and removed a little chain with a cross on it which was hanging from its upraised right hand. So now you know where it came from! I can't think why she should have done that, unless, perhaps, her first reaction was to get rid of it because crosses weren't allowed in the Shrine.

"How can you expect me to know what was in her mind? I just stood there, wondering what on earth I could say to her. Any second she could have turned round and seen me, but she didn't turn round. She got down from the chair, and then she went down on her knees.

"I watched her praying, but all I could think was that the bastard who had made the golden idol was jeering at me more than ever because now I wouldn't be able to chop up his bloody Baby after all: I wouldn't be rich. I wouldn't be anything but what I was from the word go, a born loser.

"What you have to understand is that it wasn't Rachel who

was praying there; just somebody who knew the golden Child existed, and would be able to talk about it. The one person who knew. So you can understand why I killed her.

"I had to.

"There wasn't all that much blood. What there was spattered on to one of the cloths, which I'd draped round me. Later, I cut the stained bit out and burnt it.

"She died quickly. I don't think there was much pain. Not that it mattered all that much as it wasn't Rachel. I stooped over the person I had killed, meaning to take the cross away from her. It was solid gold, after all; and besides, I wanted to forestall questions about where it could have come from.

"Only then I saw she'd changed back to Rachel, and I couldn't bring myself to touch it.

"I closed the Lady up again, put the chair back against the wall where it belonged, and got the hell out of there.

"I'd killed Rachel! Can you understand what that means? What I suffered, what I'm suffering every second of the day?

"What the hell do I care whether you understand or not?

"You'll understand all right why I killed Charlie Griffin. Lord knows how he tumbled to the Lady's secret. There was I at home that night, wondering whether you'd left any of your boys in blue watching the Shrine, and how soon it would be safe to go back there, when there's a knock at the door and Charlie practically falls in. I knew it had to be something extraordinary to get him out on his own two feet, long after his bedtime, and uphill to The Barn.

"When he'd sat down and got his breath back he stuck a bit of old paper under my nose and told me it proved Henry the Eighth's gold Jesus was hidden inside the Lady. You could have knocked me down with a daisy. I read where he pointed, and so far as I could make out it didn't prove anything of the sort—just a note of money paid to some fellow he said was a carpenter, and I said so, acting all amused and incredulous. But he insisted there was no doubt about it, and would I help him get it out because he hadn't the strength to do it himself, and there was no one else he could trust.

"That's when I first caught on to why he'd come on his own, at night, instead of sending Anguish over with a message for me to come to him at the Manor. Charlie was on the fiddle. Of course I knew he was hard up—he was always on about what he'd do to the Shrine if only he had the lolly—and what he was afraid of, he went on to say, was that if he had the Lady opened up, all open and above board, there'd have to be an inquest, and the likelihood was they'd declare the Infant treasure trove, and it'd end up in some museum. Even if they allowed it to remain at the Shrine he'd never be allowed to sell it: something, he said, he wouldn't want to give house room to. It was Henry who'd destroyed the Priory and given orders for the Lady to be burned. To keep the gift of such a man in the restored Shrine would be a bloody insult.

"It was bad enough the Lady'd had to put up with it in her belly all those years; but Sir Amyas had done the best he could in the circs, and you had to give him credit, he couldn't have dreamed up a better hiding place. Now it was only poetic justice that the Child should be turned into money, and the money used to make the Shrine more like what it was before Henry went and pulled it down.

"Charlie did say that nowadays governments make some payment to finders of treasure trove, but he was sure we'd do much better if we melted the gold down and disposed of it, and the gems, ourselves. It would serve Henry right, and besides, he needed the cash quickly. He couldn't wait for the slow wheels of bureaucracy to get rolling.

"Would I go into it with him? If I would, he'd give me fifteen per cent of the proceeds. How's that for nerve, seeing I was to do all the work? He'd have asked Anguish, he said, only I was physically stronger and the old fellow had become a compulsive gambler and he couldn't trust him to handle anything so valuable. Most of it would end up with the bookies.

"He told me that as soon as the police allowed it he wanted the Lady brought back to the Manor, and then I'd be able to get cracking—'locate the secret spring' were his words—without anyone but him and me knowing what was going on.

"Naturally I agreed. What else could I do? I think he was agreeably surprised I didn't argue about terms. He was still pretty puffed, and I suggested going over to the Manor and fetching back the bathchair and then pushing him home in it.

"He accepted gratefully, and I went off to get the chair, promising to take care nobody saw me.

"I took care all right! Anyway, there wasn't a soul about. There hardly ever is, after closing time. I heard some drunk bawling his head off in the distance. That was all.

"I brought the bathchair back and helped Charlie into it, and I pushed him home. That is, I pushed him up the Manor drive, as far as the garage where the thing's kept. I helped him out of the chair, set him on his feet, and when he turned away to go into the house I strangled him from behind with this scarf I wear round my neck. I'd already taken it off and wound it round the handle of the bathchair so there wouldn't be any fingerprints. It was very easy.

"I put him back in the chair, intending at first to leave him in it in the garage. But then I thought of the grotto. Bury him where he un-buried the Lady. A nice touch.

"So I pushed him there, keeping in the shelter of the terrace as long as I could. Chloe began to bark but I took the chance. Charlie was always complaining she gave voice if so much as a leaf brushed a window-pane, and I gathered no one ever took any notice. Anyhow, it was all right. I took the bit of paper that had somehow set Charlie on the track out of his pocket. Then I left him in the grave, brought the bathchair back and put it away; went home, burned the paper, and went to bed.

"Let me say I am moderately sorry about Charlie Griffin. Only moderately. My heart is too filled with grief for Rachel to have room for much else. After her, it didn't matter if I rubbed out the whole human race. I had to kill Charlie, otherwise Rachel's death would have been wasted, and you can't waste a valuable death like that.

"I still can't figure out how Charlie guessed the Lady's secret, but I couldn't leave him alive knowing it. And I'd have been mad to move her to the Manor where I couldn't get at her at all except for a measly fifteen per cent.

"One other thing, while I'm on the subject. I didn't go straight home, quite. You wouldn't know, you blue-arsed fuzz, but when you've killed someone, even when you haven't planned it that way, you feel kind of keyed up. It's a trip. Let's face it, you've done something pretty big. In a way, you've produced a masterpiece.

"So I found this penknife in the road, shining in the moonlight. I recognised it at once: Neil Woodgate's. We were all sick of being told Rachel'd given it to him.

"I picked it up carefully, using my scarf. My first thought was simply to chuck it in the pond. That'll teach him! And so I went out of my way a bit, to the top of the Green. But when I got to the pond, there was Oscar sleeping, and I thought of something better than just throwing the knife away. As I said, I felt high.

"I stuck it deep into Oscar's neck. I thought, if there's a lot of blood, I can wash myself in the pond. As it happened, the blood came out slow and bubbly and I didn't get even a spot on myself. Oscar just gave a gurgle and died.

"I wiped the knife thoroughly just in case, and then went home. I was very tired. It had been a long day."

## 29

"You all know that Paul Falkener has been arrested and charged with the murders of Rachel Cass and Charles Griffin. He has made a statement which may be used in evidence."

From his seat at the dining-table Jurnet surveyed his audience, disposed uncomfortably on the Hospice chairs. As host, he felt he should explain they were perfectly good chairs once you got the hang of them. The trick was to treat them the way you would nettles. Don't tickle them with your arse. Sit hard and you won't get stung.

On second thoughts, maybe he didn't want them too comfortable.

"We'll be packing up here in the course of the day. You won't be sorry to see us go. Before that, though, there are one or two things I felt that, as a matter of courtesy, I should clarify for you. And one or two loose ends you might be able to tie up for us."

Philip Cass, holding his wife's hand tightly, said: "He must be insane."

"Mr. Falkener's state of mind," Jurnet returned briskly, "will be a matter for the court. It's not something we can usefully discuss here. What we *can* discuss—" He looked round thoughtfully, his gaze coming to rest on Lydia Massingham. "Miss Massingham, for example, might have an idea of something we can usefully discuss."

"Me?" the enormous woman squeaked. "Discuss what?"

"I was thinking about that chopper, actually."

Frightened, defiant, yet above all relieved to be rid of a burden: "You know!"

"I know that a loose robe with wide sleeves is a good kind of garment for concealing one."

"You don't think I was going to kill her!" Lydia Massingham cried. "I wish he'd killed me instead!"

"Suppose you tell me what you *were* going to do with it?"

"All right. I took it out of Philip's shed." She looked across at Joanna. "Only borrowed it. I was going to put it back afterwards."

"After what?" asked Jurnet.

"After I'd chopped up the Lady."

"My dear madam!" The exclamation came from Professor Diefenhaus.

"Chopped her in pieces!" Lydia Massingham persisted obstinately. "She's been nothing but trouble since the day Charlie dug her up. Pity she wasn't burnt four hundred years ago after all. Beastly sex object!" The woman took a breath that set her breasts wobbling. "Sunday was a marvellous opportunity. All that free publicity. We'd have been in all the papers and on television. I didn't care if I went to prison. It would have been worth it!"

Again she looked at Joanna, as if beseeching her approval.

"I hid it under my robe," she went on, "and waited till I saw the procession well on its way. Then I nipped round to the cloister door."

Jurnet interpolated: "Did you see anybody coming out?"

"Paul, you mean?" Lydia Massingham shook her head. "Nobody. I was all set to smash the glass to get in, but someone had left the key in the door. I didn't expect to do a proper job— I knew the Lady was made of some terribly hard wood—but I thought if I could cut her about a bit, knock her head off or something—"

The Professor's resounding "Tut!" was more eloquent than words.

Jurnet asked: "What did you find inside the Shrine?"

In a voice that quavered almost out of control Lydia Massingham answered: "I found Rachel lying on the floor. Her head—oh!" The woman's face contorted with remembered horror. "I knelt down beside her. I called her name. But she was dead, quite dead. There was nothing I could do." Again it was Joanna she was addressing. "Had there been anything, I'd have run for help, even though I could never have explained what I was doing there. But there was nothing. And then I saw there was blood on the chopper blade—blood and hair. I'd dropped it on the floor beside her. And I got frightened people would think it was me who killed her. People," she explained without self-pity, "always think the worst of me. So I hid it behind the Lady and got away, back to the Market Cross, as fast as I could."

She concluded with a childlike simplicity: "Though even then I hated to leave her, dead and all alone."

Joanna Cass disengaged her hand from her husband's, got up, walked over to Lydia Massingham and kissed her. An expression of unbelieving joy spread over the older woman's face.

The Reverend Lionel Persimmer inquired with diffidence: "The Infant Jesus—I saw the pictures in the paper. Are we to be allowed a sight of it?"

"It isn't here any more," Jurnet said. "Security. One of these days, I imagine, they'll put it on show, in the Castle, or the V. and A. Somewhere like that."

"It's an image of Our Lord. It belongs in a consecrated place."

"Speaking for myself, I'd say a steel safe," Professor Diefenhaus put in robustly. "Fitted out with every modern anti-burglary device and preferably buried deep in the bowels of the earth. Unlike you, sir, I have seen this remarkable artefact, and I can safely say that never in my entire life have I set eyes on an article more calculated to arouse the basest instincts of man." Turning to Jurnet he continued: "What I cannot for the life of me puzzle out is how you—and for that matter, Mr. Griffin—ever guessed it was inside the Lady."

"I can't speak for Mr. Griffin," replied Jurnet. "But so far as I'm concerned, it was all your doing."

"Mine!" the Professor cried. "But I had no idea!"

"You showed me the records of Sir Amyas Griffin's payments of hush money to John Gastard, carpenter."

"Yes, but—"

"As I pointed out at the time, I didn't see how it could be blackmail for hiding the Lady of Promise because, in that case, Mr. Griffin would undoubtedly have told you all about it. So I had to ask myself, for what else, to do with the Lady, might John Gastard, carpenter, four hundred and fifty years ago, have put the bite on Sir Amyas? Something which was still important to Sir Amyas's descendant in the twentieth century, but something Mr. Griffin wouldn't want you to know?

"All I really knew about Mr. Griffin, apart from the Shrine, was that he was hard up, that he cheated at cards, that he had a ripe old pirate for an ancestor, and that he was partial to the works of an Ancient Greek writer by the name of Agathias Scholasticus. I even had a go at the Greek gentleman myself. In translation, of course."

"I still don't see—" said the Professor.

The detective picked up a small book from the table.

"As I said, it was all your doing. You were the one who told me about Henry the Eighth and Jane Seymour and the Holy Child made of gold. Then, after you'd put me in the picture about Gastard, and while I was still trying to work out why Mr. Griffin should have stayed mum about him, I asked you to go over that last evening in the Muniment Room once again."

"Yes—"

"And one of the things you mentioned was Mr. Griffin recommending a Greek book to Mrs. Diefenhaus to read in bed. That same Agathias Scholasticus you and your wife laughed about, in the privacy of your bedroom. I laughed too when, on top of all I'd just learnt from you, I suddenly remembered something of the old chap's I'd just read."

Jurnet leafed through the book until he found the page he was looking for. Then he read aloud:

"*Trumpets! Lightnings! The earth trembles! But into the Virgin's womb thou didst descend with noiseless tread.*'"

He looked at the intent faces all about him, and repeated: "*Into the Virgin's womb!*' Not meaning to be blasphemous, where better to hide an Infant Jesus? You'd need a carpenter, of course, if it was a wooden Virgin, and you weren't much of a one for do-it-yourself."

"John Gastard!"

"John Gastard. With a secret like that to hold over his boss the man must have thought he was made for life. As in a way he was."

Professor Diefenhaus quoted sonorously: "*Waylaid and slain by miscreants unknown.*'"

"Exactly. Epitaph for a blackmailer." After a moment Jurnet went on: "Well, that was a long time ago. I wasn't here in Mauthen Barbary to find out who killed a blackmailing carpenter in the reign of Henry the Eighth. But if my theory was correct, that Charles Griffin had rumbled the secret of the Lady of Promise, he was going to need the services of a carpenter just as much as his ancestor Sir Amyas—only, this time, to get the Infant out, not put it in. And then I realised I already knew he had been in touch with one."

"Already knew?"

This time the question came from Neil Woodgate, forlornly spruce in his business suit.

"Already knew. Monday afternoon, when the Superintendent and I were in the Shrine, Falkener came in—to collect an electrical fitting, so he said. In the course of our conversation he informed me that because of Rachel's murder Griffin had let him know he wanted the Lady of Promise moved back to the Manor House."

"That's right," Alice Diefenhaus said. "Mr. Griffin said the same to us."

"Ah—but how did Mr. Griffin let Falkener know? From the time of Rachel's death Falkener paid no visit to the Manor. Anguish carried no message. He wasn't on the phone."

The detective looked at Philip Cass.

"That telephone call, the condolence one which puzzled you—that, I believe, was Mr. Griffin trying to find out, without actually asking outright, if Falkener was over at your place. To all appearances there had been no contact between the two of them since the night of Mr. Griffin's party—that is, Saturday. Yet Falkener knew Mr. Griffin wanted the Lady moved."

"I suddenly realised I'd known all the time who Mr. Griffin went to see the last night of his life. He went to see his carpenter."

"What I still don't understand," said Philip Cass, "is how you knew Paul would be raiding the Shrine the very night you had your men in place to receive him. He might have come that night, sure. But he might equally have waited a week, or a month. What made you so certain? Or were you planning to have the police in position every night till he showed up, and you just had the luck to hit the jackpot first go?"

Jurnet grinned.

"Police budgets don't run to operations of that kind, I'm afraid. I indulged in a little deception myself, to get things moving. What I did was send P. C. White over to The Barn to request Falkener's help next morning moving the Lady to Norwich. Reason I gave was that we, the police, were pulling out of Mauthen Barbary and wanted to guard against vandals breaking into the Shrine. I knew that by Wednesday Falkener should have received a cheque he was expecting—he had to have some ready cash. Breaking up the Infant was going to take time, and he would be rarin' to get away. I just wanted to make sure he got on with it."

"You seem to have made sure of everything," Mrs. Diefenhaus commented admiringly.

*If I'd charged Barney Smithers and sent him to Norwich he might still be alive today. If I'd shown Charles Griffin the little gold cross it might have set him thinking. Put him on his guard. Saved his life.* Aloud, Jurnet answered with becoming modesty: "Nobody can make sure of that."

Shrugging off the failures, he smiled at Neil Woodgate.

"Some things you can, though. Take this young fellow here. If I hadn't phoned his mum and found out he was a poet in his spare time I'd still be having dark thoughts about how, Sunday night, he came to know a song he never had a chance to hear to the end, if the story he told us was true."

"A poet!" Alice Diefenhaus exclaimed. "But that's marvellous!"

"A poet. He's the one who wrote the calypso for those ladies from Brixton. Could have come straight from the Carribean." Jurnet sounded like a proud father. "So of course he didn't need to hang about to learn the words. Open the Manor gates and go back home, just like he said."

Neil Woodgate had gone bright red with embarrassment. But there was also, the detective noted approvingly, a brightening of the eye, a flash of boyish pride. Life reasserting itself.

"Another small footnote to history, Professor," Jurnet said. He tipped the contents of a small envelope into his palm, and proffered his hand for the American's inspection. "And I mean footnote."

The Professor peered.

"It seems to be a thorn of some kind."

Joanna Cass said: "It must be barberry."

"Spot on. Dr. Teago took it out of Falkener's foot. He must have picked it up when he took Griffin's body out to the grotto. No place to walk barefoot, that's for sure! I noticed Monday afternoon he was limping. By the time we arrested him it had turned distinctly nasty."

He said, taking no pleasure in it: "It's still touch-and-go the foot may have to come off." He returned the barb carefully to its envelope. "The revenge of the Barbrés, eh? What you might call a delayed reminder of the rightful owners of Mauthen Barbary."

"How horrible!" Mrs. Diefenhaus shivered. "And not very

grateful of them, or their ghosts, seeing the man Falkener killed was the last of the Griffins."

"There was Rachel to be paid for as well," Philip Cass reminded her, tight-lipped.

Joanna cried: "Just the same, not crippled! I can't bear to think of him crippled!"

"Rachels come high," said Philip Cass. "Rachels come very high."

The telephone rang, a welcome diversion. Jurnet reached for the receiver and listened, his heart jolted by joy at the sound of the voice coming over the wire.

"Hi!" said Miriam. "I'm back!"

"Shalom!" said Detective Inspector Benjamin Jurnet.

It was more like July than October.

As they left the church path and the shadow of the yews Joanna fretted: "In this heat they won't last twenty-four hours."

Her husband, who was carrying a large vase, glanced down at the sheaf of scarlet gladioli cradled in her arm.

"Then we'll bring more tomorrow. I'm glad she's out here. She belongs on the bright side."

"Yes," Joanna agreed readily. "Once the headstone's up we'll be able to plant things that love the sun." She looked about her, at the flint church, the lichen-spotted tombstones. "It's funny. I always thought it sinister. Now, only four months later, it seems a place of peace. And even, incredibly, happiness."

"Yes." But Philip Cass frowned. In the distance a dark figure was kneeling beside a grave. "I wish he wouldn't do that!"

"He's only praying."

"Let him find somewhere else to do it! Next thing you know, he'll be reporting miracles." He started forward. "I'm going to tell him, once and for all."

"You can't do that!" Joanna caught her husband's arm. "You'll upset him terribly. Go and fill the vase. He's just going."

With reluctance Philip obeyed instructions and made for the stand-pipe set in an angle of the church wall. Joanna, one hand shading her eyes against the sun, watched as Lionel Persimmer rose to his feet, dusted his knees, and made the sign of the cross. He took a roundabout route back to the church, as if he wished to avoid the interrupters of his meditations.

Philip came back with the brimming vase, and the two

walked on together, out into the heat of the day. The grass-covered grave looked cool, almost inviting.

"You notice how he kept out of our way?" Philip wedged the vase into position and stood watching as his wife, seated on the ground, arranged the flowers to her satisfaction. "He knows what I think, all right."

"And we know what he thinks." The gladioli in place, Joanna sat still. The sun shone on her hair. The sight of her filled Philip Cass with a great thankfulness.

"Trouble is," he said, "you think the same."

She looked away, out to the burnt stubbles and the wide sky. "I'm not sure."

Philip Cass gave a little laugh.

"Our good Inspector Jurnet solved every mystery except the greatest one of all."

"He did what he was here for. As it turned out, he said, it wasn't a police problem."

"As it turned out! He and the Superintendent were very decent, the way they kept all mention of it out of the inquest and the court proceedings. Justice with a human face."

"They didn't know what to make of it, any more than we do." Joanna smiled up at her husband. "You don't believe, in your heart of hearts, that Rachel ever went to bed with any man."

Philip settled himself down on the warm ground beside her. He broke off a blade of grass and chewed on it absently.

"I have to believe it. There's no other possible explanation."

"Didn't somebody say that when you've exhausted the possible explanations you're left with the impossible ones, however unbelievable they seem to be?"

"To wit, Lionel Persimmer's crackpot theory of a failed madonna. The Messiah who didn't quite make it!"

Joanna said: "There's one thing I'm not clear about. Never mind whether you believe it or not—take the Gospels, the basic story. God becomes man. But when? What was the exact moment it was supposed to happen?"

Philip Cass looked puzzled.

"In the stable at Bethlehem, I suppose. The minute he was born."

Joanna shook her head.

"Nine months earlier than that, surely. Mary was an ordinary human being. She carried Jesus like any other pregnant woman. So the moment her child was conceived it must have been human, and vulnerable."

"So?"

"So, think of all the things that could have happened, especially in those days. She might have had a miscarriage, she and Joseph might have been killed by robbers on the way to Bethlehem. In that filthy stable she might have caught something and died, and her baby with her. They were human—that was the whole point of the exercise—and so they had to take their chances like everyone else. In Mary's case it came off. Who knows if there weren't other Marys who weren't so lucky?"

"And Rachel was one of them?"

Joanna nodded.

"You realise it's a very fallible God you're postulating?"

"I know." She smiled. "It's a great comfort."

"Not to me it isn't! An Almighty with a run of bad luck is all we need! If you're going to save mankind, get on with it, I say! Don't turn it into a lottery, depending on whether some virgin mother-to-be does, or does not, get run over by a bus—or killed by a Paul Falkener."

He got to his feet, pulled his wife up gently, and held her to him.

Joanna Cass looked down at the burgeoning curve of her belly, and felt the child move inside her.

"So long as He keeps on trying," she said.

## ABOUT THE AUTHOR

S. T. HAYMON has, in *A Very Particular Murder*, brought us her most dazzlingly rich novel yet, the fifth featuring Inspector Benjamin Jurnet. Born in Norwich, England, the author now lives in London.

If you enjoyed this Inspector Jurnet mystery, you'll enjoy S. T. Haymon's fifth dazzlingly rich mystery, A VERY PARTICULAR MURDER, in which Inspector Jurnet must make quantum leaps in intuition to solve the myriad mysteries of God, love and particle physics—and the complex relationships among them.

Turn the page for an exciting preview of A VERY PARTICULAR MURDER, coming soon from Bantam Books.

# 1

Darkness had almost filled the canyon at the foot of the castle mound when, moving at snail's pace, they came, little by little, over the fine bridge which sprang across the chasm separating the Norman keep from the rest of the city. At the rate the line of cars was moving the two had plenty of time to admire the great stone bulk directly ahead, by day brutish but turned by floodlighting into a fairy palace, spun sugar against the velvet sky.

The Superintendent leaned forward in the passenger's seat of the Rover, pulled down the sun visor with its inset mirror, and made minute adjustments to his already impeccable black tie. The bugger looks pleased with himself, thought Jurnet, piling additional fuel on to the anger already burning inside him like indigestion. Did the little tin god really have to leave it to the last minute to let his underling know that his presence was required at the castle that very night; a night, moreover, when, if the bloke at the hire agency was to be believed, Angleby was into the *dolce vita* like nobody's business, everybody from the masons to the model railway club descending on the racks of dinner jackets like a plague of locusts? For the umpteenth time Jurnet moodily swivelled back into place the made-up bow which had worked its way up his left ear, feeling as he did so the jacket too tight across his shoulders, too short in the sleeves; wondering for how long his braces were going to be able to support the tonnage of trouser tailored, at a guess, to accommodate a woman eight months gone with quads.

Wounded vanity? Not a bit of it—or only a little bit. Jurnet had long accepted his superior officer's effortless elegance as a cross he was doomed to bear. The wound was deeper. All day long, whatever had occupied his surface attention, the detective had felt vibrating through his whole being the slow march of minutes progressing like troops at a state funeral towards that moment in the evening when Miriam had arranged to telephone from Israel. As it was, in six, no, five minutes—Jurnet glanced at his watch to confirm the crass inhumanity of time—whilst he looked like being still marooned on this stone raft in space, the telephone would ring out in his flat, and go on ringing until, incredulous, it petered out, unanswered. From the moment he had opened his eyes that morning Jurnet had anticipated that call, until he had come almost to believe that, lifting the receiver, he would feel desert heat on his face and the brittle air of the development town at the back of beyond where Miriam was engaged in setting up the knitting project which was to be an extension of her thriving business in Angleby. Listening, he felt, he would have to screw up his eyes against a sun which must surely have brought out the delicious freckles on her nose and bleached the red lights in her hair to gold.

He would hear her voice. Most of all, he would hear her voice.

Instead of which, here he was, stuck on the castle bridge till the small hours, in all probability, all to celebrate the three hundredth anniversary of the birth—or was it death?—of that long-haired oddball in baggy breeches who sat in bronze in the Haymarket holding a skull in his hands like he'd just finished his dinner and wasn't sure what to do with the bones: Sir Thaddeus Brigg, scientist, philosopher and almost everything else you cared to think of, proof at least that not everybody born in Angleby was thick as two planks.

It was, as Jurnet for all his carry-on very well knew, his mates, his own unique species, who were holding up the cavalcade, busy where the bridge debouched on to the wide gravelled space which lapped the castle walls; checking invitations against lists fastened to clipboards; lifting boot lids; opening rear doors for a brisk but comprehensive once-over of the back of the car. The Superintendent, peering upward through the windscreen at the sculpted battlements, commented: 'Room on that roof to land helicopters by the gross. I only hope the Chief was right in deciding six sharpshooters were enough.'

'So long as he hasn't forgotten the paras,' Jurnet growled, letting the frayed hems of his patience hang out without caring who saw them. In his inner ear the phone had already begun to sound its forlorn tocsin. 'Someone on the Council gets this brilliant idea there's money to be made out of one of our ancient eggheads, and we end up lumbered with a major security operation. We don't go to all this trouble for the royals.'

The Superintendent lowered his gaze to his subordinate, and said in tones of rebuke: 'We have some very valuable lives here.'

The subordinate, who harboured the quaint idea that all lives, even the lowliest and most alienated, were of equal value, managed with difficulty not to say so. Instead, with a pretence of sweet reasonableness: 'I wouldn't mind betting, back in their colleges or research institutes or whatever other mousehole they've crawled out of, they go about their business like any other citizens.'

'Very likely,' the other conceded. 'That doesn't absolve the city of its responsibility.' Taking care not to disturb the set of his dinner jacket, the virgin crease of his trousers, the Superintendent twisted round in his seat so as to confront his companion more directly. 'It's the very number of them, don't you see? What you have to realize is that by the time they've all got here Angleby will contain within its boundaries a significant percentage of the people upon whose mental processes in the years to come may depend the very survival of the planet as we know it.'

Or its destruction, thought Jurnet, bloody-minded but again with the sense to keep his mouth shut.

'Think what a single bomb might do, dropped on such an assembly!' The Superintendent, carried away by his vision, sounded almost enthusiastic. 'Alter the history of the world! Or then again, consider the opportunities for hostage-taking! What, relatively speaking, is the worth of another Einstein?' At this gem of wit, Jurnet forced his features into the expression of appreciation clearly expected of him. 'Agreed,' the Superintendent continued, acknowledging the tribute with a gracious nod, 'the Council had no idea what they were starting—the Lord Mayor told me so himself. Who would have thought old Sir Thaddeus was held in such esteem abroad? Of course one knew about his *Religio Aleatoris,* that masterpiece of moral philosophy—'

'Of course!' agreed Jurnet, not bothering to disguise his mockery. *Religio what*? 'All *I* can remember about the geezer is that he once gave evidence in court against two poor old women that got them hanged as witches.'

'He was a man of his time,' the Superintendent observed indulgently. 'But also, it now appears, a man of our own, equally. He seems, quite intuitively, to have discovered the essentials of quantum physics all of three hundred years before anybody else thought of it; though of course he didn't call it that. Now that he has come into his own at last it's not surprising that physicists the world over are eager to come and do honour to his memory.'

'Pity they couldn't do it in their own backyards.'

The Superintendent said coldly: 'You've no local pride, Ben, that's your trouble.'

Fortunately for Jurnet, who loved his native city to the point of idolatry, the car in front moving off at that moment gave him something else to do beside reject the unjust accusation in terms he knew he would immediately be sorry for. Only a grinding of gears betrayed his anger.

His desolation.

The telephone had stopped ringing.

Jurnet inquired, taking care: 'What you haven't told me, sir, is what I'm actually here *for*. I take it we're as thick on the ground indoors as out?'

'Quite the contrary! We want our visitors to enjoy their stay in Angleby. We've gone on the principle that so long as we've made absolutely certain nobody can possibly gain unauthorized entry, there's nothing to stop a happy and relaxed evening being had by all. Naturally, we've shut off the rest of the museum.' The castle, having long outlived its original function as the symbol of a hated despotism, to say nothing of later incarnations as a gaol, a barracks and stabling for Oliver Cromwell's horses, had, with the mellowing of time, evolved into the repository of the city's corporate soul. 'We turned everybody out at three o'clock sharp and went over the place with a fine-tooth comb. That little coxcomb, the curator, wasn't best pleased. Acts as if the place is his personal property, only lets the public in as a favour. By the time we finished, if there was so much as a black beetle left wandering about without a pass, I'd be surprised. I'm only here tonight to keep a benign eye on things, and you, as ever, to support me in that worthy enterprise.'

Jurnet sighed, then got down to cases.

'What about the caterers?'

'Ah! The proverbial weak link, eh? I can only say that Palmers have been most co-operative. As they should be. They've catered enough civic functions'—again a little simper signalled an imminent *bon mot*—'to know on which side their bread is buttered. No waiters—only waitresses of an age beyond the seductions of perfidious foreigners. And no casual labour in the kitchen. Just the same, we've got a few men back of the swing doors, if only to make sure the food handlers wash their hands when they come back from the loo.'

The Superintendent tenderly found a new position for his superbly clad buttocks.

'The chief thing,' he announced, not batting an eyelid at the gargantuan fib, 'was that I didn't want you to feel left out. Somebody, after all, had to mind the shop—but, from one or two comments you let drop, I couldn't help wondering whether you didn't feel a little peeved. After all, intellectual giants such as Angleby is privileged to entertain tonight aren't likely to pass this way again in a hurry. It's like seeing Halley's comet. You'll be able to tell it to your grandchildren.'

If—Jurnet made the silent qualification—the intellectual giants haven't vaporized us all into interplanetary dust before I've had a chance to beget any. Aloud he said, scarcely damping down the irony: 'Very kind of you, sir. What I'm not sure of, though, is exactly what *is* this knowledge these men possess which makes them such potential targets for the villains.'

'I'm not sure I'm the one to ask,' the Superintendent responded with what was, for him, an astonishing modesty. 'Subatomic particles and all that. You ought to get a book out of the library.'

'If it's all down in black and white for anyone with a library ticket to get hold of, why should anybody bother to hijack them?'

'For what they may come up with next, man! One of

the faculty up at the University told me there's a rumour going about that one of the papers to be delivered during the week will be another of those milestones in the history of mankind like Newton and gravity, or the Earth going round the sun instead of vice versa. These chaps, let me tell you, are getting close to the core of things. Don't tell me the thought of probing the ultimate doesn't excite you, Ben, even a little?'

'Brings me out in goose pimples. Only wish it was Rotary here tonight, or the nnual convention of pincushion manufacturers.'

The Superintendent frowned his disapproval. 'Not like you to run away from a challenge.'

'Anywhere to run, you wouldn't see me for dust! That's the trouble with these know-alls. Never think of asking first who wants to know.'

# 2

In the castle vestibule the air was a jangle of voices being jolly in several languages. The men laughing, embracing, slapping each other on the back, did not look the kind to pierce through the last veils of illusion to ultimate reality. It could equally have been a gathering of accountants, wholesale grocers, or manufacturers of National Health dentures. Jurnet could not decide whether this appearance of ordinariness was reassuring or deeply disturbing. What lethal extravagances of cerebration were massing like storm clouds behind those unremarkable brows?

Their womenfolk, so far as the detective could glimpse them among the press which filled the space wall to wall, looked a pleasant enough bunch. The sole beauty in Jurnet's line of vision—a slim blonde whose aura of incense and lilies was belied by eyes of a startling darkness, was escorted by a gangling man wearing clerical grey and a dog collar, and by a blond boy, not quite a man, evidently her son and very like his mother except for eyes that, whilst dark as hers, were bright and demanding. When Jurnet by chance met his roving glance, the boy held the confrontation boldly, did not look away.

There was something vaguely familiar about the clergyman, so that when, a lank strand of sandy hair falling over one eye, the latter made his way towards Jurnet, threading himself between the merry groups with practised meekness, the detective was not unduly surprised. By the time the man had reached his objective, he had got him taped.

'Feldon St Awdry, isn't it?' Jurnet got his blow in first. 'Have I got it right?'

'You have indeed!' The clergyman smiled, disclosing large teeth set rather haphazardly into an expanse of pallid gum. 'Simon Maslin,' shaking hands. 'Our chalice and paten, if you remember—'

'I remember all right! We never recovered them for you.'

'Not your fault, Inspector!' The Revd Simon Maslin returned earnestly. He had more the air of a curate than an incumbent. Impossible to imagine him higher up the ecclesiastical tree than its lowest branches. 'I'm sure you did everything that could be done.' The man actually blushed as he came to the matter in hand. 'I know it's not something to take up a police officer's time with. It's only that I can't find anybody else to ask—'

'What's the trouble?'

Mr Maslin pushed the hair away from his eye with a knobby hand. He had a way of bobbing about that was neither a tic nor a twitch.

'The thing is, we have Professor Flaschner with us—' the clergyman pronounced the name with reverence, clearly convinced that Jurnet would recognize the hallowed syllables. 'In our care, so to speak. He has a heart condition, you know, and I really don't think he should attempt the stairs. I was wondering if there was a lift anywhere' . . . voice trailing away, 'though he keeps telling me not to fuss . . .'

Jurnet looked across to the noble flight which led up from the vestibule directly to the Great Hall. People—including the Superintendent, in urbane conversation with a Japanese gentleman as well tailored as himself—were already beginning to make their way up; a way Jurnet had looked forward to following. Ever since he was a boy, when the Great Hall with its display of armour had been his favourite place in the whole museum, he had longed, once through the turnstile, to spring up those stairs two at a time, the shortest distance to his destination. But no. The powers that be in their stony unreason had decreed that the stair was to be labelled Way Out, a stair no more to be ascended by mere mortals than Jacob's ladder. Visitors to the museum wishing to reach the Great Hall were obliged, whether they would or no, first to trek through the flora and fauna of Norfolk, its geology, agriculture, industries; past paintings of the Angleby School, mementoes of the county's worthies, as well as the lovingly assembled gleanings of local middens Paleolithic, Bronze Age, and medieval. That night, coming into the building, Jurnet had taken in the situation at a glance, and rejoiced. For once he was going to be allowed to go up the down stair.

'There *is* a lift,' he admitted, abandoning his childish dream. 'I'll show you.'

'No, no! If you would just tell us where—'

'Doubt you'd find it on your own. Anyway, the museum's shut off and you'll need a bit of clout to get through.' On a sudden thought: 'Hang on a minute, will you?'

Leaving the clergyman standing uncertainly, moving his hips and elbows in a manner that suggested he could do with a restringing, Jurnet edged his way neatly to the mahogany counter which stood alongside the vestibule entrance. He noted that with true Norfolk prudence the lady who had charge of the pamphlets and postcards had removed every last one. Evidently, in her book, the new magicians were no more to be trusted than the old. At the back of the counter, however, the folding wheelchairs were stacked as usual.

Mr Maslin looked unhappy when he saw what the detective had brought back.

'Oh dear! I doubt whether the Professor—'

'That's OK. If he doesn't need it, he can push *me*. I warn you, it's quite a walk.'

The crowds were thinning, moving steadily towards the stairs. Ahead, Jurnet could see, intermittently visible, the ashen-gold hair of the woman with the dark eyes. The answer to the question of whether its owner wasn't a bit long in the tooth to wear it the way she did, spread out over her shoulders like a young girl, the detective set aside until he could get a good look at her face.

The woman moved with her son down the length of the vestibule. The detective could see no one with the pair who might be the mythical professor; only, as he and the vicar drew near, Alistair Tring, the curator of the museum, the man whom the Superintendent had earlier characterized as 'that little coxcomb', could be heard complaining shrilly to somebody out of sight: 'Get up, sir! Get up at once!'

'Oh dear!' The Revd Maslin, with a despairing glance at his companion, darted ahead. Jurnet heard his voice raised in an introduction he evidently expected to put all to rights: 'This is Professor Max Flaschner—'

'I don't care if he's bloody God almighty,' retorted the curator, his small beaked face red with passion. 'Nobody sits on the exhibits in *my* museum!'

At the far end of the vestibule Jurnet now saw that the Buddha was still in place. Well, of course. Enormous, of some black basaltic rock dense enough to lend mass a new meaning, it had obviously been too much of a job to move just for one night, the way the smaller bits and pieces which normally cluttered the vestibule had been cleared away. Jurnet both knew and did not know the statue, since, on his juvenile visits to the museum, its impassive, inward gaze had always disconcerted him, made him hurry past without really looking. Seated in the capacious lap was a large man who had been larger, his skin no less than his elderly dress clothes proclaiming that, once, additional flesh had filled out that powerful frame, filled in the grooves in the cheeks, the hollows under the eyes.

Eyes that twinkled with a mischievous humour, however.

'My good sir,' said the large man, in a heavily accented voice that illness had not deprived of its authority, 'you have my permission to put here a small plaque, nothing fancy, to say that here rested the celebrated bum of Professor Max Flaschner, physicist, Nobel Laureate and clown.' Dismissing the small man from his attention as one might dismiss a fly with a well-directed flick of the wrist, the man tilted his face upward and, in a different tone, spoke to the Buddha. 'I thank you for your courtesy, Master.' A pause, then, lower: 'And for your strength.'

'The fellow's drunk!' Alistair Tring pronounced, looking at Jurnet for support. He adjusted his gold-rimmed spectacles and looked again, closer, at the lean Mediterranean features which were such a trial to their possessor. 'You're police, aren't you? I know I've seen you before somewhere. Can't you do something about this buffoon? I told the Lord Mayor what would come of using the castle—but would he listen?' Puffed with the self-satisfaction of having been proved right, the coxcomb looked ready to crow. 'And your lot's not much better! D'you know what they've gone and done upstairs? Only taken the helmet off every suit of armour and left it upside down at its feet like a ruddy piss pot, that's what, on the chance there's a terrorist inside!'

Jurnet said: 'Sounds a reasonable precaution to me.'

'Balls!' The curator's invective resembled his clothes; an advertisement that, anno domini notwithstanding, he was still up front with the trend-setters. 'You've no idea how stupid they look, standing about without their heads, like something out of a song by Gracie Fields.'

'Better them than the visitors, I should have thought.'

'Hm!'

It dawned on Jurnet that it was less a protective love for his artefacts than a consuming jealousy which motivated the curator's attitude towards his unwelcome guests. *Who did they think they were*, the lucky buggers whose exhibits needed no dusting, no labels, no glass cases for children to foul up with snot and time-expired bubble gum?

'I am refreshed,' announced Professor Flaschner, carefully lowering himself from the Buddha's lap to the floor. The boy came forward to take his arm.

'Christopher!' The Professor lovingly cupped a hand

along the soft curve of cheek. 'So tall! Tawno will be amazed!' Smiling: 'All the same, when you see him, round your shoulders a little, eh, or he will be jealous.'

Professor Flaschner seated himself in the wheelchair without having to be persuaded. He leaned back, drew a trembling breath. Then: 'Tawno's going to be angry I drove.'

'You *were* naughty.' It was the first time Jurnet had heard the blonde woman speak. Now that he saw her close to he had to admit that, even next to her teenage son, she looked OK with her hair streaming over the simple shift of some grey, silky material which came down to her ankles but left her arms bare. Extremely OK. The voice, however, a little girl's voice, was a whit discomforting. It was a long time since Mrs Maslin had been young enough for a voice like that. She said to the Professor: 'You know we'd already arranged to meet the train.'

'From Cambridge to Angleby is not far. Tawno would have hated to be here for three days without his own car to get about in.'

'He could always borrow ours. Tawno knows that.'

'He knows.' The man still had a powerful charm. He reached for Mrs Maslin's hand, bent over it and kissed the slender fingers lightly. 'Thank you for everything. It is lovely for him to be among old friends. But still the rascal would not be happy without his toy.' Again the laboured breath. 'One day soon he will have to grow up, won't he? Forty-seven—it is more than time.' Twisting to look over his shoulder: 'And who is the kind gentleman to whom I am indebted for this fine chariot?'

The Reverend Simon Maslin effected another of his introductions, all elbows and stumbling compliments.

'Detective Inspector Jurnet has been kind enough to say he'll show us to the lift—'

'Us? My dear people, please! When it is time for my

cortège I will let you know. Meantime, please, the rest of you, to go the same way as everybody else and keep an eye out for Tawno. If he doesn't see me the moment he comes into the room he will be anxious. An inspector!' This time, with an effort which set a vein in his forehead visibly throbbing, the Professor swung his whole body round, so as to get Jurnet squarely in his sights. 'A detective inspector! It is too much honour!'

'Happy to oblige.'

Claire Maslin and her son looked at Jurnet as if seeing him for the first time. It was as if only the Professor's attention had made the detective real to them.

The boy looked puzzled by what he saw, a reaction to which Jurnet, whom many years in the Force had reluctantly convinced that he did not conform to most people's idea of what a police officer ought to look like, was quite accustomed. Not for nothing, he had to acknowledge, did his mates, even if carefully behind his back, call him by the hated nickname of Valentino.

The woman was less puzzled than puzzling.

Jurnet was not a vain man. On the contrary, his looks were an embarrassment, an involuntary deception he sometimes felt ought to be actionable, if only he knew in what court, and against whom, to institute proceedings. It was simply that he had lived with them long enough to know their effect on women. Most were attracted by them, a few dismayed; but none was indifferent unless her attention was already spoken for elsewhere. Mrs Maslin, having been made aware of the tall, dark man waiting behind the wheelchair, glanced at him briefly, and away again.

At the Revd Mr Maslin she did not look at all.